Perhaps She Will Die

Joe Scipione

This is a work of fiction. Names, characters, places, and incidents are products of the author's imagination or are used fictitiously and are not to be construed as real. Any resemblance to actual events, locations, organizations, or persons, living or dead, is entirely coincidental.

World Castle Publishing, LLC
Pensacola, Florida
Copyright © Joe Scipione 2021
Paperback ISBN: 9781955086486
eBook ISBN: 9781955086493
First Edition World Castle Publishing, LLC, July 19, 2021
http://www.worldcastlepublishing.com
Licensing Notes
Cover: Karen Fuller
Editor: Maxine Bringenberg

For Mandy, who never gave up on this story.

CHAPTER 1

Every time her teacher walked to the front of the class, twelve-year-old Barbara thought it was going to be the time she fell through the hole in the floor. But Ms. Wabash never did. She always managed to step right over the hole and continue on like it wasn't even there.

It was the end of another long day, and although Barbara loved going to school more than almost anything else, she would be happy to be out of the dilapidated old building and back into the fresh, cool air and the warm sunlight. So, when Ms. Wabash skipped over the hole and turned to dismiss the school for the day, Barbara was one of the first students to pack up and make her way out the door. The school she attended with her older brother, Peter, and seven other kids of various ages that lived out in the country, wasn't much, but it was her favorite place on earth. A lot of parents had pulled their kids from school to help with work around their farms or shops, but her father was different. He wanted Peter and her to get a good education so they could do something other than farm with their lives. Therefore Peter, fifteen now, was the oldest in school, and he wasn't leaving until he graduated, even though all the other fifteen-year-olds were out working and making what little money there was to make. Father made him go to school every day.

"It's almost 1940," Father had explained to them one night after dinner. "The world won't always be like this. One day there will be lots of jobs, and the people with the best educations are going to be the ones doing them. Get your education, then make money to help our family. But if you get a chance to have a job where you wear a suit and tie every day, take it, and never look back. Because that's how you'll turn your life around. You'll get out of this place; you won't have to farm, and you'll be somebody."

Barbara's parents were different from most of the other kids' parents. They were willing to work harder so that their kids could go to school instead of getting the kids to work to help out the family. She always wondered why her parents were different, but she never really questioned them. She loved school and didn't want to stop going. It was her way to escape and learn about new and different things. Every day was an adventure.

The school wasn't much to look at from the outside. It looked just like any other house in the area, and if it wasn't for the sign that hung out in front, anyone would have walked right by. People might start walking by too. The sign was on its last legs. It was supposed to be anchored in the ground by two posts, but one of the posts had rotted away down near ground level, so it was only held up by one post now. The sign leaned to the side, and on windy days, it wiggled back and forth. It was only a matter of time before the other post snapped, then no one walking by would know the building was actually the Roberts School.

The building itself was in pretty much the same shape as the sign. The loose cinder blocks piled in front of the door were beginning to crack and fall apart. A few of the windows were broken, and the glass had never been replaced. During the warm months of school, it was good because the broken glass would let some air into the school. But during the winter months, the teacher had to board up the holes in the windows to keep the warm air in and the cool air out. The wooden boards on the side of the school were starting to fall and hung at odd angles on every side, and the shingles on the roof were not much better. And, of course, that hole in the floor. It was a good thing Ms. Wabash knew where every leak in the roof was so she could put buckets on the floor the moment it started raining. It may not have been the greatest looking place Barbara had ever seen, but when she was there, she had a hard time thinking of a place she would rather be.

It was good to get outside on days like today, though. The sun was warm, and although the air itself was cool, the schoolroom didn't cool off much. There wasn't any ventilation either, other than the broken windows, so all day, the school just got hotter and hotter. Barbara was happy to get outside and cool off in the spring air.

"Goodbye, Nancy! I'll see you tomorrow, Albert!" Ms. Wabash called from the school's door as the kids filed out and walked their separate ways back home. "See you tomorrow, Barbara Whitehurst!"

Barbara turned back and waved, flashing a grin at Ms. Wabash. It was the same grin she gave every time Ms. Wabash used her full name. It had been a running joke for a while. There were two Barbaras at the school—Barbara Cherry, who lived a few miles away, and Barbara Whitehurst. But Barbara Cherry was older and had been at the school a few years before Barbara. So at first, whenever Ms. Wabash called on Barbara, they both spoke or answered the question. Out of necessity, Ms. Wabash had gotten into the habit of saying Barbara Whitehurst when she was calling on her, and just Barbara when she was calling on Barbara Cherry. She didn't know why, but it always made Barbara smile.

"Goodbye, Peter Whitehurst!" Ms. Wabash called as Peter walked up behind his sister.

"Bye, Ms. Wabash," he said, then turned back to his sister. "Barb, I'm going on ahead. Father had a few things he wanted me to help him with when we got out, so I want to make sure I have enough time to get them all done. You're okay walking home, right?"

"Pete, I'm twelve now," Barbara said. Her birthday had been less than a month ago. "Of course, I'll be fine. Go ahead, I'll see you at home."

"Okay!" Pete yelled. He had started running as soon as Barbara told him she would be fine. He was different than Barbara. While she always thought about what else she could do with her life, other than live on a farm, all Pete ever talked about was working on the farm with his father.

She watched as he sprinted down the dirt road toward home and out of sight.

It was a tough time for farmers in all parts of the country, and their little corner of Illinois was no different than anywhere else. But Father had had some luck the past few years. While much of the middle of the country was facing a drought—a dry spell, as Father would call it—they had been lucky. The past few years, the corn had been growing almost as well as it ever had. With corn being her father's major money-making crop, he was doing pretty well for himself, considering the shape most farmers were in. She was proud of her father. Proud that he pushed her and Pete to do more than what he did. He could have easily done what more of her friends' parents had done and put Pete and her to work in some way, anything so the family would have more money coming in. But he never even thought of it, or if he did, he never mentioned it to her. He just let them continue right on going to school, only worried about what they were going to do in the future.

She waved goodbye to a few of her friends in class, and they each headed off in different directions. Nancy O'Hara and Albert Whistle were neighbors, and they walked to and from school together every day. Barbara thought of them as her best friends. Nancy was a year older and Albert a year younger, but they were the closest in age to Barbara. They were almost always working on the same things at the same time in class. It was natural that they became fast friends once they started going to school together. It was only about a twenty-minute walk to get to either of their houses from Barbara's, so on the weekends and sometimes after school, she would walk over, and they would play until it started getting dark. She gave each of them a big wave.

"Bye, guys!" Barbara yelled to her friends, walking in the opposite direction.

"Bye, Barbara!" Nancy yelled, and both she and Albert waved back at Barbara.

Barbara turned back and began her ten-minute walk home. Pete was nowhere in sight and, if he wasn't home yet, he could probably see it as he continued running. They almost always walked to and from school together. She always thought of Nancy and Albert as her best friends, but that was only because she didn't include Pete because he was her older brother. But he was in many ways her best friend too. She looked forward to their walks together before and after school. He wasn't like so many older brothers she had read about in books or even heard people talk about. Sure, he teased her sometimes, and when they were younger, he'd gotten annoyed with her, but when everything boiled down, he was the best kind of big brother. He protected her when she needed protecting, he helped her when she needed his help, and most of all, he laughed with her when something was funny. She couldn't wait to see what it would be like when they were older. She always envisioned him getting married and living in Mother and Father's house and her marrying someone who bought a piece of land right next to Pete so they would stay close forever. She knew it probably wouldn't happen that way. Mother had an older brother she wrote a letter to once a week but almost never saw. Father had two sisters that he wrote letters to also. One lived here in Kankakee County, and they only saw her a couple of times a year. But still, Barbara could dream if she wanted to. Who knew where they might end up?

She did like the idea of walking home on her own also. Her parents had told her it would be okay to do it a few times now that she was twelve. Nothing bad had ever happened when she and Pete made this walk, so she didn't think anything was going to happen if she did it by herself. They never saw any dangerous animals, just a few deer on early winter mornings sometimes. No one that lived in the area was very dangerous. Her parents knew all the neighbors and went to church with most of them. They were all good people, so she was sure she didn't have anything to worry about.

The dirt road toward their house took her through an open field — this was where she and Pete had seen the deer every time. She always looked for them, but they weren't usually out at this time of day. Just past the field was a grove of trees. She had to walk down the long sloping hill in the field before she got to the trees, then the road went back up out of the trees, and it was a quick five-minute walk to their road. Then another three or four minutes down their street to her father's farm. It really was a quick walk.

As Barbara approached the trees, a flock of birds came flying out. She couldn't really call it a forest because the group of trees was not that large — the trees stretched less than a mile in either direction, with the road cutting right through them. The ground here was also lower than the grassland on either side of the trees, creating a little valley. On rainy days this part of the walk was muddy, and they had to slog through a small pond covering the road just to get past. Today wasn't rainy, and there hadn't been any rain for a few days, so when Barbara noticed the puddle in the trees just off the side of the road, it made her think for a moment. She didn't remember it being there when she and Pete walked by this morning, but maybe it had been. The grass had been wet this morning — she'd thought it was just morning dew, but maybe it had rained last night while they were asleep, and she didn't notice it. Either way, it wasn't a big deal, and she just continued to pass through.

It was always a little dark when they walked through the trees. She remembered Pete one time calling it the tree cave because — well, it looked like a cave made of trees. The high branches on either side of the road grew together up above their heads, and you really couldn't tell the difference between branches on one side of the road and branches on the other side. They all looked the same from the ground. The angle of the sun at this time of day lets very little light in through the trees, just like a cave.

Barbara walked through the tree cave and gave a cursory glance at the puddle along the side of the road. The water in the puddle rippled as if a frog or something had just jumped into it. She smiled, thinking about how happy the frogs must have been to have a small, muddy puddle to play in. She turned her attention back to the road in front of her and continued on her way up out of the tree cave to the higher and drier grassland on the other side.

Barbara took a few more steps and thought she heard shuffling behind her like someone was walking on the road just behind her. No one else at school lived in this direction, so she wasn't sure exactly who might have followed her. She hadn't seen anyone on the road as she walked, and there was nothing between the tree cave and the school. Maybe it was just the wind blowing leaves or an animal or something. Or it was just her imagination. She didn't usually walk home from school by herself — maybe she was a little scared and just didn't realize it. Whatever the reason, she decided not to look behind her but picked up her pace instead. The shuffling continued, also at a faster pace to keep up with Barbara

Attempting to show off her lack of fear, Barbara whirled around to face who or whatever was following her. When she spun, there were two yelps — the first was from Barbara, and the second was from the dog about ten feet behind her. The noise that escaped Barbara's mouth startled the dog, which provided one of its own. The girl looked at the dog, who, after his yelp, seemed to want to follow her still. The dog looked up at her, its tongue out and its mouth open. Dogs couldn't smile, but if they could, this one would have been smiling at her. The dog took slow steps toward her, and she took two equally slow steps toward the dog, crouched, and then knelt with her hand out as the dog approached her. She loved animals, and although her family never had a dog of their own, she always felt a special connection with them when she did have a chance to be with one. This dog seemed no different, coming right up to her. Its cold nose smelled her hand and then licked it. It was as if the dog knew her.

Barbara knelt on the ground, patted the dog's head, and scratched its neck. The dog liked it, pushing its head against her hand whenever she stopped scratching or petting for a moment. She liked it too. They were still in the shade of the tree cave, although just by a few feet. The ground was already headed uphill, and the trees were not above them, but the sun, low in the sky, cast the shadows of the trees outward. She rubbed the dog's head some more, laughing as the dog tried to lick her hand with each pat.

"I think he likes you," a scratchy voice said.

Barbara jumped and looked up to see an older man walking up out of the tree cave. He was older than her father, or at least he looked older. He wore an old black ivy cap that looked a bit too small for his head. Either that or the disheveled gray hair that covered his head wouldn't let the cap sit right. He wasn't clean-shaven, but he didn't have a beard either, just a good amount of gray stubble covering his face. His clothes were old and worn, as were his shoes. They were outside, and he was too far away for Barbara to know for sure, but she was positive if she got closer, he would have smelled like something close to horse manure.

"Oh, is he yours?" Barbara stood up but kept her hand down so the dog could lick it.

"Yes, yes. It's okay, though. He really does like you, it seems." The man smiled but showed no teeth, his lips remaining pressed together. The smile looked forced.

"I think he does." Barbara smiled back. Her parents had always taught her to be polite to adults. The man still stood about ten feet away, watching Barbara and his dog. "What's his name?"

The man put on the forced smile again. "Rufus." At the mention of his name, the dog turned to look back at the man, then returned his head to Barbara's patting.

"He's really nice. You must have trained him well," she said, not sure what else to say. She looked at the man and noticed his eyes now for the first time — they were green. Not a light green she had seen in other people with green eyes, but a darker shade of green. She had never seen eyes like his before. "Well, I've got to get going. My father's waiting for me. It was nice to meet you and Rufus."

Barbara gave the dog a final pat on the head and started to turn.

"Yes, of course. It was nice to meet you, Barbara," the man said.

Barbara started to walk home and then turned back around. She hadn't told him her name. How did he know who she was? Rufus was walking toward the man.

"How did you know my name? Do you know my parents?" Barbara asked. She took a step backwards as she spoke. The guy already made her nervous, and this wasn't helping.

He opened his mouth to speak as Rufus approached him, but no words came out. At first, Barbara didn't notice what was happening — her eyes were on the man, not the dog. Movement from the dog caught her eye, and she looked down at him. Rufus began to break apart before her eyes. What was happening? She couldn't really tell, but starting at its tail and moving at a slow pace up its body, the dog was breaking up. Millions of pieces were coming off it and moving toward the man. She looked closer, trying to get a better idea of what was happening. Flies? Flies. The dog was turning into flies, and…she watched the flies approach the man, and they flew right into his open mouth. All of them. His eyes remained on her. His grotesque mouth hung open as millions of the small insects filled it.

The dog was gone, and the air around the man was filled with flies as they continued pouring into his mouth. Barbara screamed and turned toward home to run, but when she turned, she ran right into the man. He looked down at her and smiled as one final fly walked along the edge of his lips and into his mouth.

"No!" she shouted at him and turned again back toward the tree cave. But he was there in front of her again. This time the smile was gone from his face. He reached out and grabbed her by the arm. Barbara twisted and jerked her arm, but the man's grip was too strong. She couldn't move her arm at all.

"Come on. It will be okay, Barbara," he said. She kicked his legs, his crotch, anything to get him to let her go, but he didn't move. He pulled her toward the tree cave as she tried to yank and pull against him. He wasn't that big, and he was old, and she felt like she should be having more of an effect on him, but nothing she did seemed to stop or even slow him down.

"Help! Help me!" she shrieked, hoping someone would hear her, maybe Ms. Wabash at school or anyone within earshot. But it didn't look like anyone was coming. They were now under the shade of the cave — she could feel the cool air under the trees. She continued to scream and fight against whoever, or whatever, this thing was pulling her back under the trees.

"It's going to be okay, Barbara. Trust me," he said. The smile returned to his face, but Barbara thought she liked it better when he didn't smile. The smile made things worse.

"No, I don't want to. I don't want to!"

Barbara pushed and fought against him until he held her

still by both arms. He looked angry as he held her shoulders tight and wouldn't let her move. She squeezed her eyes shut but could feel and smell his breath. She wanted to know what was happening, so she opened her eyes and then regretted it. Just as the dog had done, the man was falling apart. The cap on his head, his hair, the hands that held her were turning into flies, just like the dog. She was surrounded by flies, and she thought she could move, but somehow, she was still held in place. The flies swarmed around her. She could feel the pressure against her body—the flies were holding her in place.

Barbara wanted to throw up from the feeling of them against her skin. The sound of millions of flies surrounding her, their wings buzzing as they flew, was too much. She wanted to scream but clamped her mouth and eyes shut as the swarm got closer, tighter around her. They were on her nose—she could feel them landing on her, the tiny legs everywhere—then inside her nose. Exploring.

"No." Barbara let out a small, short protest, but it was just what the flies were hoping for. A few went into her mouth at first, then a few more. She tried to push them out with her tongue, but they kept pouring in until her mouth felt full, and they were going deeper. The movement of them on the insides of her cheeks and forcing their way down her throat made her gag, but they didn't stop. She tried to clamp her mouth shut, but there were too many of them—they held her mouth open. The buzzing of the flies was everywhere—she couldn't get away from it. She opened her eyes but saw nothing but the blackness of the flies that still engulfed her.

Barbara tried to scream, but the sound was muffled by the flies—they were everywhere. Barbara struggled for another second, then realized there was no use fighting back. She thought of Pete, at home, so happy to be helping their father out. Why hadn't she just run home with him?

Everything went black.

CHAPTER 2

"It will be okay, I promise." Lisa Ewing looked next to her and then in the rearview mirror at her twelve-year-old son Matthew and her ten-year-old daughter Olivia while they sat at the stoplight. Olivia actually didn't seem too upset by the move. She was taking it in stride and even showed signs of excitement when they talked about their new house in an actual neighborhood. The same couldn't be said for Matthew, and Lisa understood why he was upset. He was twelve years old and had been to school with the same kids since he was in preschool. He might not have had a lot of close friends, but he knew everyone he went to school with, and now they were moving him to a new town where they didn't know anyone. A move like this could be hard on a kid that age. But Lisa and her husband Tim knew this was the right move for their family.

"Yeah, right," Matthew said. He had been facing forward but now turned to face the window as the red light turned green, and Lisa pulled the car forward. She checked her side mirror, and the U-Haul Tim was driving was still behind them.

"I know it doesn't feel this way right now, but I think, in the long run, it will be better for us. We have a lot more space at this house—you'll have a whole extra room in the basement just for you and Liv. We'll be able to set up a TV, and you can have your video games down there and use it whenever you want. It'll be a space just for the two of you," Lisa said, still trying to talk him into moving even as they made the final trip from their old duplex to the new house.

"Our rooms are bigger too, Matt. You should have come with me and Dad last week to see the new house. It's really nice," Olivia said from the back seat.

"I know. I like that part, I guess. It's just my friends and stuff. Why couldn't we at least stay in the same town? What's so great about Medville?" Matt said.

They'd left their old town of Wrighton for Medville for many reasons, the biggest of which was the schools. Medville had one of the best school systems in Illinois and was always on different lists for the best places for a family to live in Illinois. It was also a lot safer. Wrighton was a small town, but the crime rate had gone up every year for the last fifteen years, and it didn't seem like it was slowing down or stopping. It would also cut forty minutes off Tim's commute to work each day.

When Lisa and Tim bought their duplex just after getting married, it was never meant to be the place where they raised their kids. They had made plans to move once already, just after Matthew was born. But when Lisa tried to go back to work after maternity leave, there was a reduction in force, and she was asked to leave. It seemed illegal to her at the time, but she also felt like there wasn't much she could do, so she stayed home to raise Matthew, and then Olivia came along, and she just never went back to work. It would have been hard to buy a house with only Tim's salary back then; they were in a different spot now. Tim's hard work the last fifteen years had paid off, and he was now making a lot of money. They were able to be more comfortable with just his salary. Matthew wouldn't understand all of those reasons, of course—he just knew he would miss his friends.

"It'll be hard right now, Matthew, but in the long run, it'll be better for us. You've just got to trust me and Dad. We know what we're doing. You'll make new friends, and you'll still be able to see your friends from Wrighton. It's only a forty-minute drive back there. So if you want to go see them on the weekends, we can drive back and see them."

Lisa knew he would probably never ask to go back and visit friends in Wrighton—he never saw kids outside of school, to begin with. He had friends at school, but that was it. He would make new friends at his new school, and maybe living in a neighborhood instead of on a main road like they did in Wrighton, he would see kids outside of school and make some real friends.

"Just give it a chance and have an open mind. We've got two weeks before school starts, so we can get comfortable in our house and meet some of our neighbors, and then you'll start up at school. Also, remember if you went to middle school in Wrighton, there would be a lot of new kids in your classes that you might not know. Five elementary schools fed into the middle school, and you don't necessarily see people you know. You'd probably be making new friends either way. It is a good time for you to move."

Lisa and Tim had been repeating the same thing to Matthew since they told him they were definitely moving more than a month ago. The duplex had sold, and they found a house they liked in Medville less than a week later. They had closed on the new house a week ago and would close on the duplex in a few days. With a little help from Tim's brothers, they were able to get the U-Haul packed up last night with all of their stuff, which wasn't much from the tiny duplex. Tim's brothers were going to meet them at the new house this morning to help them unload the truck, and then the real work would start.

Lisa took a few turns off the main road, slowing her speed as she entered the small neighborhood, then turned on Molly Lane and pulled up in front of the new Ewing residence. She parked on the road in front of the house, leaving the driveway for the U-Haul, which was now a few blocks behind them.

Olivia got out of the car first and ran up to the front door. Lisa watched her turn the doorknob and push her shoulder against the door before realizing she didn't have a key. Matthew was the only one who hadn't been in the house yet, mostly due to his apathy about the move, and he was sluggish getting out of the car. He did, though, and Lisa put an arm around him as they walked up to join Olivia.

It was a Colonial-style house perched up on a small hill. The driveway sloped up to the garage in the front, but just a little. The backyard was flat, large, and fenced in, just what Lisa and Tim had always wanted. The lot was big too, almost a full acre of land. At the very back of the lot was a small grove of trees that would provide them shade in the afternoon when they sat out on the back deck. The inside was also just what she always dreamed she would have — granite counters and new appliances, big bedrooms, and an even bigger living room. Tim had already picked out the perfect spot for his new TV. She was excited to begin their new life in this house. She hoped their excitement about the house would start to rub off on Matthew at some point, but he still stood there with his head hanging down as she pushed the door open so he could get his first look at his new house.

"Matt, come on." Olivia pushed past them. "I want to show you our new rooms."

Lisa watched Matt's eyes when he walked in. There was a stark contrast between their old duplex and the new house — there could be no way he wouldn't see this as an upgrade. He looked around at the double-story entryway, and Lisa thought she saw a smile, but then it was gone.

"Okay, fine," Matt said and trudged up the stairs, with Olivia watching and smiling from above.

"I already picked mine, but there are two others you can pick from," Olivia said as she walked to the side of the house with the kid's bedrooms.

Lisa watched them and smiled, hoping Olivia would rub off on him a little.

"Guys, a couple of minutes and then we're going to have to start unloading the truck."

Lisa took off the light sweatshirt she was wearing and set it on some boxes they'd already brought over and left just inside the front door. She walked around the downstairs and listened to the sounds of the kids moving around the upstairs. She couldn't wait until Matthew saw the basement when it was all set up. It was going to be a separate area just for the kids. The finished basement was beautiful when it was empty, but Matthew might lose his mind when they set up the TV and gaming systems. There was no way he would still hate this move when he found out he could sit down there and play video games for two straight days over the weekends if he really wanted to.

Her footsteps echoed through the empty house as she went back to the kitchen and just looked. There wasn't much about it she didn't love, from the island to the breakfast nook that overlooked the backyard. It was the ideal kitchen. She couldn't help but smile as she took it all in. It was the first time she had been at the house since it became officially theirs.

The beep-beep-beep of the truck backing into the driveway took her attention away from the kitchen. She would have more than enough time to enjoy it soon. She watched through the front windows as Tim backed the truck in. She heard the truck grind and crank as he secured it.

Tim got out of the truck and had the same look on his face that Lisa had just a minute before when she got out and looked at the house. It was theirs. Their house. The thing they had worked so hard for. The thing that they had wanted twelve years ago was now a reality for them, and they were both happy and excited to start this new chapter.

"Now the work really starts," Lisa said, leaving the house and joining him out front.

"Yep. My brothers will be here in a little bit," Tim said. He pulled out his phone and looked at the screen, then returned the phone to his pocket. "In about twenty minutes or so. They're getting coffee and donuts for us too. How's Matt?"

"Well, he didn't cry on the ride over, so I guess that's better," she said, thinking he really was getting a little better about all of this. "Liv is giving him a tour, and I think everyone else's excitement might rub off on him. Once his stuff gets off the truck, I was thinking of letting him just start on his room instead of helping to unload. Just let him set up his room how he wants—maybe it will help him out."

Tim nodded, then put his arm around her shoulders. "Look at this. We did some good work, Lees." He pulled her tight against him and kissed her on the forehead. He had done that forever, and she loved it every time—the pulling tight, the kiss on the forehead, not quite at her hairline, just below it, but he always managed to get his lips right on her skin without any hair getting stuck to him. It was one of those things she always wanted as a little girl; a husband who would do cute things like that all the time to show they loved you. He didn't even have to say it as long as he kept on kissing her forehead—she knew how he felt.

Tim let go of her and went to the back of the truck and opened it. This was the largest truck they could get. The good news was, everything they owned, except for the few things they'd already brought over, fit inside of it. The bad news was, now they had to unload everything they owned from the back of this truck. It was going to be a long day. Lisa had already been told multiple times that she didn't need to lift or move anything. She could direct them when they got in the house and make sure everything ended up where it was supposed to, even unpack if she wanted, but no lifting. The three men had packed the truck, so they already knew they could lift and move everything.

Lisa watched Tim lift up the back of the truck, then saw

someone behind him in the next yard waving.

"Oh, a neighbor!" Lisa smiled and waved back. "Are you all set here for a minute? I'm going to go introduce myself."

Lisa went down the slight slope in their front yard, across the grass, and then onto their new neighbor's yard. The older man who waved at her stood by his front door on the porch, smiling as she approached. He was on the short side, and had a head of stark white hair that was difficult to miss. He wore a button-down short-sleeve shirt and a pair of perfectly blue jeans, which he probably called dungarees. The exact clothes Lisa would expect an old man like this to wear.

"Hi, I'm Lisa," she said before she arrived at the porch.

"Hi there," the old man said as Lisa reached the step up onto the covered front porch. He put out his hand. "John Holland."

Lisa shook his hand and then said her name again. "Lisa Ewing. That's my husband Tim," she said, pointing over at Tim as he stepped out of the back of the truck with a small box in his hands.

"Nice to meet you, Lisa. Welcome to the neighborhood. You got kids too?"

She thought it was a bit of an odd question to ask someone he just met, but then she just passed it off as a curious old man wanting to learn about his neighbors. For all she knew, the family that was there before them had been there for thirty years. They never met them and only worked directly with the realtor. They had moved to Florida to retire, so the chances that John Holland had the same neighbors for a long time seemed high. He was just a nosy old man, nothing wrong with that.

"Yes, two kids. They're inside already picking out their rooms." Lisa smiled and laughed. "Do you like this neighborhood?"

"Oh yes. It's the best," the old man replied. "I've been here for almost forty years. I guess it is now. My wife and I raised our kids here. They're all married and moved on now, but we never saw any reason to leave, so we stayed. She loved it here. She passed on about, oh, fifteen years or so now."

"I'm very sorry." Lisa had not wanted to hear the old man's life story, but she couldn't get away now.

"Oh, it's okay." He crossed his hands across his chest, another old man maneuver. "We knew it was comin'. Cancer. It doesn't make it easier, but at least we were ready for it."

"That's so sad. You must miss her." Lisa couldn't stop herself. Now that she was here talking to the man, she wasn't about to cut it short, so she kept talking to him even though she just wanted to be back in her new house and wished she had never started this conversation.

"I do. But my kids come by enough, so I'm not too lonely. Plus, it's such a great neighborhood, you know? Everyone is real friendly—always wave and stuff when you drive by, and we all watch out for the kids, you know? Most everyone had kids or still has kids, so we just watch out for each other. If anything is out of place, someone will notice and call the cops quick. It really is a safe place to live."

"Thanks. That's one of the reasons we chose this house. The neighborhood looks awesome, and our realtor said it's one of the best in the area. And the schools are great too. It's really an upgrade for us."

The old man nodded and watched as Tim brought another box down out of the truck. "Well, let me know if you need anything, you know? I can't help bringin' the stuff in the house for you, but if you need anything else, I'm right here all the time."

"Thank you so much." Lisa smiled and shook his hand again. "It was nice to meet you, John."

"Nice to meet you too, Lisa. Don't be a stranger."

Lisa stepped down off the porch and back over to the truck, where Tim was getting another box out. Lisa looked at it and decided it wasn't too heavy. She snatched it from him and brought it inside. It was marked kitchen, so she brought it right over to the kitchen and left it on the floor. She had a plan, and it involved no boxes being left on the counters. With the help of Tim and Olivia, she hoped to have the major areas unpacked by the end of the day. If the bedrooms, living room and kitchen were unpacked, it would make everything that much better in the morning.

"Looks like you made a friend already," Tim said. He put the box he was carrying down on the kitchen counter.

"No, down there." Lisa pointed next to the box she already put on the floor. "Nothing on the counters. Yeah, he's a nice little old man. John Holland. He's a little bit nosy, but I think he just wants to be able to look out for us."

"Oh yeah?" Tim looked at her as he placed the box on the floor next to the one she'd just brought in.

"Yeah, just little stuff. Did we have kids, stuff like that. But then he started telling me about how he raised his kids here, and everyone in the neighborhood watches out for each other and watches out for the kids. I'm sure he's harmless." Lisa spoke as she looked through the drawers in the kitchen to make sure they were all empty. They had done a walk-through right before the closing, but they had only been on the lookout for the big stuff they didn't want. The small things that might be in drawers and could easily get thrown out in the trash if it wasn't wanted were easy to overlook at the walk-through. She also thought there could be a few surprises in the drawers, which was always kind of fun. Kind of like a treasure hunt. It would be an even better treasure hunt when she sent Tim up into the attic. Who knew what he would find up there.

"Yeah. I mean having a neighborhood where everyone looks out for each other and keeps an eye on everyone else. That's the kind of place we've been talking about for so long, and now we're here. How long did we live in the duplex? We had only two neighbors the entire time, and we hardly spoke five words to them the entire time we lived there. Neither of them wanted anything to do with us. This is the opposite of that. I hope we find some friends a little closer to our age, though," Tim said. Lisa laughed. Then he pulled a knife from his back pocket and sliced open the two boxes on the floor of the kitchen for her. He placed it on the counter. "I have another one in the truck, and this way, we don't have stop and open boxes for you. You can just go at your own pace."

"I'm going to get it all put away, I'm telling you, as long as no one gets in my way." Lisa pointed at him, a smile on her face.

"Hey, don't look at me. It's the two upstairs that are going to slow you down, not me."

"Well, they're going to do their rooms, and if they need a break, he's got his video game thing, and she has her tablet. They can help, or they can deal."

"That's the spirit, Lees," Tim said.

The sound of two car doors closing told them Tim's brothers were there and ready to either work or eat. She knew they would do a lot of both throughout the course of the day — she just didn't know which would be first. The counter was clear, so whatever food they came in with, she was ready for it.

CHAPTER 3

"Matt, let's go!" Lisa called from the kitchen up the stairs in the general direction of Matt's bedroom.

For all of Matt's issues with moving and the problems that had surrounded that part of his life, he was always very good about going to school. He said he liked school, and it showed. As with any twelve-year-old, Matt was sluggish getting out of bed on some mornings. This was one of those mornings. His body was still getting used to going to bed early and waking up early for school, unlike the summer when he stayed up late and slept late.

"I'm coming," Lisa heard his muffled voice call from up the stairs. He was going to get ready. He was always ready on time—sometimes, he just needed some extra motivation. When he was younger, Lisa used to wake him up and make him eat breakfast in their tiny little kitchen, then go back upstairs and get dressed for school. Now that he was older, she felt like he should be able to get himself ready on his own, so she let him. He would sleep later, take a shower, and eat a quick breakfast on the way to school. It wasn't the way she would have done it, but it worked for Matt. His grades didn't suffer, so she didn't care.

Olivia was the exact opposite of Matt. Matt didn't want anything to do with other people in the mornings. Olivia came down dressed and ready for the day every morning at 6:30. She even started setting her own alarm. Tim would come down ready for work some mornings and find Olivia sitting at the kitchen table eating a bowl of cereal by herself. Once there were other people around, Olivia would be talking to them non-stop. Lisa liked to listen to the morning radio talk shows, and Olivia would always be ready with a comment or a question about the news topic being discussed on the show. There were times when Lisa just wanted to listen to the radio, but she knew Olivia was learning just as much in the hour with the radio on as she was the entire day at school. She always answered her questions, and they had lots of interesting conversations because of the radio.

"Mom, when you were my age, what kind of music did you listen to?" Olivia asked while a classic rock song played on the radio. Lisa couldn't remember the name of the band or the song's name even though she must have heard the song a hundred times in her life and could sing every word.

"Actually, the same exact stuff I listen to now. It's called classic rock, and mostly music from the 1960s or the 1970s."

"My friends' parents all like country music. Do you ever listen to that?"

Olivia was so mature for her age, sometimes Lisa forgot she was talking to a ten-year-old. There were many occasions when she acted much older. She was never sure if Olivia was just mature for her age or if it was a male/female thing. There were times when she acted older than Matthew, even though Matt was two years older than her. Maybe it just took longer for boys to mature. Or maybe Olivia was just a more mature person in general. Either way, there were questions that came out of her mouth from time to time that reminded Lisa that her daughter had only been around for ten years. This was one of those times.

"Lots of people listen to country music. You've heard it. It's a lot like these rock songs, but it's usually a little slower, and the singers usually have an accent. I just don't like it that much,"

Lisa said. She never wanted to influence her kids' opinions. She hoped her dislike of country music wasn't rubbing off.

"Cool," Olivia said and returned to her bowl of cereal, finishing it up as Matthew came downstairs.

In his typical outfit of black sneakers, matching black jeans, and a black T-shirt to go with his black hoodie, Matthew came into the kitchen. He had one earbud in his ear with the wire leading down to his pocket. The other earbud dangled at his chest. He seemed much happier since the start of school. Tim and Lisa had been worried about him when school first started, but he settled in and even made some new friends. One of the best parts, they told him, about moving to a new town was that if you didn't like your old friends or who you hung out with at your old school, you could just make new ones. It was a way to start over from scratch. Either there were more kids like Matthew in Medville, or he was making friends with different kinds of people. His grades were good so far, and he was happier now than before they moved. It was like he was a new kid.

"Hey, Matty," Lisa said when he came in and slumped down on the chair opposite Olivia. They had about ten minutes before they needed to leave for school. Lisa knew he wasn't going to talk much to her—he just couldn't do it this early in the morning—so all her questions to him were of the yes/no variety. "Banana and a bar?" she asked. It was already out on the counter.

Matt nodded, and she dropped them in front of him. He unzipped his backpack and tossed the granola bar in the front section, then peeled the banana and ate it at the table with his eyes closed. Lisa could hear the music coming from his earbuds, but she couldn't make out what it was. For a while, she and Tim didn't like the music he was listening to—death metal, he called it—but they let him listen to whatever he wanted. Lately, he had started listening more to older music, and Lisa and Tim always tried to give him more choices and stuff to listen to, but with his MP3 player always on and in his pocket, they had a hard time keeping track of exactly what he was listening to at any given time.

Lisa cleaned up Olivia's cereal bowl when she finished and checked the time.

"All right guys, let's go," Lisa announced.

Matt got up first, followed by Olivia. Lisa followed the two of them after grabbing her purse and throwing on a pair of sunglasses. The schools were only about a five-minute drive, close enough that the kids could walk if they had to, especially Matt. But they were still getting used to the new place, and Lisa and Tim weren't quite ready to have the kids walking to school by themselves. They went through the house, past the front door, and through the door to the garage. Matt got in the back, and Olivia got in the front. The rule was whoever was in the car the longest got to ride in the front, so that meant Olivia in the mornings and Matthew in the afternoons.

***

At some point since the kids went back to school, Lisa had gotten in the bad habit of eating a quiet breakfast at the breakfast nook in their kitchen. Not that a quiet breakfast wasn't a good thing—she loved it—but another habit she picked up she knew was bad, but she didn't feel like she was able to stop it. She watched. The breakfast nook was located in an alcove in the kitchen and surrounded 180 degrees with windows. It was great in the mornings because she could sit there in the morning sunlight and plan out the day in her head. The plan lately involved opening and unpacking boxes, but still, it was a good idea to start thinking about the day before just jumping in full speed. At first, that was all she did. But then there was more.

The woman with the white, perfectly groomed poodle would walk by every day between 8:15 and 8:30. She had not missed a day yet unless it was raining. Trash day was on Wednesday, and everyone put their trash out the night before, except for the people across the street a few houses down. They always rushed to get their trash cans out five minutes before the truck came by to pick it up. At some time before nine, an older gentleman would come by on his daily jog. So far, he didn't care if it was raining or not. He ran by the house every day with his headband on and listening to his music or whatever he listened to while running.

At least once a week, the guy around the corner had a brush fire in his backyard. It wasn't always the same day, but it was at least once a week. She didn't know where he got the brush to burn that much. Lisa couldn't always see the guy, but she always saw the flames of the fire, sometimes shooting high up into the sky, he was so close by. It reminded her of her brother when they were younger, and their father would have a big fire. Her brother would use paper cups and trap ants in them, then tossed the cup into the fire. At the time, she thought it was gross—looking back on it now, he might have had more than a few cruel tendencies—but he turned out to be a great husband, father, and uncle. He wasn't a serial killer—at least, not that she knew of. She smiled at the thought of her brother, and then her mind drifted back to the neighborhood.

The younger couple right across the street always left in a big rush right around 8:30, with their twins in car seats. Lisa assumed they were heading to work but had to drop the kids off at daycare or a family member's house before then. She didn't know too many of the people that lived in the neighborhood yet. She waved hello to the people that she recognized but wouldn't have called anyone that lived around them friends. Because she didn't know anyone, it was easy for her to watch what she could see of their daily routines and make up stories about them, like the couple with the twins.

John Holland, of course, she had met, but she was starting to understand why John was so nosy the first time she met him. He sat at home all the time too. Lisa knew because she could see most of his backyard and all of his front yard from her breakfast nook, and he never left the house as far as she could tell. He must sit by his front window or something and do the same thing she did, keeping track of the people that lived around them. She knew what he would say about her already. "She leaves around 7:45 to drop the kids off at school, then comes home for a little while. At some point around lunchtime, some days, she leaves and comes back with groceries. Then she leaves again at 2:30 to get the kids." She was no more or less predictable than anyone else, but she understood a little bit more about John Holland because of her new, bad habit.

Lisa tried to justify it to herself. It wasn't like she watched people all day. She listened to the radio for a half-hour, drank her coffee, and had a small breakfast before getting to work unpacking and cleaning up the house. She didn't watch the street that whole time, just when she was sitting eating her breakfast.

It just happened to be Wednesday, and Lisa sat in the breakfast nook as poodle lady walked by. The poodle had pink bows in its hair today. Yesterday they were blue, so Lisa didn't know if the dog was a male or a female. She needed to know. She took a sip of her coffee as the DJ on the radio sent the broadcast over to Janie at the news desk. It was the same news Lisa had heard twice this morning before dropping the kids off, so she turned it off. She watched all the regular stuff happen on the street and finished her coffee. She got up and put the empty mug into the dishwasher, then went on with her day.

The kids' bedrooms were unpacked. That part of Lisa's unpacking plan went the smoothest. She told the kids to unpack while Tim and his brothers brought the boxes in, and they did an incredible job. Neither of them wanted to do it at first, but when she told them they could set up their room any way they wanted, and if they didn't, she would do it the way she wanted, they jumped at the chance to have things their way. Any time they didn't have to do things the way their mom wanted, they jumped at the chance.

If you walked into their house, you wouldn't have known they moved in a little over a month ago unless you went down in the basement. On the first floor, they were unpacked. No boxes anywhere. Everything had its place—there were even pictures on the walls. The upstairs was more of the same—no boxes, everything in its spot, and pictures hanging on the walls. One of the good things about moving from a small duplex to a much larger house was that all of your stuff fit neatly, and it did for the most part. But they had a garage that they never parked the cars in at the duplex, so they used it for storage. At the new house, they said they wanted to start using the garage for the cars, which meant they needed to put everything they'd had in the old garage somewhere else. It led to a very full basement. Although they called it a finished basement, it was really only half-finished. The half that was not finished was used for the furnace and the hot water tank, and the electrical equipment, but there was also a lot of storage space.

Lisa went down and looked at the boxes and bins stacked up in the finished part of the basement, along with a futon they had bought specifically for the basement and the TV and Matthew's video game stuff that still needed to be set up. She had done a quick, fast job with the rest of the house and had been avoiding doing this. The amount of stuff to be put away was daunting.

Lisa exhaled and shook her head, looking at the stuff that needed to be put away. Part of her problem, she supposed, was that she wasn't the biggest fan of bugs, flies, and spiders, and although Tim assured her it was fine, she couldn't get past the fact that the unfinished part of the basement might be crawling with any or all of them. Lisa opened the door to the unfinished half of the basement and looked around. Above her hung a pull string. She tugged gently on it and illuminated that half of the basement. She didn't look up on purpose, knowing there would be cobwebs. The less she looked up, the better. She went in and looked around, deciding where everything was going to go. There was an area under the stairs where she thought the cardboard boxes would go. They were filled with various holiday decorations. The bulk of them were Christmas decorations, but there was one box marked Halloween and another marked Easter/Thanksgiving. They didn't use the decorations every year, but maybe they would now that they were in a house.

She backed up and went over to the other side of the unfinished area. There was even more room over there, but a lot of the space was already filled with Tim's tools and stuff. He had not organized those and just dropped them off when the stuff was brought in. She wasn't about to move any of that stuff around, but it was all off to one side and pushed against the wall. She was pretty sure the bins that were left would fit along the opposite wall. The bins were filled with stuff they hadn't looked at in years. Some of the bins were filled with the kid's stuff from when they were babies, others with the kids' school work. Not all of their school work, just the stuff they thought they should keep.

Then there was the bin of Tim's baseball card collection. He had at least four or five large bins full of the things. When he was a kid, he and his father would go to baseball card shows and shops almost every weekend, collecting the cards they thought were the best. He'd spent a good deal of money on the cards growing up. When Tim's father passed away a year or so after he and Lisa got married, he spent an entire day going through all of the old cards on the floor of the living room in the old duplex. Although Tim didn't collect baseball cards anymore or even look at the ones he already had, neither of them had the heart to sell the collection or get rid of it. Even with the move, when they were tossing box after box of things from the duplex, neither of them gave a second thought to the fact that the baseball card collection, all of it, was making the move with them.

Lisa gave one final look at the area where the bins would go and then went back out to the finished part of the basement.

"All right, here we go," she said under her breath. Lisa hefted the first box up. It was heavier than it looked, but she managed to lift it up, bring it through the door into the other part of the basement, and drop it down on the floor underneath the stairs. She continued like this until all of the boxes that needed to be back and hidden from sight were out of the finished part of the basement. Sweat dripped down her forehead, and she was breathing heavily. Lisa checked her phone, which she had put on the futon while she worked, so it didn't get cracked in the process of moving the heavy boxes and bins. It was almost 11:30. She'd been moving boxes back and forth for two hours.

A quick survey of the basement told her she was almost done. There were still a few boxes in the room, but they contained the wires and remotes and video game systems that were needed in this part of the basement. The TV sat on the floor, and the futon was tucked in the corner. It wasn't really set up for use just yet, but it was closer now than it was two hours ago. Lisa wasn't sure what she was going to do this afternoon, but she wanted to take a shower before she made that decision. She bunched up the bottom of her T-shirt and lifted it up to her face, wiping the sweat. Then Lisa went back to examine her stacking job, first looking at the stack of boxes under the stairs. She would have rather had all of these things in the same type of bin because they would stack a lot better, but it still looked neat and organized. The bins on the other side of the stairs looked neat and organized also. They were lined up along one wall, with Tim's tools lining the other wall. They would have to be something Tim did one of these weekends.

She admired her job for a few seconds and heard and faint buzzing noise above her. It made her jump. She didn't know if the sound was a bee or a fly or what, but she thought it was better to play it safe and ducked down low, hoping to stay out of the range of a bee's stinger. She looked up. It was only a couple of flies circling around the ceiling. Lisa looked around for a magazine or a piece of cardboard she could use to swat them, but there was nothing she could see.

"You're lucky this time," Lisa said, waving a finger at the flies.

She nodded and smiled at a job well done and went back through the finished part of the basement and up to the first floor. She got a drink of water and sipped it as she looked out the front window. It was a nice day, and she hadn't spent much time outside since the move. Part of her brain told her she should get back down in the basement and try to put the room together. Get the TV in the right spot, hook up all of the various electronics, and move the futon into position. Even if it wasn't perfect, at least the room would be usable. The other part of her wanted to sit outside on the front porch or the back patio and just enjoy the sunshine. Her stomach grumbled.

Lisa was about to turn around and go take a shower before she found herself some lunch when she saw movement across the street. It piqued her curiosity, and she couldn't help but turn back to her window, careful not to be seen. The young couple, the ones with the twin babies, were home again. They weren't usually home at this time of day—it was different from their normal routine. They got out of their car but didn't go to the back seats to get the babies. Maybe the kids were still at daycare or wherever they brought the kids in the mornings?

The guy got out first and slammed his door. Lisa couldn't hear, but it was clear he was yelling. The woman got out next, also yelling, and slammed her door too. They both walked up to the front door of their house, still arguing about something and yelling. The woman fumbled in her purse—it looked like she was looking for her keys but couldn't find them. Both were still yelling at each other—Lisa wished she could hear what they were saying. The guy put his hand on the woman's shoulder and moved her out of the way while she still looked through her purse. He had his keys in his hand already. He opened the front door and went in—the woman followed, shaking her head. The door slammed shut behind her so hard that the screen door flipped open a bit before closing and settling back into place.

"Well, that was interesting," Lisa said to herself as she took a long sip of water. She stayed at the window a few more minutes, waiting to see more. She half expected to see one of them storm out of the house, get into the car, and drive off. Someone would have to leave at some point to go get the twins. It reminded her that even though a marriage looked perfect, it didn't mean that was true.

When nothing happened across the street, Lisa moved on with her day. She made a mental note to check in on them later to see what time they went and got the kids; it was just something to entertain her a little bit more throughout the day. Lisa finished off her glass of water and left it on the kitchen counter, and then went up to take a shower.

After her shower, Lisa ate some lunch and decided it would be better to finish getting the basement organized, so she did that until it was time to pick Matthew and Olivia up from school. The little incident she watched across the street was all but forgotten until the kids were up in bed and Lisa and Tim were sitting on the couch watching the news before they went up to bed themselves.

"So, remember I told you about the couple across the street, with the twins?" Lisa said. She turned down the volume on the TV so it would be easier for them to talk.

"Sort of, yeah," Tim said. When he got home from work after being on the phone or in meetings all day, he wasn't usually in the mood for long discussions. He didn't mind hearing about her day, but he wasn't going to share too much about his own. That was fine with Lisa, who, after fifteen years of marriage and Tim working in the same office, although in different jobs, she had heard most of the stories he could tell about work already.

"Anyway, they usually leave the same time every morning.

They put the twins in the car, and then I think they take them to daycare or wherever." Lisa relayed her assumptions about the couple as if they were true.

"Oh yeah. I remember you telling me about them. What were their names again?"

"I have no idea. Anyway —" Lisa was about to go on, but Tim cut her off a smile on his face.

"You don't remember their names?"

"No. I don't know them. I've never met them." She swung her feet up on Tim's lap so she could look at him while they talked.

"But I thought you told me about the twins and daycare, and they both work or something like that."

"Well, I just…I figured that's what they were doing." Lisa waved her hand; this was not the point of the story. "Anyway, they came back today around lunchtime, I guess it was, without the kids. And they were screaming and yelling at each other out in the driveway. Then they slammed the car doors and went in the house and slammed the front door of the house too. It was crazy. They both looked really pissed. I didn't see them leave to go get the twins, but I'm sure they did at some point. I just missed it."

"Lisa." Tim just looked at her. He had that twinkle in his eye that told her he wasn't being too serious. She could see the sides of his lips curling, trying not to smile. Most people wouldn't have been able to pick up on it, but she could. It was the little something extra only someone who was talking to their best friend would really have been able to pick up on.

"What?" She looked back at him, not trying to hide the smile on her own face.

"You can't do that kind of stuff."

"Make sure my neighbors are okay, you mean? Watch out for others?"

"No, Lees. You can't spy on the neighbors. It's bad enough

you're learning their schedules — so-and-so does this at this time. And this guy does that then, and the people across the street take their kids to daycare. You have no idea what these people are doing. You're just watching them for no real reason."

"No. It's not for no reason. Remember John said that everyone in the neighborhood watches out for one another. I'm just doing my part." Lisa still had a smile on her face, and Tim was smiling too.

"Oh, I see," Tim laughed. "But still, we don't need you making up all sorts of stories about all of the neighbors. We've got enough to worry about around here without having to worry about made-up neighbor stories."

"Yeah, I know. You're probably right. I should probably just go introduce myself over there one of these days. Then I can stop making up stories about them. I'll know the real story. That might be even more fun."

"Listen," Tim said, and put a hand on her calf and looked at her, the smile gone from his face. "I know there are more people around us, and it's easy to fall into the habit of people watching. But I don't think it's always the best thing for people. That's why the old guy next door is so nosy. All he probably does is watch people from his windows. He doesn't have anything to do or anyone to tell him it's not a good idea. It's not good for him, and once you start doing stuff like that, it's hard to stop. Just promise me you'll try to do it less. Okay?"

She understood what he was saying. He didn't even need to give her that last little speech because she understood it in her head. She didn't want to become one of those people that was always interested in what everyone else was doing. She had always been independent, and she wanted to stay that way. In the duplex, they'd lived on a busy road and rarely saw their neighbors — here, it was the exact opposite. There were people to see and meet and watch, and it was easy just to hang out at the windows to see what people were doing. It was something new for her, and it was, at least at the moment, fun for her. But she didn't want to be that person. In her head, she decided she would try to cut back on the people watching. Noticing people going by the house when she was home was fine, but keeping track of the schedules of people she didn't even know was not okay.

"You're right. It's probably not the most healthy thing in the world to people watch from the windows of the house," Lisa said, looking at him.

Tim nodded. "I'm not mad. I think it's interesting. Especially the coming home in the middle of the day to fight. Not sure what's up with that."

Lisa nodded. They watched the end of the news and went up to bed around eleven. Lisa fell asleep, thinking about what the two people across the street could have been arguing about.

CHAPTER 4

"Hey Ben, wait up!" Twelve-year-old Harry Blighton called as he swung his leg over the frame of his bike and pushed off the sidewalk, then started to pedal. Ben never slowed down — it felt like he was always moving. If Harry walked out of the house, Ben would run, and if Harry ran, Ben would sprint. He was also moving faster. Harry wasn't exactly a slow mover himself; he and Ben were always the ones the teacher had to say "sit still" to during class. It was just that if Harry was running at one hundred miles per hour, it felt like Ben was going one hundred and ten miles an hour. There wasn't that much difference between the two, but Harry could always notice it, even if no one else could.

It was the summer, though. That meant no more teachers or anything much other than playing outside for the next few months. It was their favorite time of the year. Their bedtime got moved back, so they stayed out almost every day until it was almost dark, sometimes even later than that. But they were always together, Ben and Harry, Harry and Ben, the duo that would make summer great.

"Hurry up then, Harry!" Ben called back. He looked over his shoulder at Harry with a grin on his face.

Harry knew Ben wasn't going to slow down now. If anything, his request would only make Ben pedal that much faster. The only saving grace for Harry was he was taller and a little more athletic than Ben, meaning he could keep up with his more energetic friend. Once he got the bike going, he would be able to catch up.

Harry pedaled hard and caught up a little way down the road. They were both out of breath, and now that they were together, they both slowed down to recover.

"Asshole," Harry said between breaths.

The pair had just discovered the joy of swearing at each other when there were no adults around. They had heard their fathers do it with friends and just picked up on it. The curse words, forbidden at home and certainly in front of their mothers and sisters, were becoming more commonplace when it was just the two of them. Harry had to catch himself a couple of times from swearing in front of his mother when he banged his foot or his hand on the side of the kitchen table. If she heard him let those kinds of words out of his mouth, he would have caught a beating for sure.

"Well, maybe I'm not an asshole, and you're just a pussy, Harry," Ben said as they reached the end of the street and turned right onto Molly Lane.

"Shut up. You're an asshole and a pussy." The two of them laughed.

They didn't even have to talk about where they were going. Even though they'd just left Harry's house for a day of fun, they both knew where the first stop would be. There was a lean-to that they had put together the first week of summer out in the small patch of woods near the school. Ben's father had put a fence up around their backyard in the spring and had three extra fence panels left over. He told Ben he could have the panels and do whatever he wanted with them. Both Ben and Harry figured it wouldn't be much fun if they just used the panels at one of their houses, so they made three trips out into the woods with the panels and made their own space, away from everything else. Neither of them really wanted to call it a fort or a treehouse because it sounded a little kid-like, so they just called it The Spot. They had been spending the whole day every day there most of the time for the last few weeks. Harry even snuck a box of matches from his house, and they had made a campfire out in the woods the week before. It wasn't totally planned out because they didn't have anything to douse the fire, but it never got out of control, luckily for them.

The two turned left off of Molly Lane and onto Mayflower Road. At the end of Mayflower, they turned off the road and onto a small dirt path that led them through a field. The grass was tall. On the other side of the woods, the grass was always cut because it was closer to the school, but this side wasn't really used for anything, and the grass was just left to grow. It wasn't too bad in the fall, winter, or spring because there weren't too many bugs out, but the summer was a different story. The tall grass was like a magnet for the bugs, and although the path was wide, it was surrounded by them. Harry could hear them buzzing and flying through the waist-high grass on either side as he rolled his bike down the path. Sometimes a huge dragonfly would whip right by his head, so he had learned to ride with his mouth closed as they whizzed down the hill toward the woods.

"My dad wouldn't stop talking about Kennedy again last night," Ben said over his shoulder as they went down the hill.

"Oh yeah?" Harry said, his mouth mostly closed. He stopped pedaling. Ben did, too, and they just coasted.

"Yeah," Ben turned again. He didn't care about the bugs; they never flew into his mouth, and he didn't even seem like he was worried they might. "He loves the guy. He's certain that if he's the next president, we're all gonna be okay. I guess he's done all sorts of good stuff. My mom likes him too. They said they would never vote for Nixon."

They got to the bottom of the hill and skidded to a stop with the trees on either side of them. There was a sort of path they took most times when they got there, but it was covered with water today—there was no way they could get through on their bikes. It wasn't a big deal. A thunderstorm had come through the night before, and this, being the low spot in the area, was where the water was going to collect.

"Looks like we gotta walk 'em around," Harry said as he lifted his leg and got off his bike.

Ben did the same and followed Harry around the puddle. It was larger than he expected and looked more like what he always thought a swamp would look like than just a puddle. As they got a little further into the woods, the water was still there, just underneath the layer of grass and leaves. Harry thought the puddle was gone and then would catch the glistening and rippling of the water as it continued to stretch on. He kept walking his bike, looking back at Ben every so often to see if he was there, but he was never more than a step or two behind him.

The puddle seemed to dry up, and the packed path they usually took through the woods reappeared. Harry walked his bike onto the path and then looked back but couldn't even see the path they had turned off of. The puddle was much longer than he had thought. He kept walking but slowed down. The path through the woods was wide enough for them to ride next to each other, but they usually rode one in front of the other. But since they were walking, it made more sense to be side by side.

"My parents told me they're voting for Nixon no matter what. Said there was no way they would ever vote for a Democrat from Massachusetts," Harry said as they walked, the lean-to now in view though still a bit of a walk away.

"I don't really know what any of that means," Ben said with a laugh.

"Yeah, me neither. Whatever though. Whoever is president, we'll still be stuck in school with teachers telling us to sit down and do our homework. Nothing will really change for us, I guess." Harry laughed too. In the back of his mind, he knew

someday he would be old enough to vote, and then he would try
to care more about the stuff on the news that his parents talked
about. But until he was old enough to vote, he didn't know why
he should care about that kind of stuff. He would have the rest
of his life to worry about adult stuff. It didn't affect him now, so
he didn't care.

They arrived at their lean-to. Harry parked his bike against
the same tree he always did — Ben did the same. Then they flung
down their backpacks and kicked the remnants of the fire they
had started.

"I brought a surprise," Ben said as he sat down on one of
the rocks they had dragged through the woods to use as a seat
inside the lean-to. He unzipped his backpack and started digging
around.

"What is it?" Harry asked. He sat on the rock next to Ben
and tried to peek around his shoulder and into the bag. He knew
he wouldn't be able to see. Ben's bag was an eternal mess — it
always took him forever to find stuff in there during the school
year. And that was when the teacher and his parents were on him
every day to keep it organized. Now that it was summer, no one
cared about his organizational skills, and his bag was proof.

"You'll see. I found them in the desk drawer. There was a
bunch of them, but I just took two for now. I don't even think my
parents know they're in there," Ben said, still looking, his head
buried in his bag.

"What is it?" Harry repeated. Then after a moment of
watching Ben dig, he said, "Seriously, how much shit do you put
in there?"

"Fuck off," Ben said. "Ah! Here they are."

Ben pulled his head, then his hand, from his bag. Between
his fingers, he held two short white sticks. Both of Harry's parents
smoked — the whole house smelled like cigarettes most of the
time. Even when his parents cleaned the house because it was
a holiday or someone was coming over, the smell of the smoke

was never really gone. He knew what the sticks were right away. Although he'd never had a strong desire to smoke one, he often wondered what it would be like to light one up and breathe in the sharp, acrid-smelling smoke.

"You never tried one, right?" Ben asked.

"No," Harry shook his head. "You either, right?"

"No. My mom hates that my dad smokes. She would kill me, but you've seen my dad. He smokes all the time. He must have forgot he put these in the desk whenever he did that. There was a whole pack of them. If it's good, I'll go back and get us some more." Ben smiled.

"Did you grab more matches?" Harry asked, grabbing one of the cigarettes from his friend. He put it between his fingers and put the end with the filter in his mouth, pretending to puff on it.

"I did better than that." Ben flashed a smile and pulled out a small lighter.

"Was that with them?" Harry asked, leaning forward on the rock.

"Nah, my dad keeps like twenty of them in a drawer in the garage. There's no way he'd miss this one. I pulled it from the bottom of the pile too. We're all good."

Harry snatched the lighter from Ben and leaned forward, cupping his hand around the lighter and the end of the cigarette. Not because he had any idea what he was doing, but because he had seen his parents do it this way for as long as he could remember, so he knew it had to be the correct way to light a cigarette.

Harry lit one end of the cigarette and sucked in through the other end, not inhaling but just filling his mouth with smoke. He felt like it was lit and handed the lighter to Ben as he blew the smoke out of his mouth. He put his mouth back on the end of the cigarette and inhaled, feeling the burning sensation as smoke filled his mouth and then his lungs. He coughed just as Ben did the same, smoke spewing from his mouth and out his nose at the same time.

"Oh, man!" Harry said when he was able to catch his breath.

"Yeah, wow," Ben replied between the coughs.

"I guess the first few times it's like that, and then you get used to it," Harry said. He lifted his cigarette to his lips again and sucked, not as hard as last time. The burning sensation in his lungs returned, and he tried to hold the smoke in as long as he could. His eyes watered, and he looked over at Ben, who had already taken a small drag and let it out. Harry exhaled and coughed, but not as much as the first time.

"Hey, not so bad, Harry," Ben said. They leaned back a bit on the rocks and smoked, listening to the silence of the woods.

"It's not too bad now." Harry took another drag and blew the smoke out. There was no coughing now for either of them. Harry couldn't help but think about how cool he must look, smoking a cigarette while sitting on a rock in the middle of the woods. Why else would people smoke other than to look cool? That first drag was awful—he wouldn't want to do that again. But now, he was used to it.

"You think we're the first ones in our class to try this?" Ben looked over at his friend.

"Maybe, I don't know. Neil Packer?" Harry said the name of the only other kid in their class that he thought might have smoked before. His parents were both big smokers, like Harry's, and he was always bullying other kids. He was basically just an asshole all of the time. That was the only criteria Harry used.

"Nah, I don't think so. Only because he has such a big mouth. If he smoked, the whole class would know about it because he would never shut up about it."

The ash on Harry's cigarette got longer and longer, and he flicked it off. He was more than halfway finished with his. He looked at Ben's, and his was more than halfway gone too.

"Too bad you didn't bring that whole pack," Harry said.

"I know. I was just thinking that. You want me to fly back and get some more? My parents aren't home today. They're both at work."

"I'd go grab some of my parents', but they're both home. Yeah, go! I'll hold down the fort," Harry said, realizing he'd just referred to their lean-to as a fort. It would have made him feel like a little kid if not for the cigarette in his hand.

"All right. I'll try to get a full pack, but I'll get what I can. I'll be back soon." Ben handed Harry his nearly gone cigarette, ran, and hopped onto his bike. He rode off toward the main path.

Harry had a thought just as Ben was riding off. "Don't forget about the water!"

Ben raised his hand, letting Harry know that he'd heard him. Harry didn't know if Ben was going to try to ride through it or ride around it, but he wouldn't be surprised if Ben was dripping wet when he got back, hopefully with more cigarettes for them.

With Ben gone, Harry sat inside the lean-to and finished his cigarette. He felt much more comfortable by the end of the first one than he did after the first puff. He closed his eyes, and it felt like the world was spinning around him. *It must be the cigarette*, he thought. It was a weird feeling but also kind of cool. He opened his eyes and stood up. The dizzy feeling was still there, but on his feet with his eyes open, the effects weren't as bad.

Harry walked around the outside of the lean-to. There was grass growing in some areas up through the leaves that covered most of the ground, but the area around the lean-to was mostly all matted down from the constant traffic it had seen on a daily basis this summer.

Then he heard a rustling in the leaves behind him, coming from the direction Ben had just gone. Harry turned around and smiled, expecting to see Ben walking his bike back, dripping wet. There was no one there, but he heard more rustling coming from the other direction, and he turned around again. Still nothing.

Harry was sure it was just the cigarettes making him feel weird. The leaves probably rustled all the time, and he just didn't notice it because he was there with Ben, and they were always talking about something. But he was sure he had heard the sound of someone coming through the woods. That was a sound he'd heard lots of times, and it always sounded the same. Even in summer, there were enough leaves on the floor of the woods that someone walking through them would make an unmistakable sound.

Still feeling dizzy, Harry leaned on a nearby tree for support. His head snapped around. There it was again. He focused as hard as he could on what he saw around him—a squirrel, a bird, anything that might rustle the leaves like that. But there was nothing.

"Hey there," a voice called from behind him. Harry turned to face whoever had called out to him. An older man was walking toward him from the direction of the main path. Out of reflex, Harry dropped the cigarette butts that were still in his hand and was quick to cover them with his foot, stomping them out. He would have done it with any adult coming along—the fact that he didn't know this man didn't change how he should act.

"Uh, hi." Harry was unsure of what to do, but his father always said to respect his elders. The old man was still far enough away from him that he couldn't see him as clearly as he would have liked to. Plus, the hat on his head made it hard to see his face. He didn't know if this guy was someone he knew, or maybe someone his parents knew. It could be anyone—someone from the neighborhood or just someone walking by. He had no idea but remained calm, more worried about the fact that he smelled like cigarettes and his light-headedness than anything else.

The old man continued walking toward Harry, but without saying anything. Harry thought he saw the man smile as he took slow steps toward the lean-to. Harry needed to break the silence.

"Did you see my friend Ben on your way in here? He just

left; he should be right back," Harry said.

The old man didn't respond, just shook his head and continued to walk closer to him.

A fly flew past Harry's head; he waved a hand at it and squinted at the old man. He was closer now, and Harry could see the white hair underneath the hat that looked just a little too small for the man's head. A few more flies buzzed around his head, and he waved a hand at them again.

"Do I know you?" Harry said, now feeling more nervous than before. The guy was getting closer and not really talking. Why did he need to be there? Harry took a step back.

"No, I don't think so. I was just passing through," the old man said. His voice was gravelly, and the words came out slow and measured.

It looked like the guy was smoking. Harry could see a dark cloud of smoke escape the man's mouth when he spoke. He didn't see anything in his hands, but he was still far enough away. He could just be holding a cigar or something so that Harry couldn't see it from where he was. More flies flew past him, and Harry waved at them again. Where did they come from?

"I don't know you, Harry, but it's okay. Everything will be fine," the man said.

At first, Harry didn't catch the fact that the old guy had used his name, but when he realized it, it was too late.

"What did you say?" Harry asked. He tried to back up another step, but there was a tree behind him—he had been backing up as the man drew closer without realizing it. More flies swarmed around him. The man's legs were gone. Harry stared in shock. The man was disintegrating right in front of him. Harry squinted, trying to see what was happening. There were more flies around him, and he tried to lift his hand to swat them away again, but his hand wouldn't move. He looked down and saw that his body was wrapped in flies from his knees to his chest. How had he not noticed? He pushed hard against them, but the millions of small bugs pushed against him, and he couldn't move. He looked back at the man, now just a head as the rest of him turned into flies.

Harry could feel the pressure of the flies against his body — they pressed into him. He could feel them against his legs, his stomach, his chest. They surrounded him and made their way further up his body. He felt them against the skin of his neck and around his ankles. The noise was so loud he could barely hear his own screaming. He lifted his head up toward the sky, trying to keep the flies away from his face. The rest of his body was paralyzed, covered on all sides by the flies. They crawled closer and closer to his face.

"No, no, no. Please," Harry begged when they crawled along his chin. He felt them push their way into his mouth and up over his head. He closed his eyes, but the flies forced them open, and then he could feel them on his eyeballs, crawling in his ears, covering his head and forcing him down. There was nothing he could do; he couldn't fight back, so he just let it happen. The flies covered him, and then he saw nothing. Heard nothing. Felt nothing.

CHAPTER 5

Of all the holidays, Lisa liked Halloween the least — or she did now that she had kids. Before kids, she didn't really mind Halloween. If she had wanted to, she could get dressed up — there were always adult Halloween parties they were invited to, but they didn't have to go. Sometimes she liked putting on Halloween costumes, but most Halloweens before kids were spent sitting on the couch with a bowl full of candy by the front door and getting up whenever the doorbell rang. When she was done handing out candy, the bowl was still more than half full, and the next three weeks were spent either eating all of the leftover candy or trying to figure out a way to get rid of it all.

After kids, it became her least favorite holiday. The kids usually got hyped up for it, which was never a good thing, although as Matthew got older, he seemed less and less interested in dressing up. It was always on the 31st, which meant she still had to take the kids out trick-or-treating even if it was Wednesday night. They usually had school unless the day gloriously fell on a Saturday. That meant they had to come home and do homework right away, which they didn't do on any other day. Then she had to find something quick for them to eat so they weren't walking around cranky and hungry. And last but not least, her kids never chose easy Halloween costumes. There was always make-up, or hair that needed to be done, or elaborate costumes that took time to get the kids into. After all that was done, Tim would get home from work just in time to take them out, meaning Lisa could stay home and hand out candy. But getting to that point was a lot of work.

That had all been in the duplex, of course. Two weeks before Halloween, she was already feeling different about the holiday in her new home. The kids were settled into school, and both of them were bringing home work with A's and B's on it, so that made her relax a little about everything. Before the move, they told themselves as long as the kids made a good switch, it was worth it. So far, both kids had made new friends, and now that the good grades were starting to roll in, they both felt they made the right decision. But that wasn't the reason Lisa was starting to think about Halloween differently. One Sunday afternoon, after the Bears football game ended around three, she and Tim noticed most of the neighbors out in their front yards working, although they couldn't tell what they were doing. The Ewings usually went out for dinner as a family on Sunday night. When the family left the house, the neighbors were still working, and when they got home, they saw what everyone had been doing. They were decorating their houses for Halloween.

"I guess this is what they were all doing this afternoon," Tim said as he inched the car forward down the street.

"I guess so. I've never seen a whole neighborhood do this much work for Halloween. Usually, it's just a house or two," Lisa said, her face against the glass of the window, looking at all the different decorations.

"Look at that house," Matthew said from the back seat.

Lisa looked back as Matthew pointed to a house just around the corner from theirs. At least three zombies inhabited the front yard, pushing their way out from under tombstones, and another three standing up on the grass. Complete with strobe lights, it offered a freaky image for someone with a bit of imagination.

Tim turned the car slowly onto Molly Lane.

"Wow, look at that." Olivia pointed to the house across the street, the one with the couple with the twins that Lisa had still not met yet. Thirty or forty bats hung from their trees, again illuminated by multiple strobe lights to give it that little extra scare factor. Some of the bats dropped quickly from the trees and then went back up—it would have been scary if you went up to the house trick or treating. "Mom, Dad, we've got to get some Halloween decorations. Please. Let's make our house the scariest one!"

"Oh, I don't know," Lisa said. She still wasn't sold on Halloween, but seeing the other houses decorated was kind of neat.

They pulled into the driveway, and she noticed John Holland's house was one of the few not decorated. She understood why it wasn't, but his house looked out of place now. Then she realized her own house was also not decorated. She gave Tim a look as he pulled into the garage and put the car in park.

"It might be cool to be one of the scary houses," Tim said, returning her look with that half-smile of his. "Come on, Mom. It'll be cool," Tim said, looking back over his shoulder at the house across the street, then back at her, the teasing smile on his face. He knew she hated when he called her mom.

"Oh, all right. We have Halloween decorations in the basement, but nothing like these. I guess I can go get some stuff to decorate with while you're at school tomorrow," Lisa said.

"No!" Both kids shouted at the same time.

"We'll go with you, Mom," Olivia said.

"Yeah, no offense, Mom. You're just not the best 'cool scary decoration' person. I think you might need some help with this. Is there one of those party stores around here? They always have cool Halloween stuff," Matthew added, looking a little too excited about the prospect of decorating his front yard for Halloween.

Lisa laughed. "Hey, I think I could do scary on my own if I really tried. But that's fine. I'll wait for you guys, and we can go right after I pick you up tomorrow. Then Tuesday after school, we can work on getting all of the decorations up. Sound like a plan?"

Both kids nodded, and Tim laughed. They all climbed out of the car and went into the house with their leftovers from dinner.

***

After she dropped the kids off at school the next day, Lisa sat down to eat her breakfast. She wanted to take Tim's advice and meet the neighbors instead of just watching them, but it was easier said than done. She was hungry by the time she got home from dropping them off, and she needed to eat. It just happened to be the time that a lot of people went by the house in the mornings, so she fell back into the same routine of eating and watching people as they started their own morning routine. She really did try to stop, but with the radio on, there was not much else for her eyes to do, and she just looked out the window while she ate. She justified it in her head by telling herself she wasn't watching them—she was just looking out the window when these things happened to be going on.

She searched on her phone for the name of the party store so she would know where she was going later. It was only about three miles away, but she also found one of those seasonal Halloween stores that was a few more miles away. The party store would have been good enough, but she thought the Halloween store would have a lot more stuff for them to choose from. If this was going to turn into a competition for the kids, she wanted to give them the best chance to have the scariest house on the block.

Lisa smiled to herself as she locked her phone, the address of the Halloween store saved in her Map App.

"No!" Lisa heard someone shout from outside. Even with the windows closed, the shout was as clear as if the person was in the house. She held still. Who had said that?

"No! No!" she heard again. It was definitely someone outside. Lisa went over to the window and moved the curtains to the side just a bit so she could get a look outside. She realized she was doing it again, but she was just checking on her neighbor.

John Holland was out in his backyard. Lisa had not seen him back there once in the two months they'd lived in the house. His hand was up against his ear, and the old man was pacing, his right arm swinging back and forth while his left hand was pressed against his ear. She couldn't tell for sure if he was on the phone or not, but from this distance, it looked like it.

She watched him for a few minutes, his right arm swinging back and forth as though he was imploring whoever he was talking with to reason with him. Almost like he was explaining something to them, but John kept getting more and more frustrated as time passed. He didn't shout again, but he became more animated. Lisa was worried for the old man, and she wondered if whoever he was talking to knew how old and frail the guy was. Could it be a telemarketer or one of those IRS scams? She watched for another minute, deciding that if this continued much longer, she would go over there and talk to whoever was on the other end of the phone.

"I said no! Not this time," John said, louder than any of his other shouts. He marched back toward his house from the middle of his backyard. He went into the house, his hand still against his ear.

Lisa still wasn't sure exactly what she had just witnessed. It could have been anything, really. One of those scams, or even a call from a friend or relative—there was really no reason for her to read too much into it other than that. She was sure she had yelled at someone on the phone before, and maybe people had overheard it, but that didn't make it their business. The fact that she overheard John yelling in his backyard on the phone didn't make it her business. For all she knew, he did it all the time, and this was just the first time she happened to catch it — they were the new family in the neighborhood, after all.

The event stuck with her for the rest of the morning but then was gone from her head by lunchtime.

***

The next few days went by without much incident for Lisa. She didn't even think about the strange incident with John Holland. It just blended in with some of the other things that happened in the neighborhood from time to time. The kids picked out Halloween decorations, and they set them up in the front yard as a family. They even got a wave from a few neighbors, including John, who was out checking his mail as they worked. The final result was not the best in the neighborhood, but it was better than nothing, and it helped Lisa get more into the spirit of the holiday.

The Ewings felt more like a part of the neighborhood with every day that passed.

A few days after the Halloween decorations went up, Lisa was out in the front yard raking the leaves. They never had to worry about raking leaves at the duplex. They didn't own it, and the owners wanted to make sure the yard was taken care of, so they hired a lawn company to mow the lawn in the spring, summer and fall, get the leaves in the fall, and shovel and plow in the winter. They didn't mind doing these things and would help out as much as they could, but it was good to know if they didn't want to do it, they didn't have to.

It was still early in the morning, and she looked up when she heard footsteps across the street. The couple was loading the twins in the car. Lisa had still not introduced herself to them, but she had seen them a few times. Her eyes met the wife's, and they waved and smiled at each other. If it had been a different time, Lisa might have introduced herself to them, or maybe they would come over to say hello, but the couple had been there with two little kids getting ready to go out somewhere. It wasn't easy.

And if they were both trying to get to work on time, they didn't have much time for more than a wave at this point anyway. But a wave was good enough for Lisa. She had a friend that lived close by and didn't necessarily need more friends. The wave was enough for her to feel more comfortable.

She returned her attention to the leaves. In retrospect, she should have raked right before getting the decorations down on the front yard, but she did her best to rake around the evil doctor and his bloody nurse, piling up all of the leaves in one corner of the front yard. When most of the leaves were up, Lisa got some brown paper yard waste bags from the garage. The town would pick up three bags a week during the fall to help residents get rid of their leaves. There were lots of good things about Medville, and the way the town helped the people keep their yards looking nice was certainly one of them.

Lisa opened the first bag and set it on the grass. At first, she tried to lift the leaves up into the bag, but it fell over or closed up on her each time she went to put more in. So she laid it on its side and pushed leaves in until it looked to be about half full. With weight in the bottom of the bag, she could stand it up, and it would stay open without falling over. She filled the first bag and brought it down the curb. Then, she laid the second bag down on the ground and knelt to push the leaves in like she did with the first. Then, she heard a familiar but disturbing noise.

"No!"

It was John Holland again. Lisa knew it without even looking up. She tried to ignore him and continued filling the bag, but she heard it again.

"No! No!" John said again. Now that she was outside, she could hear just how loud he was yelling. There must have been other people who heard him, either in their own houses or outside. This was the second time she had witnessed this, but it couldn't have been the only two times this happened. Someone else must know about this.

Lisa couldn't see much of Holland's backyard from where she was in her own yard, but she didn't need to see to have a pretty good idea of what was happening. He was probably back there, holding a phone or something to his ear, shouting and swinging his arm back and forth. It sounded the same. Lisa assumed it looked the same too.

Lisa continued to fill the bag, but all of her attention was focused on listening to John. She was outside this time, so maybe she could hear more than just the yelling, she thought. She stopped moving because the rustling of the leaves made it difficult to hear, but she heard nothing else. No more yelling, nothing at all. She resumed her work, assuming whatever she had heard was just a shorter version of the conversation she'd heard a few days before. Then a loud metal clang made her jump. The neighborhood was quiet most of the time, and the loud noise had come out of nowhere.

Lisa held still again, listening. It was clear the clang had come from John's backyard — there was no doubt in her mind. She didn't really know what to do. Part of her, the part that wanted to take Tim's advice, knew she should just leave the old man alone, finish her work, and go back in the house. John could do whatever he wanted in his backyard — she didn't have to give approval or even know about it. The other part of her, the new Lisa, wanted to know what was going on in his backyard. Also, and she wasn't just using this to justify her curiosity, John wasn't a young-looking guy. She didn't know him that well, didn't have any idea how old he was, but it was clear just by looking at him that he wasn't the kind of person who should be doing hard work in his backyard by himself.

It happened again, a loud clang followed by a dragging sound, almost like he was shoveling. She waited a minute, maybe more, and it happened again. It was too much for Lisa. Her curiosity was going to win out. She left her rake and a half-full bag of leaves laying on the front yard, brushed her hands off on her pants, and went inside the house. She thought about kicking her shoes off at the door, her own rule, but decided she would vacuum later that day and just went into the kitchen. She stood up on the far side of the table away from the windows and crouched down, peering through the window into John's backyard. He did have a shovel, an old metal one with a wooden handle. It looked a lot like the one Lisa remembered her father having when she was growing up. It had a rounded front, and Holland was right up against the side of his house, digging into the grass. She couldn't see how far down he had dug, but it couldn't have been very deep. He stood in his bathrobe and slippers, shovel in hand, digging. She watched him plunge the spade of the shovel into the ground, push down on the side with his slipper-clad foot, and then lift the dirt out and dump it into a small pile behind him.

Lisa found herself almost unable to move. What she was watching was not normal, but she didn't know what to do. She thought about calling the police, but there was no real reason to do that. If she had known the number of one of Holland's children, she would have called them, just to let them know. If she knew any of the other neighbors a little better, she would have asked them if this was normal behavior for John, but she didn't really know anyone. Instead, she just watched. Dig, dig, and then every so often, the scraping sound of the metal shovel against the concrete foundation of the house.

He moved along the house as he dug, almost as if he was digging a trench around his house. Lisa guessed that was fine. There wasn't really a problem with it, except for the fact that he was doing all of this work in his bathrobe and slippers. She continued to watch. For forty-five minutes, he dug, and for forty-five minutes, she watched the old man dig. When he decided to go in, she had no idea if he was done or if he just needed a break, but there was a good-sized hole in his backyard.

She had originally thought it was a trench he was digging, but when she moved up to Matthew's bedroom to get a better view, she realized it was a perfect square. It was fascinating, scary, and confusing at the same time. *Why is he doing it?* Lisa was interested now. She knew Tim would find it interesting—at least she hoped he would. They wouldn't mention it to the kids, though. If there was something wrong with John Holland, she didn't want them to worry about him.

***

When Lisa and the kids came home from school later that afternoon, Matthew went right to his room. She was never sure of the order of things, but he listened to music, played games on his phone or on his laptop, and did his homework. She didn't really care when it got done, as long as everything was done by six-thirty when Tim arrived home from work so that they could all eat together.

Every afternoon Lisa would start to think about what she was going to make for dinner. Growing up, she was lucky enough to have a family that ate dinner together every single night, and she was glad she was able to give her family the same experience. They liked being together, so it was easy to get them all to come together at dinner time. Sometimes Tim would call ahead and tell her he was going to be late for dinner. Sometimes they waited for him, but most times on those nights, they just couldn't hold out and ate without him. It was one of those nights. Lisa didn't mind. She realized he was the only one in the family bringing in money, and if he needed to work late every once in a while, it wasn't going to be a big deal to her. It was all part of what she signed up for, and she'd known it ahead of time. If Lisa could pick the best night for Tim to work late, spaghetti night would be her choice. It was easy for her to make him a plate, wrap it in plastic wrap, and throw it in the fridge for later.

The kids had eaten, and Olivia was up in bed getting ready to go to sleep around eight when Tim finally got home. Matthew was on the couch in the living room watching some science TV show.

"Hey, Dad," Matthew said.

From her chair in the reading room, Lisa heard the door to the garage shut and then heard Tim kick off his shoes. She put down her book, went to the fridge and pulled out the plate of spaghetti, put it in the microwave, and set it for two minutes.

"Hey, Matty. What's up? How was the day?"

"It was fine." Matthew gave his usual response to how the day went. If you asked him more specific questions, he sometimes surprised you with a more specific answer, but even then, it was rare.

Tim went across the living room and into the kitchen. "I can already smell it. You know how much I love your sauce, right?" Tim said.

Lisa smiled at him as he walked up to her and slid his arms around her waist, kissing her gently on the lips. She smiled and looked up at him.

"You know I love when you work late on spaghetti night. It's the easiest to reheat." She kissed him on the lips again, the sound of the microwave filling the quiet kitchen.

"Well, I'm glad it's quick to reheat because I'm starving," Tim said. He went to the fridge and pulled out a bottle of beer and the parmigiana cheese, then got himself a fork and a napkin and left everything but the beer on the table. He opened the beer and took a sip. "So, how was the day?"

"It was fine," Lisa repeated Matthew's answer, then kept her voice down so Matthew wouldn't overhear her. "Actually, it was interesting."

"Oh really?"

Tim raised his eyebrows when he spoke. Interesting was a word Lisa never used to describe her day. Maybe Tim would find it interesting. Either that or she was going to hear about her past time of keeping an eye on people in the neighborhood.

"Yeah, it was, actually." The microwave beeped, and Lisa opened it and grabbed the plate. She brought it over to the table and sat down with him while he ate.

"What happened then?" Tim asked as he sprinkled the cheese over his steaming hot pasta.

"Well, okay," Lisa started and figured she give him the play-by-play as best she could then tell him why she was watching John Holland dig a hole. "I was outside raking leaves and heard this crazy sound, but I wasn't sure what it was. It was like a metallic sound, you know?"

Tim nodded and took a few bites of his spaghetti; he was looking at her and nodding. Either he was into the story or just pretending to be while he ate.

"Anyway, I didn't know what it was, so I went looking around. Turns out it was John Holland digging a hole in his backyard."

"Really? He's so old, though. What was he digging it for?"

"Tim, he was digging in his bathrobe and slippers." Lisa looked at him. "I know you said it was probably a bad idea to keep watching the neighbors all the time, but I was worried something was wrong with him, so I just kinda kept an eye on him while he dug. At some point, he just stopped and went inside."

"Really?" Tim put his fork down and took another sip from the beer bottle. "Are you sure he wasn't in just regular old guy clothes that looked like a bathrobe?"

"No, I'm sure. I saw him in the same thing the other day when the mail came. We were both out getting it at the same time. He shuffled out in the slippers and the bathrobe and shuffled back."

"Jeez, that's a little weird," Tim said, and shook his head.

"I know, right." Lisa laughed. "I wish I knew him better. Or we knew the number for his kids just so we could tell someone, you know. I do kinda feel bad watching him like that, but what else was I supposed to do, you know?"

"No, no. I agree. You know I would tell you if I thought otherwise. He should have someone keeping an eye on him, even if you're just watching from afar. If something happened, at least you could call him an ambulance. Maybe I can talk to him this weekend, get the number for his kids in case something ever does happen. There might be something going on."

Tim looked worried. She couldn't tell if he was worried for John or for her. She was, after all, home by herself all day. It was one thing if he assumed everyone that lived around them were good people, but they didn't know John for more than the minute or so that she talked to him the day they moved in, and then the occasional wave after that. Who knew what was actually going on inside his head? She was more nervous now about the old man than she had been earlier.

"I'm sure he wouldn't hurt anyone, though," Lisa said, trying to convince herself as much as she was Tim.

"I'm sure he's a nice guy, Lees. I'm not saying he's not, but we don't know what's going on with him. I'm worried for you more than him, really. I'm not here during the day. You've heard about those people in nursing homes—they don't really know what's going on and end up attacking a nurse or something. It's not that they are violent people. Something just happens to their brain. I'll see if I can talk to him this weekend. Until then, just don't let him in the house or anything, and come inside if you see him outside. Please."

Lisa nodded. Tim had done a good job of making her nervous. He would try to talk to John this weekend, but she was going to be a nervous wreck until then.

CHAPTER 6

"Hi, there!"

Lisa jumped and snapped her head around at the sound of the voice behind her. She was adjusting the Halloween decorations after dropping Matthew and Olivia off at school and hadn't seen anyone outside when she pulled in the driveway.

"Oh, I'm sorry. I didn't mean to scare you." It was the mother of the twins across the street. Lisa recognized her immediately. She looked young from across the street but seemed even younger now that Lisa could see her more clearly. They must have gotten married right out of college or something and then got pregnant right after that, Lisa thought, her imagination running wild again.

"It's okay. I'm Lisa. Lisa Ewing." Lisa stuck out her hand to her neighbor.

"Marie Shaw." She shook Lisa's hand. "My husband is Mike. You've probably seen us with Emily and Avery, our twins."

"I have," Lisa smiled. "They must keep you busy. Tim is my husband, and Matthew and Olivia are my kids, but they're a little bit older than yours."

"Yes, definitely," Marie laughed, and Lisa could see the genuine smile on her face. "Well, I always feel really bad. We try to wave whenever we see you out, but with the twins, we felt like we never have a second to come over and introduce ourselves. Mike took them to daycare, and I'm working from home today, so I figured I'd come over and say hi finally."

"Oh, that's so nice of you. I really appreciate it."

A car drove by, and Marie turned and waved. Lisa followed suit but didn't know who she was waving at.

"People in this neighborhood are so nice. I don't know who you've met, but they are all really nice." Marie turned back to look at Lisa.

"Oh, not that many, actually. I've been so busy between getting unpacked and getting the kids settled in school. It's been crazy. The last few weeks, though, I've started to feel a little more settled. We've only met John Holland," Lisa pointed her thumb at John's house, "And now you."

"Well, that's a good start." Marie squinted one of her eyes just a little bit. Lisa wasn't sure if something was in her eye, but she didn't know her well enough to know why she squinted like that. "It's hard right now. People aren't out very much in the fall and winter, but when the weather gets nice, people are outside all the time. We haven't lived here that long either, but I feel like we know so many more people already."

"Oh really? How long have you been here?" Lisa liked Marie so far, and it would be good to have a neighbor across the street that she liked.

"It will be two years in December, so not all that long. But like I said, you get to know people so quick once the spring and summer roll around."

"Awesome. If we have a cookout this summer, we'll be sure to invite you," Lisa said.

"Yes. Definitely," Marie answered. "I've got to actually do some work since I haven't even looked at my emails since yesterday at three. It was so nice to meet you, Lisa."

"Yes. You too, Marie. Please don't be a stranger." Lisa smiled as Marie crossed back to her side of the street.

"I won't. You either."

Lisa shook her head, went up to the front door of the house, and let herself in. She was happy with herself, although she hadn't really done anything. She'd met the neighbor across the street, and she was nice. Maybe the next time she talked to Marie, she could tell her, or ask her, about John Holland. It was good to have someone she knew in the neighborhood that wasn't a strange old man. A few more chats like that, Lisa thought, and she would have a new friend to add on all of her social media sites.

***

Later that afternoon, Lisa was putting laundry away when she heard the now all too familiar yell of John Holland in his backyard. She was upstairs in the master bedroom, which was on the opposite side of the house from Holland's property, and she could still hear him. She took a small pile of Matthew's clothes and went into his room, threw the clothes down on the bed, and went over to his window. Very carefully, she lifted up one of the closed blinds—not a lot, just enough for her to see out and into Holland's backyard. At least this time, he was dressed—jeans and a sweatshirt, but what she always called a grandpa sweatshirt. No hood, and although she couldn't see from here, she was willing to bet there was a small sports logo on the left breast. There was one other major difference, and it made her worry the most. John did not have his hand up against the side of his face. Instead, he had both hands on his shovel, digging again in his backyard.

"No! No," he yelled into the air as his shovel struck down into the earth.

Lisa watched with only one thought running through her head—was there ever a phone? The other two times she had witnessed the yelling, his hand was up against his face. It looked like he was holding a phone to his ear, but she never saw one. The way society was right now, her mind just placed the phone in his hand because what else could it have been? But did she ever see an actual phone? Any sort of device in his hand? She didn't think so.

He never looked up, so she was sure he didn't know she was watching him. She kept an eye on him. The old man was losing his mind. She didn't know him that well, but it was the only explanation for what he was doing. He was making the small square of dirt in his backyard larger and more rectangular in shape. He had already dug from the corner closest to the Ewing house, about two-thirds of the way across his house along the foundation, and now he was digging back away from the house. All the grass that had been there was gone—it was just a layer of dirt. He lived on a half-acre lot, and right in the middle of his yard was a large maple tree. He was nearly there.

"No! I don't want to!" John Holland yelled up into the sky, then he stopped and turned. He looked right at Lisa. Even at this distance, she could see his eyes. They looked right at the lifted-up blind and straight into hers.

Lisa jumped back, dropping the blind. She regretted it instantly. If she hadn't moved, he might have thought it was just the blind hanging funny—there was no way he could actually see her from the ground. He just saw the blind up. But now that the blind had dropped, he knew someone was watching him. She chanced another peek, this time barely lifting the blind. John was walking toward his front yard, shovel still in his hand, and he did not look happy. Was he coming to her house? Why was he still carrying the shovel?

Lisa left Matthew's bedroom and crept to the top of the stairs. She couldn't see the front door, and no one looking in the house could see her from where she stood, but she could hear if someone came up on the front porch or knocked on the door. She held her body still. The house wasn't that old and didn't creak or groan like an older house would, but she didn't want to take any chances. She already knew she wasn't going to answer the door. If John ever asked her what she was doing, she would act like she had no idea what he was talking about. As soon as she thought John was gone, though, she would call Tim. Hopefully, she could convince him to come home early.

There was a loud bang on the front door—three bangs, actually. He used the shovel to knock on the front door—the metallic sound of the spade hitting the door that hard was unmistakable. Lisa held her breath and waited. The guy had a shovel; there was no way she was going to answer the door.

Nothing. Silence. Then he banged again, three times like before, but louder.

"Who's home?" John called from behind the front door. Lisa didn't move. She barely breathed as he stood just outside her home.

"Lisa? Are you home?" Holland said.

She heard the niceness in his voice. It was not the screaming, yelling voice she'd heard coming from his backyard. It was the voice of the nice, nosy old man she met the day they moved in. She wanted to believe he was that same person, but she didn't know for sure and wasn't about to open the door to a guy with a shovel.

"You know, I keep a pretty good eye on everything, Lisa, and I know you dropped the kids off at school earlier, and I didn't see you go back out. I know Tim left for work this morning, and he hasn't come home so that just leaves you," John said.

Lisa took a deep breath in and put her hand over her mouth. She wasn't the only person in the neighborhood that kept track of everyone's schedules.

There was silence again. Did he leave? The silence continued. Lisa was about to move, thinking John was gone when the shovel slammed against the door three more times. She couldn't see the door, but she wondered what the front of it might look like after this.

"I don't know if you're hearing me or not, Mrs. Ewing," the nice John voice continued, but it was a marked distinction to the shovel slamming against the door. "I don't know if you saw me outside. I just came over to say you don't have to worry about me. I'm okay. I'm sure if you saw the shoveling and the yelling and stuff, you might think something was wrong with me, but it's not. I'm okay. I'm having some work done in the backyard, and the doctor told me I need to get some more exercise, so I figured I'd help out, doing as much of the work as I can."

Another long silence. Lisa didn't know what to think. He didn't sound crazy. Lisa second-guessed herself. She couldn't be sure he had the shovel now. Part of her wanted to open the door to check. That was the wrong decision though, she knew that much.

"Okay. I guess that's all I have to say then."

His feet clopped against the wood of the front porch as she heard him leave. She wanted to go back to the window and look down at his backyard to see if he gave another look up at the window. See if he was really still carrying the shovel. If he wasn't, it would change the whole dynamic of this situation. John didn't sound crazy. He didn't sound like a guy who had been yelling up into the sky while he dug up most of his backyard. At the door, he didn't act like the guy who a few days earlier had been outside yelling in his bathrobe while he started to dig up his backyard. No, the guy who was just at her front door sounded a lot like the guy she met the day they moved in. Maybe a little too nosy. Maybe he knew a little bit too much about the people that lived around him. But Lisa could relate to that—she knew a little bit more about the people who lived around her than she should have too. If the situation were reversed, she probably would have known who was home and who wasn't at most houses in view of her own. She felt a lot like John that way. The man she saw out the window and the man talking at her front door did not match.

She swung her legs around and sat on the top step of the stairs. What she really wanted to do was go back to the window and have another look, but she knew she couldn't. Not without him seeing her again. So she stayed there. She didn't move for at least ten minutes.

The sound of the shoveling in his backyard returned, along with the yelling. Now she could move. She went downstairs and got her cell phone, then tried Tim, but there was no answer. He rarely answered his phone during the workday — he had no way of knowing what was going on here. Lisa knew some wives who would get angry at their husbands if they didn't answer the call from them, even when he was at work. And she knew some guys who would expect their wives to answer no matter what as well. Lisa was not like that. She knew Tim would probably not answer his phone. If he saw it was from her and didn't answer, there was usually a reason. She also knew she didn't need to leave a message. When Tim saw the missed call, he would call her back. That was really all there was to it. It was just the way it always was with them. It took trust, but she didn't have to worry about if he knew she called or not. He would know she called, and he would call her back as soon as he could. That was the way it always was.

But today was different. Today freaked her out, so she stood in the middle of the kitchen and called his phone again. If she wanted to, she could have leaned over the table and looked outside to see what John Holland was up to. But she didn't want to now. Her urge to keep track of everyone in the neighborhood was suppressed a little bit.

There was still no answer on Tim's phone. Not surprising. She ended the call as Tim's voice-mail kicked over. She switched over to a text message and typed one out to him. *Call me as soon as you get a chance.* She was about to hit send and then added one more thing just so he knew, at least a little, about what was happening. *John Holland.* She stuck the phone in her pocket and tried to get back to work.

She brought more clean laundry up from the laundry room and folded it, and put it in the appropriate place, but her thoughts kept drifting back to next door. It was easy when every few minutes, John yelled "No!" at the top of his lungs. Whenever she went into Mathew's room to put some clothes away, her eyes drifted toward the window. Each time she had to stop herself from taking another look outside. Leave it alone, she said to herself over and over again. Eventually, all of the clothes were put away. Then, she returned downstairs to do something she rarely did; sit on the couch and watch TV.

It wasn't that she never watched TV. It was just that she tried to save those kinds of things for when the family was all there. The kids were at school, and Tim was at work. When they were all together, she would sit and watch TV with them. If they weren't home, there was enough other stuff she could be doing. But she needed to get her mind off John, so she changed her normal routine and flipped the TV on, hoping to find something that would catch her interest. After flipping around a few stations, and checking her DVR and finding nothing she wanted to watch at the moment, she realized it might be a futile effort. She was about to give up on the TV situation when her phone rang.

Lisa pulled out her phone—it was Tim. "Hey," Lisa said after putting the phone up to her ear.

"Hey. Is everything okay?" Tim asked, worry in his voice.

"Well, I guess it's okay now," Lisa said. "John was outside digging and yelling again and—"

"Did he see you or something?" Tim asked. He knew her too well and figured she wouldn't have called him if the old man was just out in his backyard.

"Yeah. I was up in Matthew's room putting away clothes, and I heard the yelling again and just looked outside for a second when I heard him. But the blinds were down, so I just lifted one up a little bit, and when I did, he saw me."

"That's not really that bad. At least he knows we know he's acting weird."

"No, but then he came over," Lisa said.

"He came over? Did you let him in the house?" Tim said, the worry in his voice turning into a concern for her.

"No, no. Of course not. He knocked on the door a few times. But I think he brought his shovel with him. And he was at the door for a while just kind of talking at me through the door."

"What? With his shovel? Shit, Lees. The guy is crazy."

"I know. But he sounded so normal when he was talking at the door. He said he knew it looked strange but that everything was fine. But he also talked about knowing I was home and that you were gone and the kids were at school. He didn't sound crazy, but some of the things he said just—they made me feel uncomfortable."

"Okay. I can understand that," Tim said. "Don't look, but do you know if he is still out there?"

"I...I don't know. I haven't heard him yell in a while, but that doesn't mean he's not still shoveling. At least he was wearing normal clothes this time," Lisa laughed, trying to lighten the whole situation. It wasn't like she was scared for her life or anything. She could probably overpower the old man if he tried to go after her anyway. It wouldn't hurt for her to take one of those women's self-defense classes, though. She made a mental note.

"All right. I can be done here. I'm coming home. What time do you leave to get the kids?" Tim said.

"You don't have to," she said, then answered his question. "Around two-thirty."

"Okay. No, I'm leaving now. I'll probably be home close to two-thirty. I'll try to get there before you leave. If he knows your schedule, he probably knows what time you leave to get the kids, so try to get in the car earlier than usual. I'm sure it's nothing, but just in case he is super crazy, change your routine. If you're not there when I get home, I'll go over and talk to him. I'll see if I can find any of the other neighbors around too. Maybe he's done this kind of thing before. Either way, I think he needs help."

Tim had gone from worrying husband to problem solver. He didn't always emotionally understand what she was going through, and he never shared his own feelings very much, but she knew he loved her. He was a problem solver, and this was the kind of problem that needed solving. She knew he wouldn't hurt John Holland. Tim understood that John was old and probably had dementia or something that was throwing him off. Maybe it was even undiagnosed or untreated Alzheimer's, but something was wrong with him. They would try to get him the help he needed, but their first priority was to protect their own family — then they would worry about helping John.

"Okay. I'll leave earlier than usual. Why don't you call me when you get here? I won't come back with the kids until I know you're home," Lisa said. Then after a short pause, she said, "Thanks. Sorry, you had to cut work short."

"Nah," Tim said. "This is more important than work anyways. Plus, I don't really have anything going on, so it's all good. I'd always come home for something like this. We'll get it fixed today, so there will be nothing to worry about the rest of the week."

"Yeah. Thanks, Tim."

"Of course. I've got to pack up my desk real quick, and I'm out of here. See you soon, Lees. Love you."

"Love you," Lisa said.

She ended the call and sat on the couch, wanting to have another look outside. But she didn't. She hoped John would still be out there when Tim got home so he could see the yelling old man for himself.

***

Lisa did as planned and left early to pick the kids up. There had been no sound from John Holland's house since his visit to her front door. She left the house with little snacks for both kids. Since they usually had a snack after school and they might not be coming right home, she wanted to be ready with something for them to eat. Lisa walked quickly from the front door to her car, not even looking in the direction of Holland's house. She got in the car and back down the driveway. The backup camera showed some movement behind her, and she jumped for a second before realizing it was Marie Shaw checking the mail. Lisa backed the rest of the way down the driveway and waved at Marie at the mailbox. She was about to drive off and then stopped the car and rolled down the passenger window.

"Hey Marie," Lisa said. She wouldn't have done something like this if she wasn't worried about John.

"Hey, what's up? Just getting ready to go get the twins," Marie said, closing the mailbox and walking over to the open passenger side window.

"Getting my kids too," Lisa said. She smiled and hesitated a second and then just decided to go for it. "Have you ever seen John do anything kind of...strange?"

Marie didn't answer right away, but she let the air out through her nose, and her mouth turned down. "Do you mind if I get in?"

"Not at all," Lisa said. She unlocked the door, and Marie climbed in. Lisa pulled up the car in front of Marie's house, on the side of the road, so cars could pass if anyone came by.

"Have you seen weird stuff? Has he done weird stuff?" Marie looked at Lisa, her mail on her lap. She must have seen the fear or worry in Lisa's face because she didn't wait for an answer. "Every once in a while, he goes through these spells. I don't really know what else to call them. Mr. McCoy down the street told us about them last year because he's lived here as long as John has. He just has these spells where he does things that don't make sense. We had to call the police on him last year."

"Oh my God, really?" Lisa was relieved to hear that she wasn't alone in this after all.

"Yeah," Marie nodded and continued. "He wouldn't stop knocking on our door and yelling at us. We called the police just one time. Mr. McCoy said a lot of people have had to do that. He just picks a house and does it for a little while. Then he stops and becomes nice old Mr. Holland again. It's like he's bipolar or something."

Lisa just nodded.

"What have you seen?" Marie asked.

"Well, he was out in his backyard yelling really loud and digging. I just heard him yell and looked out the window. He must have seen me because he was at my front door banging. It just scared me, was all."

"That sucks." Marie looked angry or frustrated or both. "I've got to go get my kids, and I know you do too, but just know it's not the first time it's happened. If you get scared, call the police. You wouldn't be the first person to do that either. He really is a nice guy. He doesn't have anyone to help him out around the house, and I think he's just losing it. I don't know how many calls to the police it takes for them to get him some help. But we've all kind of decided it's the best thing we can do. It just sucks because you just moved in."

"Okay. Thanks. It honestly makes me feel better knowing it's not just me." Lisa laughed, wondering if Marie could tell how relieved she was.

"It's definitely not just you." Marie pulled on the door handle, the door opened, and she got out. Then she leaned into the car. "Lisa, let's do drinks sometime. You guys can all come over one night when the twins are asleep."

"Yeah, for sure," Lisa said with a smile.

Marie shut the door and walked up toward her SUV. Lisa checked her mirrors and pulled away from the curb. It didn't immediately solve her problem—she was still worried about a return of John Holland to her front door with his shovel—but it certainly helped her feel better about the whole thing. It also made her feel bad for John. He needed help, and there wasn't anyone around to get it for him. Maybe when Tim talked to him, he could get the number for one of his kids, and they could take a little more control of the situation, instead of the people in the neighborhood having to call the police on their poor, old neighbor.

As she drove to the school to pick up Matthew, she called Tim and explained the conversation she'd just had with Marie. He felt better about the whole situation too but still wanted to talk to John face to face. He hoped he could resolve the situation without having to call the police.

Lisa pulled onto the street Matthew's school was on and ended the call. She let out a sigh of relief, happy this whole thing was going to be behind her.

CHAPTER 7

Brian and Tiffany looked back at the school as they walked away from it and down the slightly sloped hill toward the little patch of woods that separated the school from the neighborhood that surrounded it. This wouldn't be the first time they sneaked away at recess, and it probably wouldn't be the last. They were both thirteen—Brian's mother had held him back a year before entering school, so he was a year older than all of his other classmates. Except Tiffany. She was a year older than everyone else also. Brian didn't know why. He always just assumed she was held out of school an extra year like he was, but he never bothered to ask, so he didn't know for sure.

The two of them had done this the week before too, and it was awesome. After lunch was recess every day. The regular teachers were never out at recess because that was their lunchtime. Instead, there were aides who helped out at recess time to keep an eye on everyone. The problem—or the good part, depending on how you looked at it—was that the aides were always the last ones to come out for recess. If Brian and Tiffany could be the first ones out, they would have a good five or six minutes to get out of view before any adults knew they were gone. So that was just what they did. They did it one day two weeks ago, then again last week, and this was the third time. Other kids knew what was happening, obviously, but they didn't tell anyone. Brian told his friends to listen to see if anyone told the teachers. Tiffany did the same.

Once they got over the crest of the hill and couldn't see anyone out for recess, they slowed down their pace. They walked along the path that led down toward the woods. Brain reached for Tiffany's hand, and they laced their fingers together as they walked.

"This is getting easier every time," Tiffany said, walking hand in hand with him.

"Yeah, It's not even really that hard. Did they call your parents or anything either of the last two times?" Brian said. "We have art and library after lunch, and they never take attendance at either of those, and by the time the class gets back to the room, it's almost the end of the day, and Mrs. Long would never miss me."

"Yeah, Ms. Blanc doesn't miss me either. I'm so quiet in class she wouldn't know if I was there or not. And we have library and music, so we're busy too." Tiffany looked over at him and smiled.

Brian didn't think he cared about what other people his age thought. He always just did what he wanted to do. But he couldn't help but feel cool and excited as he ditched school the third Wednesday in a row. And he wasn't just ditching school. He was ditching school with his girlfriend. He felt like he had to tell his friends what he was doing, but he didn't know if he would ever be able to. At least not until he and Tiffany broke up.

The first day they found this old, falling-down shed-like structure in the woods. They sat on the rocks that were half-buried under grass and dried leaves. That was when they kissed for the first time. Not just kissed, but kissed with tongues. At first, it felt awkward, but Brian learned what she liked, and she learned what he liked. They talked about it and learned together; it was fun. The next time they kissed more, it was a lot less awkward, and he wasn't worried as much about what he was doing and was able to enjoy the moment. Tiffany even let him touch her over her shirt. He really wanted to tell all his friends about that, but he knew what would happen if he told them. Within a few days, the entire school would know what they were doing. This time he hoped he would touch her under her shirt. Neither of them had ever done anything like this before, so it was all new for both of them and, at least for Brian, well worth the risk of getting caught to spend another afternoon in the woods with Tiffany.

It was late spring, and the trees had all their leaves back. Although the leaves weren't dark green like they would be in a few months, they were closer to the dark green of summer than the light green of early spring. The last few weeks, they'd needed pants and jackets when they made their weekly trip into the woods. Today was much warmer. Brian was in a pair of jean shorts and a T-shirt, and Tiffany was in a T-shirt and pants.

They walked from the grass onto the paved path, the tops of their sneakers wet from the rain from the night before. The path led them down into the woods in the lower part of the field. There were houses just on the other side of the woods. Brian's mother had gone to the same school when she was younger and told him that the area that was all houses now had once been a big field, and they used to walk down into the woods and then back up the hill to school. Now the area they used to walk through was someone's backyard.

"Ready?" Brian looked at Tiffany as they went into the wooded area.

"Yup," she replied, and they turned off the paved path and into the woods.

There was still kind of a dirt path through the woods. It was overgrown with ferns and other small plants and shrubs, but it was very much there. Brian went first, and Tiffany followed him as they made their way through the trees, under the branches that stuck out into the path, and stepped over small rocks and the occasional tree that had fallen at some point over the years, and no one had bothered to move. Before long, they arrived at the old lean-to in the woods.

"There is it, our mansion in the woods," Brian said as they approached the spot that was now the site of many firsts for the two of them.

"Yup, I can't wait until all of my stuff is moved in," Tiffany said. She jumped up on top of a rock off to the side of the path and then jumped down, her feet clopping against the matted down dirt.

"This is so much better than school. It's really not even a contest," Brian said.

"No, definitely way better."

They were standing outside of the lean-to, and Tiffany's back was to him. She turned around quickly and threw her arms around him, and pressed her lips against his. They stayed that way for a moment, and then their tongues met. The sounds of their kissing filling the otherwise quiet air.

After a few minutes, they stopped. Brian didn't like to be out in the open like this and felt much more comfortable inside the old lean-to. The backyards of the houses in the neighborhood were only about fifty or sixty yards through the woods, and the field that led up to school was only one hundred yards in the opposite direction. Although the woods were thick, it was not as remote as it felt when you were in it. They couldn't see or hear anyone from either side, but they knew they were right there.

"Come on, let's move in here." Brain took Tiffany's hand, and they went into the lean-to.

He had no idea who had put the structure together, but it had withstood the test of time, though he didn't know how long it had been there. It was made with a few pieces of old fence pushed together to make something that resembled a fort. The wood, especially down near the bottom near the ground, was rotting. It looked as though it had been mended a few times over the years because newer-looking pieces of plywood covered what appeared to be holes in the fencing itself. The panels were also tied together with rope at various points. Brian assumed it had fallen down more than once during strong storms, but someone had gone through the trouble of tying it back together. The rope on there now had been there for quite a while, though. It was caked with dirt and looked as though it would never come untied.

It was obvious that Brian and Tiffany were not the only ones using this lean-to currently. There were cigarette butts and empty beer cans on the ground around the lean-to. These looked new and multiplied over the three weeks they had been visiting this place. Brian had an older sister, Katie, and knew that kids who wanted to drink but weren't old enough to do it legally would come out into the woods. Katie didn't come here, he didn't think, but she went somewhere on Friday and Saturday nights, that much he knew.

They moved inside the lean-to and sat down on the rocks. They sat in silence.

Sometimes Brain felt like they didn't really talk that much. He didn't really know a lot about Tiffany, and he didn't think she knew that much about him. They liked each other, but neither had spent a whole lot of time getting to know the other. He didn't put a whole lot of thought into it. He liked kissing her and touching her, and maybe that was all he needed to know at this point. It wasn't like they were going to get married or anything. At least he didn't think so. He hoped she wasn't thinking about that stuff just yet. They were only thirteen, after all. It was 1985. People didn't get married until they turned twenty-five or thirty, at least. That was more than ten years away. There was no reason for them to be thinking about that kind of stuff now.

He turned toward her, and she looked over at him and smiled. He reached up and put his hand along her jawline and tilted her head up slightly toward him, then kissed her. He had seen this move on TV the other night and put it in his memory banks as something to try. She actually made a little moan when they kissed, so he guessed it worked. He left his hand there as they kissed, tongues sliding together. This, he thought, was why he liked her. They kissed, and his hand slid down her body, touching her over her shirt, just like he had done last week. He felt lost in the moment until a sound pulled them out of it.

They both backed away from each other and looked out the opening of the lean-to. There was nothing there.

"What was that?" Tiffany leaned over, breathing heavy, and whispered in Brian's ear.

He stayed still for a few seconds, listening. There was no noise. Nothing. Not even the wind rustling the leaves on the trees. Perfect silence.

"It must have been an animal or something," Brain said. He still listened but turned his eyes back to the girl sitting next to him.

"Yeah, probably." She smiled at him. It was perfect — he loved her smile.

He leaned back over and kissed her again, without the hand on the face this time. As they kissed, his hand slipped up her shirt just a little, and he felt the smooth skin of her stomach against his fingertips. She didn't stop him, but the sound did.

It was louder this time and echoed around them. It was like one of the tall trees that surrounded them had cracked in half and crashed to the ground. They both shot up and out of the lean-to. They looked around. Tiffany stayed close to Brian and held on to his arm. Brian felt a strange feeling in the pit of his stomach. What had they heard? There were houses not far from where they were. It wasn't like they were alone in the woods, even though it felt like they were.

"Wait here," Brian said, doing his best impersonation of John Rambo. He moved away from Tiffany and looked behind the lean-to, leaving her alone for just a second.

"Brian, come back," Tiffany called from the other side of the lean-to. They weren't that far away, but it sounded like she was miles away.

Time seemed to slow down. He was nervous but didn't know why. Tiffany felt the same nervousness—he could read it on her face. Brian couldn't put his finger on it, but something wasn't right. He walked back over to the front of the lean-to and grabbed her hand.

"Do you want to get out of here? We can go back to school or just go walk somewhere or something." Brian looked at her. He didn't want to be there anymore, and he didn't care where they went. Something about these woods was wrong right now, and they needed to go. A fly flew past him, and he waved at it as it passed by.

Tiffany didn't respond but nodded and squeezed his hand tight. They turned together and took a few steps hand in hand, back toward the paved path.

Another fly flew past them. Tiffany waved at it this time. It circled her head, and she waved at it while she ducked her head, still holding on to Brian's hand with the hand that was not swatting the annoying insect. They took a few more quick steps, trying to get away from the insect. Brian remembered learning one time that flies had the memory of less than a second or something like that. Who knew if it was true or not, but he couldn't get that piece of useless information out of his head now as they moved away from the fly. He hoped by moving away a little faster, the fly would forget about them and move on with whatever it was flies did the rest of the day.

But there were two flies now, circling their heads even as they waved and ducked their heads, trying to get out of the way.

"What the fuck?" Tiffany said, her fingers still laced with his.

They walked faster, heading in the direction of the paved path. Once they got there, Brian thought, they would be able to run in one direction or the other. The flies wouldn't follow them then.

"We must have stepped on something they were on or under or something. At least it's flies and not bees. That would have sucked," Brian said. "Come on, let's get to the path up here, and then we can run, and they won't be able to follow us once we start running."

They moved as fast as they could, still holding hands and avoiding the branches and the fallen trees they'd passed on the way in. The trip seemed longer than normal, even though they were walking faster than usual. Brian still felt something strange about the woods, but he didn't know what it was. The flies around them multiplied. There were probably only ten of them, but it felt like a hundred. They moved faster.

"Come on, Tiff," Brian said.

They approached the large tree that had fallen across the path. It slowed them down. Brian climbed over first and then held out his arms to help Tiffany. But they had stopped for too long. The flies swarmed all around them. Brian looked away from Tiffany for a second and saw the dark cloud closing in around them.

"Tiff! Come on!" Brian shouted over the noise of the flies as they closed in tighter around the two barely-teenagers.

"Brian! What the hell?" Tiffany said. He held both her hands as she stood on top of the trunk of the tree, preparing to jump off.

The flies tightened around them. Brian could feel them against the skin of his arms and legs. He looked back at Tiffany and saw they were pressing up against her back too. Tiffany landed on the ground. Brian held her hands tight.

"Come on! Run!" he shouted to her over the buzzing and flapping of wings in his ears.

He tried to turn and run, but the flies pushed into him. He felt the power of the large swarm of flies against his back. They turned him back toward Tiffany.

"Brian!" Tiffany screamed his name. He looked into her eyes. There were tears streaming down her face, her lips curled back into a grimace he had never seen before.

"I don't know what to do," Brian said.

He let go of one of her hands and tried to wave at the mass of flies, but they surrounded his arm, and it was held in place above his head. The flies pushed against his back, forcing him toward Tiffany. Flies pushed her toward him. Their bodies were pressed together, flies wrapping around them like a large blanket. Her arms wrapped around him, and one of his wrapped around her, the other still held hostage above his head. They couldn't move. The flies held them still, locked in a grotesque, fly-covered embrace.

"Brian, I don't want to die. I don't want to die."

He heard Tiffany's voice in his ear, but even the small space between her and him had been filled with flies. That was right before the flies entered his nose and ears. He could feel them inside him. They forced their way into his mouth. He heard a muffled scream and knew the same thing was happening to Tiffany, and there was nothing he could do to stop it. He just squeezed her tightly to him, and the flies took over their bodies.

The sound stopped, and there was just nothing.

CHAPTER 8

"And breaking news now coming out of Medville," the news anchor said.

Lisa was half asleep on the couch, but she turned her head and sat up straight when she heard the name of her new town on the nightly Chicago news. Tim sat next to her on the couch, his nose in a book, and heard nothing. She grabbed the remote and turned up the volume two clicks, and then threw an elbow into Tim's side.

"Look at this," she said to her husband. He looked up from his book.

The reporter on the screen was standing with her back to a wooded area, but there wasn't much more in the shot that would give Lisa any clue as to where she was. The caption under her read *Missing girl in Medville*.

"The girl, twelve-year-old Chrissy Franklin, is a student here at Mason Middle school," the reporter said. Lisa and Tim said nothing but exchanged a glance when they realized the girl was Matthew's age and went to the same school as him. "She left home for school at her regular time, but she never made it to school this morning. When school officials contacted her parents to inquire about her whereabouts, the parents thought she was at school. At first, the parents and the school thought it might have just been a case of a kid skipping school. But parents and teachers both said that would be very unlike the straight-A student. Police were notified when Chrissy didn't come home after school, and they are now turning to the public and asking if anyone in and around the Medville area has seen, or may know the whereabouts of, Chrissy Franklin."

A picture of the girl flashed up on the screen. Lisa didn't recognize the girl, but she would bet Matthew might recognize her or even know her. She checked her phone for the time—it was ten-thirty. There was a fifty-fifty chance Matthew was still awake. Lisa hit the pause button on the DVR remote and got up.

"You think he's up?" she whispered to Tim.

Tim shrugged. "We need to tell him. What if he knows her? He should know before school. Should we wait until the morning?"

"If it was your friend would you want to know right away?"

"Yeah, you're right. I'll back up the story."

Lisa climbed the stairs listening for movement or electronic devices in Matthew's room, but she didn't hear any. She knocked softly on his door, but there was no answer. She waited and listened at the door but still couldn't hear anything. Conflicted about giving Matthew his privacy and wanting to let him know about the girl in his school, she hesitated, then decided she needed to go in.

Lisa turned the knob and pushed open the door. Matthew was sitting up in bed with his earbuds in his ears. He still hadn't seen her, but at least he was up. She opened the door the rest of the way and walked over to the side of his bed.

Matthew must have seen the movement out of the corner of his eye because he jumped when she moved to sit on his bed.

"Mom!" Matthew yelled. Lisa was sure it was more anger by the fact that she scared him than that he was actually mad about the intrusion.

Lisa made put her hands to her ears and made the movement of someone taking earbuds out of her ears, asking Matthew to do the same. He took them out and looked down at his phone to pause his music.

"Sorry I scared you," Lisa said.

"It's okay. I was just focusing on the music—I guess I didn't hear you. What's wrong? Is everything okay?"

Lisa was never good at hiding her emotions from the people that knew her best. Matthew, Tim, and Olivia could always tell what kind of mood she was in within a few seconds of seeing her. Sometimes they knew how she was feeling before she did—it was just part of being in a close family.

"Well, yeah. I guess so," Lisa said. "Come downstairs, okay?"

"Uh, okay." Matthew tossed the covers off him, dropped his phone on his bed, and followed Lisa down the stairs.

Lisa returned to the couch and patted the cushion between her and Tim. This was already built up more than she had wanted to build it up, but it was too late now. They would just have to judge his reaction. Either he would care because he knew her and they would be there for him, or he would care because it was a girl from his school that he didn't really know that well and he would be all right. Matthew sat down and looked from Lisa to Tim and then at the TV, which was still paused on the story right before the one about Chrissy Franklin.

"Okay, for real, what's going on?" Matthew said.

"Just watch for a minute," Tim said and pointed at the TV. Then he hit the play button.

Lisa watched Matthew as the story began, then when the girl's name was mentioned, he jumped like he had been punched in the stomach.

"What?" Matthew said, then looked back at the TV and shook his head. Lisa could see his eyes moistening. "No."

"Matt," Lisa started, but he ran out of the room and up the

stairs before she could get more than his name out.

He came down a few moments later with his phone in his hand, staring at it.

"What is it, Matt?" Tim said.

Matt pressed a button on his phone and held it up to his ear. All three of them were silent.

"It's me. Please call me if you get this," Matthew said into the phone. Then he looked at his parents. "She's kinda my — she's a really good friend of mine."

His face had changed. He was calm when he had first come downstairs, but there was worry and fear on his face now. Lisa saw his top lip quivering. It was something he had done since he was a baby. She always knew when he was about to cry because of that top lip quiver. When he was younger, crying over the spilled Cheerios or the wrong color sweatshirt, the lip quiver had been cute. She had taken pictures and videos of the lip quiver to show her parents and laugh about it. In the current situation, the lip quiver only made her want to help him as much as she could.

"It's okay, buddy. I'm sure it's just...I know when I was in middle school, I started —" Tim spoke, but Mathew cut him off.

"It's not like that. She wouldn't skip school or go run off somewhere without telling someone. If she's not home, something is wrong. I...I talked to her last night. We talk almost every night. Late. I was going to call her in an hour or so after you guys were in bed."

"Okay," Lisa, started. They all knew he wasn't supposed to be on his phone after nine except to listen to music, but they all chose to ignore that fact for now. "Did you talk to her today?"

"No, I.... We all thought she was just out sick. There's been something going around, and lots of kids have been out. We all just assumed she caught it. I would have texted her, but we can't use our phones at school. I texted her when I got home but assumed she was sleeping. See." Matthew thumbed through his phone and then turned it for Lisa and Tim to see. The last message was at four that afternoon: *Hey, you're probably sick and sleeping. Call or text when you wake up.*

"It was delivered, but I really didn't think it was anything more than her being sick."

"Matt, is she your girlfriend?" Tim asked out of the blue. He had been studying Matthew while he was talking. Lisa didn't pick up on it, but maybe it was just a guy thing.

Matthew said nothing but nodded. "Not officially. We haven't been on a date, obviously, but we both want to go out. I was going to ask her to the movies this weekend."

A tear dripped down Matthew's face. He rubbed his face with his palm and then rubbed his hands together.

"It's okay, Matt. This is going to be hard. You can't think of anything different that might have happened with her lately? People hanging around outside of school or anything? Those are the kinds of things they're looking for. It's why they put the story on the news. The police need help finding her, so they want input from anyone who might know anything." Tim offered support and put his arm around Matthew.

"No. Nothing. I…I can't fucking believe this is actually happening," Matthew said. Another rule broken and ignored by the three of them.

"Have you met her parents? Do they know about the two of you, or was it just like with us?" Lisa asked. She wondered if she should call Chrissy's parents but then decided against it. Even if they knew about Matthew, the last thing they wanted was a call from his family at a time like this. The only thing they wanted was a call telling them someone had found their daughter. Matthew just sat there. It seemed like her words didn't even register with him. He stared at his phone as if willing a response from Chrissy would help bring her back from wherever she was.

The three of them stayed like that on the couch until well after two. Without much progress and no real updates, Lisa couldn't keep her eyes open anymore and headed up to bed.

"I will do whatever you need me to do for you, Matt. Just let me know." She headed up the stairs, unsure if she would get any sleep.

"I'll stay up as long as you need me to, buddy," Tim said as she turned the corner at the top of the stairs into her bedroom.

***

Lisa's alarm went off at six like it did every morning. She had to get the kids' breakfasts ready and make sure they were all set before going to school. It was the normal morning routine, but it was also different. She didn't know what Matthew's plan was, and she didn't really have any idea of what she could do to help him. Tim wasn't in bed with her, and he usually got up around the same time she did in the mornings.

She rolled out of bed and got dressed, figuring she could shower later. When she got downstairs, both Tim and Matthew were asleep in the same spots she had left them the night before. Matthew's phone was still in his hand — he'd fallen asleep staring at it.

Lisa walked past Matthew and went to Tim. She sat down by his feet and put a hand on his shoulder, rubbing and pressing down, trying to wake him quietly to give Matthew a chance to sleep. Tim looked up at her, blinked a few times, then must have realized where he was and what was going on and groaned.

"Hey," Lisa whispered. "What's the deal? Any news?"

Tim shook his head and leaned forward. "Nothing. He was just refreshing his phone and texting other friends. No one heard anything. He says he wants to go to school today. It will be better than sitting here at home. I don't know if you want to email someone just to let them know they were close and the night he had."

"Okay. That sounds like a good idea. You were up late. Are you going in to work?"

Tim nodded again. "I have a meeting at ten. I think I'll just leave after that. I'll be home when he gets home in case you need help or something. And that way I can get to bed early." Tim stood up, his back and knees creaking and groaning. He twisted his upper body, and Lisa could hear a crack from his back.

"That's what you get for sleeping on the couch."

Tim said nothing but shook his head and made his way up the stairs to get ready for work.

Lisa checked the time and decided Matthew could sleep for another hour or so before he needed to be woken up. Lisa went into the kitchen and checked Olivia's bag to make sure her homework was done, and there wasn't anything special she needed for school that day. Over the course of Olivia's short school career, the third-grader had learned to become self-sufficient. It wasn't that Lisa didn't want to help her youngest child. It was just that Olivia had the independence thing down, and Lisa saw no reason to mess with it. If she needed something signed or if there was a project coming up, Olivia always told Lisa and Tim ahead of time. If she had homework to do, she always did it, even if it was just studying. Lisa always checked her bag just to make sure she hadn't missed anything, but so far this year, she hadn't missed a single assignment or parent signature.

Lisa hadn't been like Olivia when she was in school. It wasn't that she did poorly—she actually did quite well. But she could always find other things to do that didn't involve books or pencils and paper after school. She still did her homework; it just took effort from her mother to get her to do it. In many ways, she was a lot more like Matthew than she was like Olivia. Sure, now that Matthew was in middle school, he was pretty good about getting his work done, but when he was in elementary school, every day was a struggle. At school, he struggled, and getting him to do homework was even worse. It got better as he went through elementary school, and it seemed like everything clicked for him at the end of his fifth-grade year. The transition to his new school and the new town didn't seem to mess any of that up. He was still bringing home good grades and getting all of his homework done, although it was still very much on Matthew's schedule.

Lisa heard the familiar sound of Olivia coming down the carpeted stairs. In just a short period of time, they had all become comfortable in this house. Lisa liked that she knew Olivia was on her way downstairs before she even got there — it made her feel like she was home. Olivia turned the corner around the stairs and passed through the living room and into the kitchen. Her eyes focused on Matthew as she walked through the room.

"Mom," Olivia said, taking her regular seat at the kitchen table. "Why is Matt sleeping on the couch?"

"Oh, he just had a tough night, Liv. I'll wake him up in a few minutes. Just a little extra rest for him today," Lisa said, then changed the subject. "Cereal?"

Although Olivia was mature for her age, there was no reason to worry her about something like this. She was still only in third grade. Lisa also made the decision to find a radio station that played only music this morning. Olivia might not notice, but she wasn't sure how much to share with her.

"I have cereal every morning, Mom. And you still ask every morning." Olivia gave a big grin, made even cuter by the fact that one of her front teeth was missing.

"Well, I just like to check, Liv. What kind?"

"Just the plain flakes today, I think," Olivia said.

They sat in the kitchen and listened to the music on the radio for a while. Lisa glanced at the time around 7:15 and decided that Matthew needed to start getting ready. She padded into the living room just as Tim came down the stairs dressed for work.

"I let him sleep a little extra. Did you check the news?" Lisa whispered, not wanting Olivia to overhear her.

"I just checked. No news, and if they have any leads or anything, they are not releasing it, just the same report as last night." Tim shook his head.

"Oh," Lisa sighed. "I hope they find her. Her poor parents. Can you even imagine?"

"I don't even want to think about it." Tim put his arm around Lisa and rubbed her back, then squeezed her close before continuing on into the kitchen. "Hey, Livvy."

Lisa turned her attention back to Matthew. He hadn't moved since she came down, and she wondered what time he had finally drifted off to sleep. His chest rose and fell. He looked peaceful. Lisa knew this would probably be the last few seconds of the day that he wouldn't be worried unless Chrissy was found or he fell asleep. She watched him another few seconds and then knelt down on the floor next to him.

"Matt," Lisa whispered as she put her hand against his arm, rubbing it slowly. He didn't move, and she rubbed a little harder and repeated, "Hey Matt."

Matthew started to stir. A groan escaped his lips, then his eyes flew open, and he sat up.

"What happened? Did they find her?" He looked at Lisa and then at his surroundings, apparently just then realizing he had spent the night on the couch.

"No, Matt," Lisa whispered again, and put a finger to her lips and looked over her shoulder toward the kitchen, where Olivia sat eating her bowl of corn flakes.

Matthew followed her gaze and nodded.

"Nothing changed overnight." Lisa looked down as she spoke. "The news reports are all the same."

"Okay." Matthew looked down at his phone still in his hand. Lisa could see the screen — there were no messages that she could see.

"Dad said you wanted to go to school. Do you still feel up to it?" Lisa asked.

Matt just nodded. "It might be a little bit easier with everyone else there, you know. Everybody loves her, so it might be better that way. I might freak out and just refresh my phone all day if I'm here."

"Okay. Go get ready. If you feel like you need to leave, just have them call me, and we can get you dismissed." Lisa put her hand on his back, rubbing it.

"Okay. Thanks, Mom," Matthew said with a small smile before heading upstairs to get ready for school.

Lisa still knelt next to the couch when Tim came in.

"How is he?" Tim asked, sitting on the couch next to where Lisa knelt.

She stood up and turned to sit on the couch next to Tim. "Seems okay. I don't know for sure. You probably talked to him more than me."

"Last night, we didn't do much talking. Just a little bit about how he might want to consider going to school even though he wouldn't want to. Because everyone there will be feeling the same thing he is. We can try to be there for him, but we don't know the girl, and she has lots of friends at school. They can help more than just sitting at home could," Tim said. "Other than that, we just sat here. I guess he liked knowing I was here, but there wasn't a whole lot I could do."

Lisa nodded. She understood what Tim was saying. She didn't want to say "I'm sure she's fine" to Matthew or anything reassuring like that because she didn't know the outcome. Matthew was positive it wasn't just Chrissy being a teenager and leaving with some friend for the night. He was sure something was wrong, and that made Lisa all the more worried. When you were twelve and thirteen years old, your friends often knew you better than your parents. And if Matthew and her other friends said she wouldn't have done something like this, it made her worry a lot more than if her parents said it. Kids *always* told their friends everything — they *sometimes* told their parents everything.

Lisa and Tim did their best to keep the morning as routine as possible. Tim went back upstairs after talking with Lisa, presumably to give Matthew one final pep talk before he left for work. Then he came down and kissed Lisa and Olivia goodbye. Matthew came down and sat at the kitchen table with Olivia for a few silent minutes before the trio left the house for their morning ritual. Lisa dropped Matthew off first with a few more words of encouragement, and then Olivia with her usual request that Olivia just try her best. Then Lisa returned home. She didn't feel like going to the gym today and just showered.

Like most people, Lisa did her best thinking in the shower. Sometimes she would listen to music while she was in there. Other times she just showered in silence and thought. She just felt like she needed the extra time inside her head today and didn't even bother with the music. She couldn't get the image of Chrissy Franklin out of her head. It could have been the fact that Matthew and she were friends, maybe more than friends, or maybe just the fact that this story hit so close to home. Usually, a story like this wouldn't affect her as much as this one was. She thought about Chrissy's parents too. If something *did* happen to the girl, it could have just as easily been her and Tim up all night worrying about Matthew or Olivia. Whatever happened to the Franklin girl could have happened to either of the Ewing kids.

After her shower, Lisa got dressed and started some research. She knew it probably wasn't the best thing she could do, but she wanted to know more about this story. And if there was some sort of news during the day today, she wanted to have that too in case Matthew needed to be picked up. Lisa got her tablet from the home office area they had set up downstairs and sat on the couch. With her tablet in hand, she flipped on the TV to one of the local news stations. It was the middle of the morning, and there wasn't any local news on at the moment, but they would sometimes cut in with breaking local news, and there was always a news report at lunchtime, so she decided she would leave it on the national morning talk show just in case.

The TV on as background noise, Lisa began her search. At first, she just checked the local TV news stations online. The stories were basically the same as those she had heard last night — there was no new information. Then she narrowed her search and checked the website for the daily local newspapers in the area. Not the *Chicago Tribune* or the *Chicago Sun-Times*, because they would only have the same brief information that the local Chicago TV stations had. Instead, she looked at the local county newspapers. There was one story in the *County Chronicle* that got her mind switched into a different gear. The story was written earlier that morning, and the news about Chrissy's disappearance was no different than anything she had already read. In fact, she almost skipped the rest of the article without finishing it. But as her eyes skimmed across the words and her finger scrolled the story up, there was a line that caught her attention.

This is the latest in a string of strange disappearances of kids in the same neighborhood that spans almost a hundred years, the line stated. Lisa read on after re-reading the line. *It is difficult to call these disappearances related given the time between each of them,* the article read. *But the near exact proximity of the final sighting of each of the children who disappeared makes it almost impossible to ignore.*

Lisa nearly dropped the tablet as she read, her feet curled up underneath her on the couch. The article gave a little information about the disappearance of the children in the neighborhood. There was not much information about the first disappearance, which took place during the 1930s, only that the girl who went missing was walking home from school and never made it. Barbara was the only name mentioned — there was no last name. The article offered a bit more information about the other disappearances, probably because there were more established newspapers here in Medville starting in the 1950s. The next disappearance was in the summer of 1960. Two boys were out for the day playing. They had made a fort in the woods. One of the boys forgot something and rode his bike home to go get it. When he got back to the fort, the other boy's bike was still there, but the boy, Harry, was gone. He was never seen again. The final disappearance was in 1985. A boy and a girl, Brian and Tiffany, went out for recess one day. It was thought they might have been ditching school, but they never turned up. Gone. In each case, there were no clues or leads for the police to follow. The children in each case were never found, and all of the cases remained open.

Lisa put the tablet down and pulled on her bottom lip, as she always did when she was deep in thought. She wondered how far back newspapers could be accessed on the Internet. She thought back to her days in school before the computer age had really begun. She knew how she would have to look up old newspapers back then. Go to the library and scan through microfilm sitting at one of those big machines, hour after hour, looking for whatever information it was she was trying to find. Now, everything was high-tech. Last year Matthew had a project for homework in which he had to look at old newspapers. He had to try to find a historical event in the newspaper the day after it happened. Then he had to compare the reporting of the event right after it happened versus what was known about the event now. Lisa was really impressed with the assignment and had planned on taking Matthew to the library in order to complete it. The next page of the assignment packet revealed that the *Chicago Tribune* had all of its archives available on its website, and they could be accessed for free. The idea amazed Lisa back then, and she'd spent hours looking through old newspapers, just reading about what had gone on years ago and admiring how much life had changed.

Now, she had an actual use for the archived newspapers, beyond just her own personal fascination. She actually had something to research. She navigated to the *Chicago Tribune* website and made sure she could look at the actual newspaper with no problems on the tablet screen. She could. Then she got up and checked the time. It was almost ten-thirty. Her stomach growled, and she realized she hadn't eaten breakfast today. It was between breakfast and lunchtime, and for Lisa, it meant she could pick which meal she wanted to eat. A bowl of cereal or a salad at ten-thirty was all up for grabs. In the end, she chose a salad. She figured with lunch—and breakfast—in her, she could settle in for a few good hours of research and collect any information she could about the disappearances.

Lisa didn't quite understand why she felt the need to do this kind of research, but she wanted to know more. She ate her salad faster than normal, without bothering to put on the radio and listen to music as she did it. She thought about her research and tried to determine the best course of action. The article had given exact dates for the more recent disappearances but only gave a general time frame for the first disappearance in the 1930s. The story about that particular disappearance, the girl who left school and never got home, would probably be the most difficult to locate if there was a story about it in the *Chicago Tribune* at all back then. She decided she would tackle the biggest problem first. It would require scanning, at most, ten years' worth of newspapers for an article, even a short blurb, about a missing girl in Medville. The other disappearances would be easier to locate. She had exact dates and would probably only need to look at the papers for a few weeks after the initial disappearance to be able to follow the whole story. She could even do those later tonight.

She finished the salad and returned to the couch. Tablet in hand, Lisa began to search the *Chicago Tribune* archives on January 1, 1930. She was going to learn more about this—she felt she owed it to Matthew.

CHAPTER 9

By the time she had to leave to go get Matthew and Olivia, Lisa had looked through every newspaper from 1930 until 1936. It was a time-consuming process slowed by the fact that there were other interesting things that caught Lisa's attention as she skimmed through the papers. She found it interesting to read about the Great Depression in the words of the people who actually lived through it. Even though she had a specific task, the interest these old papers brought on was hard to pull away from.

"How was today?" Lisa asked Matthew when he climbed into the front seat of the car. His down-turned face told the story, but she wanted to ask him anyway.

"I guess it was fine. It was good to be around other people. It was still hard, though." Matthew rested his elbow against the armrest and stared out the window.

"Did...did you get any new information? I've been watching the news all day; I wish they would tell us more," Lisa said, trying to keep him talking, but knowing he might not tell her a whole lot even if he did learn something the news wasn't reporting.

"No, not really. The teachers told us if they heard anything, they would let us know. But I'm pretty sure that's a lie. They would only tell us if they heard good news. If they heard bad news, they'd just wait and let our parents tell us," Matthew said. Lisa thought he'd correctly assessed the situation.

"You're probably right. They're just trying to keep you focused on other things, though, Matt. They don't want the entire school to be focused on this. It's a hard situation for the school and for us as parents, but mostly for you guys. Her friends and classmates." Lisa didn't know what else to say. This was one of those times when it didn't matter how many parenting books she read or didn't read. There wasn't going to be a whole lot she could be taught to say in this situation. They'd had a few of them over the years — in the end, she just said what felt right in her gut.

"Yeah. Everyone had a pretty rough day. Sarah Bowers was the worst, though. She usually walks with Chrissy to school but didn't the other day because she was running late, so she got a ride from her dad. Chrissy had to...." Matthew trailed off.

They pulled up to a stop sign, and with no traffic, Lisa reached over and rubbed his back. She couldn't tell if he was crying, but she guessed he was.

They didn't talk the rest of the ride to pick up Olivia, and the car remained silent until they got home. Lisa assumed nothing was said to Olivia about any of this, but they would have to tell her tonight.

"Dad!" Olivia yelled from the back seat when they pulled into the driveway, and Tim's car was already parked in the still open garage.

They got out with their backpacks and went inside. Lisa checked the car to make sure both kids took everything they brought into the car and then locked it. They went in through the garage, and Lisa shut the garage door before entering the house.

"Dad?" Olivia called again when she got in the house.

"Hey, kiddo," Tim said from somewhere in the house. Lisa couldn't help but smile. Even with everything going on, there were some family moments that could always bring a smile to her face.

"Mom, I'm just gonna be in my room. I'll come down at some point to eat, but don't wait for me," Matthew said. He went right up to his room, and she heard the door shut. It had been a difficult day.

"What's with him?" Olivia said as she sat down at the kitchen table with Tim. Lisa shot Tim a look and then went through the task of getting an after-school snack for Olivia and Tim.

"We get to have our snack together today," Tim said.

"I know, it's awesome. Better than you not getting home 'til after bath," Olivia said.

"Hey, hey. I do what I can." Tim smiled and looked at Lisa, then back at Olivia. "So Liv, Matthew had a really hard day today. A lot of people in Medville had a really hard day today, actually."

Lisa put crackers and cheese plates down in front of them and sat down at the table. She watched Olivia as she looked, somewhat confused, from one parent to the other.

"A girl went missing from Medville. The police are looking for her. She was good friends with Matt," Lisa said, once again guessing as to whether this was the right thing to do.

"She's just gone? Like she disappeared?" Olivia asked.

"Yeah, something like that, kiddo," Tim said. "No one really knows where she is."

"Like someone took her?"

"Maybe, we don't really know. That's what makes it hard, Liv," Lisa said. "Matt was really good friends with her, and he doesn't know. And her parents don't know. So, the police and everyone are looking for her, but no one really knows where to look. It was just a hard day today for Matt and a lot of his friends. And even for us, it was hard."

"Because it's really sad to think about?" Olivia asked.

"It's really, really sad to think about, Liv," Tim said.

"I hope she's okay," Olivia said, and then after a few

seconds of silence, she got up from the table. Lisa watched her eyes. She didn't seem upset or look like she might cry, but she did look concerned. "I'm just going to give Matt a hug. I'll be back."

"Okay, but only go in his room if he says it okay, and knock first."

"We raised a nice girl," Tim said and looked at Lisa.

Lisa nodded; a tear dripped down her cheek as she listened. She heard Olivia knock on Matt's door and then yell her name through the closed door. They heard the door open but then couldn't hear anything else.

"Thanks, Liv," they heard Matthew say now that the kids were either in the hallway or his door was open again. They listened as she walked down the carpeted hallway and then back downstairs.

"...so then I told my boss that I wanted to get home early today," Tim said, acting as though he had been telling a long story and not listening to the touching moment between brother and sister. "He told me it wasn't a problem because I was caught up on everything and that he trusts me to get my work done."

"That's really great. Do you think he'll let you do it more often?" Lisa asked, playing along when Olivia walked back into the room. Her face was blank, but Lisa could see the sad look in her eyes. "You okay, Liv?"

Olivia just nodded. Tim and Lisa both looked at her, assessing if she was about to break into tears or if she really was all right.

"I just am sad for Matt and for that girl's family," Olivia said, still not crying.

"I know, honey. It's a hard thing to figure out. No one knows why these things happen. Sometimes they just do. All we can do is be as safe as we can and hope everyone else is too. If everyone is as safe as they can be, we're doing all we can to prevent things like this from happening," Tim said.

Lisa watched her, but Olivia seemed to be okay with that explanation. Lisa decided to let the moment pass and move on with other things.

"Do you have any homework tonight, Liv?" Lisa asked, looking down at the bag resting next to the leg of the table.

"Um, I think math maybe," Olivia said. "Should I just do it now and get it out of the way?"

"You know me too well, Olivia. Yes. Let's do it now, and then you can be done. Do you need help, or you think you can handle it?" Lisa asked.

"I got it," Olivia said. There was the small beginning of a smile on her face.

Lisa got up and took a pencil from the kitchen counter, and brought it over to Olivia as she reached into her backpack and pulled her homework out of her folder. It looked like triple-digit addition. They had been working on these types of problems for two weeks, and although Olivia makes a mistake every so often, she had it down pretty good. Lisa knew she didn't need help and wasn't going to offer it. If Olivia got the problems wrong, she might check them after, but she was going to let her make her mistakes for now.

"Well, listen, Liv. I'm gonna go get out of these work clothes while you're working on that. I'll be down in a few minutes." Tim left to get changed.

Lisa let Olivia alone to do her work and started getting stuff ready to make dinner. She decided to go with grilled chicken breast and broccoli because she knew everyone liked it, and Tim was home, so everyone would get the chance to eat together. She didn't think Matthew would want to come down and eat with them, but she figured if she couldn't get him to come down, Olivia might be able to instead.

Lisa pulled some defrosted chicken out of the fridge. It would be perfect and ready to cook today. She set the plastic bag they were in on the counter and got out her cooking pan. Just as she set the pan on the stove, the familiar loud yell came from the house next door. Lisa jumped and Olivia, still sitting quietly at the table doing her homework, let out a yelp.

"What was that, Mom?"

"It's fine, Liv. Just…just finish up your homework."

Lisa stood in the middle of the kitchen and listened. Was he shoveling again? What was he doing this time? A feeling of relief washed over her knowing that at least Tim was home this time. She didn't know what she would've done if Tim hadn't been there. If she had been there with both kids, she might have freaked out. Lisa took a deep breath and tried to calm herself.

"You sure it's okay, Mom?" Olivia asked.

"No!" John Holland's voice was so loud it sounded like he could have been standing inside the house.

"Yes, I'm sure, Olivia. Everything is fine. Finish up." Lisa knew that if everything was really fine, she would have gone back to making dinner. But she didn't. She stood in the middle of the kitchen, still listening to the shovel scrapes as he dug into the ground.

"No! No! I don't want to. No!" The yelling continued as Tim walked back down the stairs, still putting his shirt on when he rounded the corner. He made eye contact with Lisa and then pointed his thumb in the direction of Holland's house. Lisa didn't say anything back but nodded at him. Tim returned the nod with one of his own. He grabbed the pair of work boots he used when he did yard work and pulled them on over by the garage door.

"Be right back," he said. Lisa heard him lock the door before going out through the garage.

Just as he walked out, John yelled again. "Is that you again, Lisa?! I see you up there!"

Lisa went over behind Olivia. She pretended to look down at Olivia's homework, but she was really just looking out the window behind her, trying to see the confrontation between Tim and John. She wasn't too worried—she knew Tim could take care of himself—but Holland had that shovel in his hand, and he had banged the door with it last time, so she couldn't be sure everything was okay until Tim was back in the house.

Lisa realized Matthew was looking down at John through his window. It made sense—he was up in his room and heard the crazy old guy next door yelling, so he looked out to see what was going on. But she also knew it might only make matters worse. It was obvious John wasn't a big fan of people watching him when he was having one of these episodes, or whatever they were.

"Come on upstairs with me for a minute, Liv," Lisa said.

"Why?" Olivia asked.

Normally if it was something out of the ordinary, Lisa would have explained it, but she didn't have time to deal with it right now. Everything would be fine, but just in case, she didn't want Olivia downstairs by herself.

"Because I said. Let's go."

Lisa lowered her eyebrows and tightened her mouth when she spoke. It was all the reason Olivia needed. She put her pencil down and got up. Lisa followed her daughter up the stairs and into Matthew's room. Olivia started into her own room but then followed her mother instead.

Matthew was at his window when they went in, lifting up the blind, watching, just as Lisa had done a few days earlier.

"Matt, away from the window," Lisa said, her tone matching the one she had used to get Olivia up the stairs.

"Mom, this guy's being crazy," Matthew said. He turned to look at her when he spoke but then turned back to the window and lifted the blind back up. "Dad's out there now. Can I watch?"

"No. Away. Now," Lisa said.

Matthew must have recognized the tone in her voice this second time because he did it right away.

"Sorry," Lisa said, and took a deep breath. "I know this probably isn't the best time for us to be dealing with this, but we have to deal with it now because it's an issue. This happened the other day too, but I was here by myself. Mr. Holland next door is having some…problems. Probably because of his age. The neighbors have even called the police on him before. It happens once in a while, and he doesn't really know what he is saying or doing. He doesn't like people watching him, Matt, although I was watching him out the window the other day too. If we hear him in his yard and he isn't bothering anyone, we are just going to ignore it. If he comes over here and bothers us, we can call the police. But there is something wrong with him, and calling the police is the most we can do to try to get him help. Okay?"

Lisa didn't want a response from either child. She asked the question but wasn't really expecting to get an answer from either of them. They knew she was telling them what to do—it was just the way she ended her orders to make sure they understood the expectation.

"And that's why you didn't want me downstairs?" Olivia asked.

"Yup. We don't know him well enough, and I don't know what he would do. I don't *think* he could do anything that would actually hurt us, but I don't know for sure. That's why Dad is over there, and that's why we will give him his privacy." Lisa felt as though this pep talk was as much for her as it was for the kids. If she had been there by herself, she would have had just as hard a time not peeking outside to see what was going on as Matthew was at the moment.

"All right. I get it," Matthew said. He sat on the end of his bed; Olivia had already made a home for herself at the top. They all sat in silence, waiting for either yelling from outside or Tim to come back into the house.

"I just love you two and want to keep you safe," Lisa said, breaking the silence for a moment.

After what seemed like forever but was probably more like ten minutes, the door from the garage opened. All three of them got up. Lisa led the way downstairs, and they all looked at

Tim.

"You guys weren't watching, were you? I caught the blind move once, but that was it," Tim said with a smile. They all smiled, even Matthew, which was good to see. Tim kicked off his shoes but said nothing, then took a deep breath and exhaled. Lisa, Matthew, and Olivia didn't move.

"What?" Tim said to the three faces staring back at him. He smiled. Lisa knew he was teasing them.

"Come on, Dad," Matthew said. The smile he flashed a few seconds before was gone.

"Okay. Okay. I talked to him. He's actually a pretty nice guy. He doesn't remember the other day at all, Lees. I don't know if he really doesn't remember it or if he's just embarrassed about it, but either way, he apologizes for scaring you. He knows he has some problems from time to time, but he doesn't really know what to do about it."

"Well, what about his kids?" Lisa was not happy with the answers she'd received from Tim so far. It sounded more like the old man was just saying whatever Tim wanted him to say. She was scared, and he had come after her with a shovel. She would feel the best if he wasn't there. The next best thing was for him to start getting some help. Just saying he didn't know what to do didn't change the fact that he could come over when she was by herself with a shovel in hand again.

"Ah, he hinted at the fact that he might have exaggerated the truth about how close he is to his kids and grandkids. I don't know if he sees them at all. He didn't say it, but he doesn't really have anyone."

"Oh, that's kind of sad, Mom," Olivia said.

"I know it is, Liv, you're right." Lisa resigned herself to the fact that she was going to talk about this with Tim later. She didn't want to unnecessarily scare the kids and tell them that poor Mr. Holland might have come after her with a shovel in his hand. But she wasn't going to let it go. It just wasn't the time to have this discussion. "Thanks for going over there, Tim."

"I'm going back into my room," Matthew said.

"Okay, Matt. Dinner's in a little bit. Please don't look out the window."

"Okay," Matthew said as he started back up the stairs. Lisa didn't know what he said okay to, but she was going with an okay to coming down for dinner.

The yelling and shoveling continued most of the afternoon and into the early evening. The sun was setting, and it was getting darker out, but still, the shoveling and yelling persisted. At least Lisa knew they weren't the only ones that could hear John yelling at the top of his lungs. The neighborhood had grown quiet, and without much wind, the sound carried. She had been out at this time of early evening before, and when Matthew was up in his room, she could hear his music playing. When she went into the house, it was harder to hear his music, but outside, it had been as clear as if she was standing there next to him. She knew other neighbors could hear Holland just as well as they could. Part of her hoped one of those other neighbors would be the ones to call the police on him, so they didn't have to.

At seven o'clock, dinner was finished and picked up, the dishes were washed, and they were all in their separate parts of the house getting ready to end another day. Matthew seemed to be in a better mood, although he was glued to his phone, either sending text messages to friends for updates or watching the news for information on Chrissy's status, but there was still nothing new.

The shouts from next door became more sporadic, and Lisa thought for sure the old man was getting tired. Even if he stopped shoveling, he must have been tired of yelling non-stop for almost three hours. Then the yells changed to something new.

"No!" John shouted, as usual. "I don't want to do that again! No! Not again!" The shouts echoed through the house.

Tim and Lisa were sitting on the couch and shared a

glance. There was a long silence. It was as if the entire Ewing house stopped moving and just listened to John yell. She was sure Matthew had his headphones on and couldn't hear anything, but to her, it felt like they were all listening. Maybe that was the end of the yelling for the night, or maybe they were going to get more. They waited. And then there were footsteps on the front porch.

"Lisa!" John's gravelly voice called at the front door. There was a knock too, but at least it was the sound of a fist on the door and not the metallic sound of a shovel hitting it.

Before either Lisa or Tim could respond, Holland was yelling again.

"Lisa! I know you're home. Tim just told me you were all home!" This time instead of knocking on the door, the old man rapped gently on one of the front windows.

Lisa and Tim both saw the shovel bang against the glass. It didn't break, but they'd both had enough.

"That's it—" Lisa started to say, but Tim was already up with his phone in his hand, ready to charge out the front door.

"John, we talked about this!" Tim said. "My whole family is here. If you don't go back home, I'm going to have to call the police."

"No! I don't want to. I don't want to talk to you, Tim. I need to talk to Lisa. Lisa!?" John shouted again. He rapped against the floor of the porch with the shovel—it was the same metallic clang Lisa had heard the other day. She sat up and went to the basement door, opened it, and came back out a second later with Olivia's aluminum softball bat. Tim was there, but if the maniac broke into the house with the shovel and hit Tim with it, she needed to be able to defend her house and her kids.

Tim turned to her and mouthed the words, "It's fine." He put his hands out like he was patting an invisible dog, imploring her to calm down. But she was seeing red. The combination of fear and anger that someone could do this to them made her want to fight for her family to have the peace and security they deserved.

"Lisa! Come on out! Let's talk," John yelled again and banged the shovel against the window again.

"Dad?" Olivia called from the top of the stairs in a low voice just above a whisper.

Lisa looked up and saw the fear in her eyes. It probably didn't help that Lisa had a bat in one hand, but at this point, she didn't care.

"Go back to your room. I'll be right up," Lisa whispered back, but she had no intention of leaving until John was gone.

"John, last chance. Leave and go home or I'll call the police," Tim said.

"No, sorry, Tim. I've got to talk to Lisa," John said, and banged the shovel against the floor again, harder than before.

"Okay, then. Sorry, John." Tim turned on his phone, and Lisa watched him dial 9-1-1. "Hi, yes. I live at 27 Molly Lane here in Medville. My neighbor has been having some mental issues lately—we've spoken to other neighbors, and to him as well, about them. He is currently at my front door, hitting parts of my house and my windows with a shovel. We're all here, my wife and two kids, so if someone could come by as soon as they could—"

"Lisa! Come on out!" John slammed the shovel against the window again, interrupting the phone call. A crack appeared on the glass of the window from one corner to the other. One more hit like that, and Holland would shatter the window.

"Yes, that was him, sorry," Tim continued in a calm voice. "Yes...thank you...no, he's elderly. I could probably get the shovel away from him, but I don't want to open the door and expose my whole family to this. John Holland...right next door. 29 Molly Lane, maybe."

Tim held up his hand and showed Lisa the number five, then mouthed the words "Five minutes" as they kept talking. He answered a few more questions between the yells and clangs of a now pacing John Holland outside the front door. Lisa heard sirens getting closer.

"We can hear sirens now," Tim said. "Sure…yes, okay." They waited, and then the sirens went silent. Lisa heard car doors open on the other side of the door.

"Mr. Holland?" a voice said.

"Yes?" John replied.

"Could you come down here on the grass and have a conversation with us? And please put down the shovel."

They heard the shovel clang to the ground.

"Okay, yes, they are talking with him. Thanks for your help," Tim said into the phone and then hung up.

CHAPTER 10

The constant blaring of the alarm on her cell phone filled the darkened room. Chrissy Franklin opened one eye, reached over to her nightstand, and hit the snooze button. There were some mornings five-thirty came a lot faster than others. Chrissy knew she woke up earlier than most kids her age, but it was only because she put a lot of effort into her school work. People thought she was smart. Everyone did. Maybe she was, but she thought she just worked harder than everyone else. When the teachers told them to study their vocabulary words, even though there wasn't any written homework, she studied. When there was a test coming up—the students usually knew a week in advance of the big tests—she studied. Even if there was no written homework, she studied the old stuff. Teachers always said the tests would be easy if they had been paying attention and doing the homework, and the teachers were right. Sometimes she misread a question and got it wrong by accident, but usually, she got all the questions on the test right because they were the exact things that teachers had said would be on the test.

It was one of the days she needed to do a little bit of work in the morning before school—it was test day. On test day, she made it a point to get a little extra studying in before school. She got up at five-thirty every day, but usually, she took her time and relaxed on the couch, watching TV after eating breakfast before she left for school with her best friend, Sarah Bowers. On test day, she sat on the couch and studied instead. If she took a quick shower and ate a little first, she could get almost forty minutes of studying in before Sarah knocked on the door at six-fifty-five.

Chrissy lay in bed for another two minutes. The alarm would blare again at five-thirty-five, and she didn't feel like hearing it, so she got up and turned it off. She could hear movement downstairs, probably her dad. He left for work around the same time she left in the morning. Her mom worked during the day after Chrissy left for school and got home around four in the afternoon. Chrissy's older sister was a freshman in college, and the family was still working on their new dynamic without Alyssa with them. Before Alyssa left, it wasn't a big deal that Chrissy's mom wasn't home when Chrissy got home from school. Alyssa was home, and everything was fine. With Alyssa away, they had to figure something else out. Luckily, by the time Chrissy and Sarah walked home from school, it was almost three-thirty, so there wasn't a whole lot of time before her mom got home anyway. The final decision let Chrissy have some time at home by herself after a check-in with Sarah's mom, who was always home after school.

After getting a towel from the hallway closet, Chrissy went into the bathroom and got in the shower. She studied lots of different places in the house and at school, but the best place to do studying, she had found, was in the shower. On more than one occasion, she thought about laminating her papers so she could bring them in with her. The warm water fell over her body. In her head, she started going over the terms that would appear on her test.

"Photosynthesis. Chlorophyll. Chloroplast. Stomata." Chrissy said each word almost silently to herself and then, in her head, thought of the definition. She tried to remember all of the words on the study sheet and thought she hit all twelve of them, but she couldn't be sure. It had been the last thing she read last night before falling asleep. She went over them again and again. In a few minutes after she ate breakfast, she would go over them again on the couch, and then if she had any free time in school before science, she would review once more. By the time her teacher passed out the test, she would know everything she needed to. She would get an A on the test—most likely—and everyone would tell her how smart she was.

But she would keep on knowing that she just worked harder at having good grades than they did. It sounded conceited in her head, so she would never say it out loud, but she also knew it was probably the truth.

Chrissy got out of the shower, got dressed, made sure she had everything she needed in her backpack that leaned up against the side of her desk, and then brought all her stuff down.

"Morning, Chrissy," her father said, sitting at the kitchen table behind his morning paper.

"Hey, Dad," Chrissy said. Her dad was eating a bowl of cereal and had left the cereal and the milk out for her like he always did. She took a bowl from the cupboard and filled it with cereal, adding just a splash of milk. Then she grabbed a spoon and brought everything over to the table to sit and eat with her dad. Her dad had always read the newspaper, even as the times changed, and most people got their news reading articles on a tablet or their phones. Her dad would always rather read the paper. They had a subscription, and it came with a free digital copy; her mom only read the digital copy. Her dad only used the actual paper. She loved that about him—he was weird, and he had his particular way of doing things, kind of like she did. But he put his paper down when she sat to eat with him.

"What's going on at school today?" he said before scooping a spoonful of cereal into his mouth.

Chrissy finished chewing her first bite and then spoke. "Well, lots of stuff, but I have a science test today. That's the only test or quiz, so I've been focusing on that mostly since yesterday. I guess that's about it."

"You studied all your science stuff?" her dad asked.

Chrissy nodded and took another bite.

"I hated science for some reason. Biology was okay, but then there was physics, which was basically just another math class," he said while she chewed.

"What's physics?" Chrissy said, chewing.

"Oh, it's actually pretty neat stuff when you think about it. But you just have to be really good at math to understand it all, and I wasn't ever very good at math, so it was hard for me. Physics is like how stuff moves and what it's going to do once you put some sort of pressure on it. Like how fast your bike will go down a hill—figuring out that kind of stuff is physics."

Chrissy nodded.

"It's interesting stuff to learn but with lots of hard math stuff, so it was a hard class for me. But that wasn't until high school, so you don't have to worry about it right now."

"The test today is plants and photosynthesis and stuff like that," Chrissy said. "After I eat, I'm gonna go study one last time."

As she spoke, her phone dinged in the pocket of her pants. It was a text message. She didn't usually get text messages this early in the morning and wasn't allowed to have her phone out at the kitchen table. She looked down at her pocket after hearing the noise and almost pulled her phone out without thinking. She stopped herself and looked up at her dad. He nodded but didn't say anything. That was enough permission for her. Chrissy pulled her phone out. She looked at the lock screen, which displayed the text message from Sarah Bowers.

Running super late today. My mom is going to drive me. See you in history, the text message read.

OK, was the two-letter response Chrissy wrote back to her friend. It was only a five-minute walk to school. They did it every

PERHAPS SHE WILL DIE

day and never had a problem. She wasn't too worried about it. She'd walked to elementary school every day with Sarah or by herself since they were in third grade, and the middle school was only about one block past the elementary school. It would be fine.

"What's up?' her dad asked. His bowl of cereal was empty, and he was just sitting at the table waiting for her to be done before he left for work.

"Oh, Sarah's running late, so she's not gonna walk today. Her mom is going to drop her," Chrissy said.

"Oh. Do you want me to drop you off? I can hang around for a little bit and drop you on my way to work."

"No, I'm okay. I like the walk to school. It's good to get out in the fresh air too. We don't get out during the day now that we're in middle school. No more recess."

"Oh, it's tough to get older, isn't it?" Her dad smiled.

"Yeah, but you get to go outside at your lunch break if you want to," Sarah said, smiling back at her dad. He liked to tease her, but she could always give it back to him—at least she tried to give it back to him. "Maybe you should try working more and taking a twenty-minute lunch inside like me."

"Ah, you got me there, Chrissy!" He laughed and pushed back from the table, taking his empty bowl and folding the newspaper in half. Then he walked back over to her and bent, kissing the top of her head. "All right, hun. Good luck on your test."

"Thanks, Dad. Love you."

"Love you too." He ran upstairs to say goodbye to her mom and left for work.

Chrissy finished her cereal and took her backpack with her to the couch. She sat at one corner of the couch, lifted her feet up and curled them under her, then reached into her bag and pulled out the vocabulary words for the test. She went over them again three times and checked the time—six-forty-five, still ten minutes before she had to leave. She reviewed the words again.

Her mom came down, said good morning, noticed that she was studying, and left her alone to do her thing. After ten minutes, she packed up her bag and got ready to go.

"Mom, Sarah texted. She is running late and getting a ride, so I'm off," Chrissy said, walking back into the kitchen where her mom sat at the kitchen table. She was scrolling through her tablet, probably reading the same newspaper that sat folded up underneath the device.

"Oh, okay. Do you want me to drive you?"

Her mom repeated the question her dad had asked. She liked that they were so willing to change their plans when her walking partner couldn't walk with her.

"No. I'll be fine. Thanks, though." She went over and kissed her mom on the cheek. "Bye, love you."

"Love you. Good luck on that science test."

Chrissy nodded, threw on a heavy sweatshirt, and then slung her backpack over that and went out the front door.

It was a warm day for early November. The air reminded her more of spring air than late fall air. She didn't need the heavy sweatshirt she wore but had no idea if the temperature would drop later in the day. Since she had to walk home this afternoon, it was easier to wear more clothes and be hot than be cold later on. She pulled the front door shut behind her and started to walk down the sidewalk.

The first half of this walk she had been doing for a long time. Three houses down the sidewalk, and then she cut through the Appleton's yard and into the field behind the elementary school. When she was across the street from the Appleton house, she checked both ways and crossed the street. There were rarely any cars on the street at this time of the morning, and if there were, it was parents driving their kids to school. Chrissy knew them and usually gave a wave. This was one of the quiet mornings. No cars, no people. The warm air was stagnant, making the morning seem eerily still.

Something zipped by Chrissy's head while she crossed the street. She waved a hand around her head and kept going. The mosquitoes had all died off when it was colder at the end of September, but maybe with this warmer air, they were coming back out. She didn't think much of it.

She had been walking through the Appleton's yard for years. They were nice people. They used to have kids that went to the middle school when Chrissy was younger, but they were in high school now. They would all walk to school together. Chrissy and Sarah would stop at the elementary school, and Chrissy's older sister Alyssa and the Appletons would continue on to the middle school. They never really asked if it was okay to keep going through their yard, but it made the walk a lot shorter, and they didn't have to walk on the busier roads this way.

The Appleton's yard sloped down in the back, then there was a thin line of trees before the field behind the elementary school opened back up. Her mom told her the line of trees used to be a thickly wooded area, but over time they built more and more houses, and the woods became just a few trees separating school property from the neighborhood. The dirt between the trees was worn down from the daily traffic through the line of trees.

Chrissy felt something else zip by her ear, and she flapped her hand at it again as she descended the hill in the Appleton's backyard. It was unusually buggy out.

She reached the bottom of the hill and looked for the usual place she passed through the trees. There was a flat rock that was almost completely buried in the ground. Every day she would step right on the rock. She didn't know why other than that it was just out of habit, but when she got to the bottom of the hill, the area they usually passed through was muddy and covered with water.

"Ugh," Chrissy groaned and looked to either side to see if there was a dry spot where she could cross over, but there wasn't. This sort of thing never happened in the fall. Even if there was hard rain the night before, the low spot never flooded up like this. It only happened in the spring. If there was a lot of snow still on the ground and a heavy rain helped to melt it quickly, the mud and swamp-like ground under the trees would appear. On those days, she would wear boots, but she wasn't expecting this today and had her nicer sneakers on that she really didn't want to get all muddy.

At first, she thought of turning around, going home and getting different shoes on, or taking her mother up on the offer for a ride. But she decided against it and would just do her best to keep her shoes out of the mud. She looked for her rock. If the flat rock was sticking up out of the mud, she could step on that and then jump across the rest of the mud to the dry grass on the other side.

She scanned, but it looked like the rock was covered by the water and mud. Another bug flew by her head. She ignored it this time. Around one of the bigger trees, the ground came up, right at the base of the tree. The dirt was high enough that it wasn't too wet or muddy. If she could get her foot right in that spot at the base of the large oak tree, she could then leap across the mud to the other side. She didn't want to have to jump to the tree because there wasn't much space to land, and she didn't want to lose her balance and fall into the mud. Instead, Chrissy got close to the edge of the brown, stagnant puddle and stretched her foot over to the other side. At first, she didn't think she would be able to reach—her leg just didn't feel long enough. Then she decided to go all out. If she fell face first in the mud, she would just have to go home, shower, and change, but she was going to go for it. She leaned her body forward, out over the puddle, and stuck her foot out. It planted right next to the tree. Since her body was still moving forward, Chrissy used her momentum in an attempt to propel herself to the other side, but she chickened out halfway through and brought her foot back next to the one right against the base of the tree.

It was hard to stand there pressed against the tree, made more difficult by the fact that she was wearing a backpack full of books. It messed with her balance. Chrissy wrapped her right arm around the tree while she thought about her next move. She almost didn't make the leap over to the tree, and the leap across the puddle to the dry grass just past it was a longer distance. She didn't think she could make it, but she also didn't think she could make it back. Chrissy held on tighter to the tree and looked back behind her, then shook her head. There was no way she could make it.

Something moved against her leg. She felt it right on her ankle like it was up inside the leg of her pants against her sock. Anything could be hiding in the dark water, and she didn't want to find out. She made the decision to go for it. There was no need to stick her landing on the other side like she did against the tree—that might be the only thing that kept her dry after this jump. She prepared herself. With her left foot leading the way, she pushed off, aiming her foot for the green grass on the other side.

Something was wrong. Her right foot stuck to the tree. She turned her body, but it was too late. Chrissy went down into the mud, her foot still held by something against the tree. Eventually, she sat up and wiped her eyes. The mud dripped off her face, and she felt it falling off her hair and down her back. Her backpack was still submerged in the viscous liquid. Chrissy blinked and rubbed her eyes again, trying to see. She pulled her foot toward her, but it still wouldn't budge. There was pressure around her calf, but she couldn't see well enough to know what was happening. She blinked the brown liquid out of her eyes and finally was able to catch a glimpse of what was happening to her.

Chrissy screamed. A swarm of flies surrounded her leg and moved up her body. She couldn't hear the buzzing at first, but it grew louder as they got closer. Chrissy put her hands back into the mud, pushing hard against the ground to try to get away from the swarming insects. But it felt like they were pulling her back, keeping her in place, not letting her move.

"No!" Chrissy screamed again. She turned toward the Appleton house. It was right there, maybe someone was home. "Help!"

There was no movement or any answer from the house. Chrissy looked back at the flies. She couldn't tell where they were coming from, but there was more of them. They covered her leg up to her waist. The weight of the flies pushed her down further into the deceptively deep puddle. She could still feel them crawling against her leg even after it was submerged in the muddy water. They proceeded up higher on her body, forcing her chest down into the mud as they got closer to her face. The buzzing grew louder. Chrissy struggled against them but couldn't move.

"Help, please!" she screamed one last time. The flies moved around her head and forced that down as well. They didn't cover her face, and she did everything she could to keep her mouth and nose out of the water, but the flies were too strong for her.

"Hel—" she started to scream, but the dirty water filled her mouth. She could feel it in the back of her throat, filling her up. She tried to close her mouth, but the flies found their way in too. The mixture of flies and muddy water filled her mouth and forced her down into the puddle.

The last sound she heard was the end of her gargled scream for help.

CHAPTER 11

Lisa didn't know if John Holland's knowledge of her daily schedule pushed her toward change or if she was just getting bored with the same routine. Maybe it was a combination of both. Regardless of the reason, Lisa started getting dressed for the gym in the morning before the kids left for school. After she dropped them off, she went right to the gym and got a workout in. The elliptical machine gave her some time to think each day, and it got her out, doing something. Plus, it made her feel good about herself.

Her legs burned, but it only forced her to push down harder against the pedals of the machine. Sometimes she would hold onto the handles, but towards the end of the workout, when she felt the sweat dripping down the small of her back, and it got harder to keep going, she let go of the handles. Lisa pumped her arms and forced herself to keep going. The best way to do this, she found, was to get lost in her thoughts.

It had been a few weeks since Chrissy Franklin's disappearance. With each passing day, Matthew got more depressed. It was a different kind of depressed than he had been when he knew they were moving. Lisa worried about him. At the school, they offered counseling for kids affected by Chrissy's disappearance. The school targeted Matthew and Sarah Bowers as the two most in need of help surrounding the incident. Matthew refused help. Lisa even called the school, hoping to get them to force him to meet with someone. They did get him into the room, but they couldn't make him talk, so he and the counselor just sat there and looked at each other. His grades were slipping, and he spent most of his time at home in his room.

At first, Lisa and Tim understood why he was doing what he was doing. It was hard to make friends, let alone find someone he thought might become his first girlfriend just to have her disappear right when he got to know her. They gave him some space for a few days, but he withdrew more as each day passed.

Her heaving breath pulled her from her thoughts and back to the gym. She looked down at the monitor, which she tried to keep from watching the entire time; forty-seven minutes. The goal was forty-five minutes. She could stop and still exceed her goal, but she pushed on. When the clock read fifty minutes, she slowed her pace and cooled down for a minute or two, then hopped off the machine. People were lifting weights and doing ab workouts in the mostly empty gym. She could do more of that type of stuff after her time on the elliptical, but she wasn't quite ready for more just yet. Her almost hour workout was perfect at the moment.

She walked slowly over to the water fountain. When she got there, she pushed the button and held it down for ten seconds, as she'd done since she was a kid. It had become a habit. Lisa always thought she did it because it would get the germy water flushed out of the system. There was a strong chance it wasn't true and just something ten-year-old Lisa believed. Either way, she wasn't about to change that habit now. She bent down and took her drink, then stood back up, still working on catching her breath. Lisa put her hand on her hips, walked into the women's locker room, and got her purse and sweatshirt out of the locker, and went out to her car.

The gym was just a short drive from home, another reason

Lisa didn't mind going every day. In the duplex, the drive was twenty minutes through the busiest part of town and multiple traffic lights. It was such a pain to get to, she never went. Here, it was five minutes and one traffic light that was almost always green. Just another reason their new home was better than the old one. It was cold out, but she was hot and rolled the window halfway down as she drove. She pulled into the driveway on Molly Lane. The car was only halfway in the driveway when she heard the familiar sound that she thought would forever send chills up her spine.

"No!" John Holland yelled from his backyard.

Lisa got the car all the way into the driveway and threw it into park. Some days she would take her time getting out of the car and into the house, but not today. She put the window up and kept the door locked while she collected her purse. There wasn't anything else she needed to bring into the house.

"No!" Another yell from next door, this one louder than the first, even with the window up. Lisa focused on making sure her eyes did not wander over to John's backyard. She didn't think he could see her or that she could see him from the angle she was parked, but she didn't even want to take the chance. She unlocked the door, still with her head down, and got out. She marched, sore legs and aching body, straight for the front door, her eyes on the front doorknob the entire time, glancing away only to make sure she had the key ready for when she got there.

Just as she reached the single step up onto the porch, a hand wrapped around her upper arm.

"I've been wanting to talk to you, Lisa," John said, his mouth much too close to her ear as he held her from behind.

Lisa tried to pull away from the old man, but his grip was stronger than she would have thought just by looking at the old guy.

"No! Get your hands off me!" Lisa yelled, trying to match the volume of the yells Holland gave out in his backyard.

"Not today, I think," Holland said. His other hand clamped around her mouth, and he pulled her hard against his chest.

Lisa struggled and fought back against him, screaming into his wrinkled, dirt-covered hand. That only made him press his hand harder against her mouth, his palm muffling her scream. He pulled her back off the porch in the direction of his house. She strained against him. He looked like a frail old man, but Lisa couldn't knock him over or put up any sort of fight against him. His strength surprised her, but she still fought. She flailed her one free arm back and forth, trying to free herself, kicking one leg then the other back toward him, but the steel grip on her arm never lessened. He dragged her across her driveway and down the small hill toward his front door.

"Please stop!" Lisa shouted into his hand, but he either couldn't hear her or didn't care.

As they drew closer to his house, Lisa became more desperate. At first, the shock of being grabbed and taken from her porch like this had caused her to fight back with no real thought put into what she was doing. Now, after having a few seconds to think and react, she fought with a purpose. She still had one hand free, and she reached back behind her head and twisted her fingers into Holland's stark white hair. Lisa pulled at it, yanking his head to the side as hard as she could, hoping to weaken his grip on her enough to twist away. Nothing happened. She pulled again, harder, and tried to wrench her body in the opposite direction, but Holland's grip never wavered. How could the old man be this strong?

"There is nothing you can do, Lisa," Holland whispered into her ear.

She could feel his chin moving against her skin as he spoke and smelled the toothpaste he used to brush his teeth.

"No!" Lisa shouted.

Her hand moved from his hair to his face. Her thumb felt the bridge of his nose and then one of his eyes, and she dug it in.

Lisa pressed as hard as she could, clawing at his eyes. Holland clenched his eyes closed — she could feel the muscles of his face squeezing tight, trying to stop her, but it only made her push harder. She wanted to push her thumb right through his eyelid and into his eye — that, she thought, would break his grip on her. But even as she dug her thumb as hard as she could into his eye, his grip didn't waver, and the distance between them and the front door of Holland's house grew shorter.

Lisa realized she didn't have much time left. The last thing she wanted to do was end up in Holland's house. She didn't know what he had in mind, but she knew she didn't want to be there. Her eyes darted back and forth as she still pushed her thumb against Holland's face. There wasn't anyone outside. With most people working, no one was around to see what was happening. She hoped someone was looking out the window right now, seeing what was happening and calling the police. It might be her only chance of getting out of this.

They made it to Holland's porch. He stopped dragging her for a moment and pulled her tighter to him. The hand on her mouth let go only for an instant.

"Help!" Lisa screamed before his hand tried to clamp back down around her mouth. She slid her own hand away from his eye and in front of her mouth, pushing his hand away, and twisted her body away from him in another attempt to stop the abduction. The old man was still too strong. He laughed and wrapped his arm tight around her head, pressing her own hand against her mouth and nose.

Lisa couldn't breathe with her hand covering her nose and felt the effects quickly after the exertion of fighting back against Holland the entire trip from her front door to his. He squeezed a bit harder, and her arms and legs weakened. They stayed that way for what felt a few seconds. He let go of her arm, and she heard the door open, but there wasn't anything she could do to stop this. Her arms and legs felt like concrete. Her eyes began to close, and she couldn't catch her breath. The last thing she saw were the walls around Holland's open front door, the light from the outside contrasting with the dark interior of the house.

***

When she came to, a chain was wrapped around her leg, and her hands were held together with a zip tie. At first, she had trouble focusing on anything more than a few feet away. She could see the chain around her leg and her hands in front of her but couldn't see what she was chained to or where she was — it was still a blur.

Her body hurt. Her arms and legs were sore. Her head pounded. She turned to look around, but that only made every inch of her body hurt more, so she collapsed and lay flat on her back. There was a light off to her right, but even a quick glance in that direction made her head worse, so she closed her eyes.

***

She could have fallen asleep or passed out, she didn't know, but when she opened her eyes again, she wasn't alone. Lisa still couldn't see much farther than three or four feet in any direction — everything beyond that was blurry. But she saw the feet standing at her head. Standing over her. She assumed they belonged to Holland, but she had no way to be sure.

Her hands were still bound together, the chain still around her leg.

"John?"

Lisa pushed the single word out of her mouth, but she could barely hear it. She couldn't even be sure she said the word or if she just thought about saying it. She blinked, hoping for some sort of response. For a long time, there was nothing but silence, but the person standing over her didn't move. She blinked.

She might have passed out again. She couldn't be sure. When she opened her eyes, the feet were still there.

"John?" she repeated. At least this time, her words were loud enough that she could hear them. She blinked again, faster this time, trying to clear her vision so she could know what was around her instead of just guessing.

"They're not always in charge, you know," the gravelly voice of John Holland said. The clear, loud voice that yelled in the backyard was gone, and the old man's voice was back. Lisa still couldn't see his face, but at least she knew who it was.

"What?"

Lisa had no idea what he was talking about. She blinked a few more times, each bringing the world back into focus a little bit more. The walls were concrete, as was the floor. The light she could focus on more now was in the corner of the small room. There was a pole just at her feet, the chain around her legs wrapped around it to keep her in place. There was nothing else in the room—nothing on the walls, no windows. The door behind Holland looked to be the heavy metal type as opposed to wood or fiberglass that were in most houses. Her eyes scanned around the room once more, looking for anything that she could use as a weapon to get out, but the room was bare. If there was a good thing in all of this, it was that when she turned up missing, Tim knew the number one suspect right away.

"I said, they're not always in charge of me. Sometimes I'm in charge of myself." John just stood over her, looking down at her. His legs looked weak. Even looking up at him, she wondered how the old man had managed to get her from her front door all the way here into what she assumed was his basement.

"John, you need help." She didn't know what he was talking about, but whoever "they" were, it was clear he didn't think they were in charge now. Maybe she could reason with this part of him. "Let me go, and we can get you help. You know you won't get in trouble for this. They're going to put you in the same place to get help whether you do this to me or not. So why don't you let me go? We can call you an ambulance and get you to a place where they can help you."

John laughed. "If I was just crazy, I'd gladly get in an

ambulance and get some help. But it's past crazy, Lisa. You wouldn't understand—not yet."

"Help me understand. You can't just keep me here."

Lisa was starting to feel more like herself. Her vision had cleared, and although she was still sore, she felt like she could use her arms and legs however she wanted. Before, it had hurt to even think about moving them. It must have been from passing out and lack of oxygen, but she felt better now. She twisted her body so she was sitting up, then pushed herself back so she could rest against the pole. Her legs turned awkwardly to accommodate the chain, but it felt much more natural.

"I *can* just keep you here, Lisa. And we will," John said. His feet still hadn't moved. He looked down at her, and she stared right back up at him. "And no one will find you. You're here as long as I—as long as *they* say you're here."

"John, you were arrested two weeks ago for harassing my family. I'm sure they told you to leave us alone after you made bail. You were calling my name at our front door. As soon as I'm found missing, which could be right now since I have no idea what time it is, you're going to be the first one they look at. They are going to search your house, and they *are* going to find me." Lisa stared at him, her lips pressed together, waiting to hear his reply to what she had said. He stood looking down at her, a small smile on his face. When he didn't respond, she continued. "You think this little basement room with the metal door is going to fool them? Keep them out? This will be the first place they'll look."

John burst out into laughter again and took a shuffling step toward the corner of the room where the light sat.

"Lisa, my little basement room with the metal door is more than what it looks like from the inside. The fact is, the police have already been here. They have already searched the house, and they did *not* find you. I might still be a suspect. Your husband has been watching my house non-stop for the two days you've

PERHAPS SHE WILL DIE

been missing. But I will not lie to you. No one will ever find you in here. And there is no way for you to get out."

Lisa watched him. She assumed she had only been out for a few minutes, an hour at most, but not two full days. Was he just messing with her head? She supposed anything was possible. But she would never give up hope that help was coming.

"You can't lie your way into me giving up hope. I'll get out of here."

"Think what you want, Lisa."

John shuffled the rest of the way over to the light in the corner. It was only then that Lisa realized it was a battery-powered light. It looked like a kerosene lamp, but it was battery-powered. She had seen lights like this before, mostly used by people going camping. Tim had bought one to go fishing a few years ago but only used it once. It was metal but housed an LED light that could stay bright for hours without needing new batteries.

"But I'm not lying. They've come, they've gone. You're still here. I'll bring the light back later with some food."

John took small delicate steps back across the small room. The moving light changing the shadows that covered the walls.

"I don't believe you," Lisa said, with less conviction than she'd had a few seconds earlier.

"Believe what you want, Lisa," John said. He pulled at the door, struggling to get it open. He put the light on the floor outside the room, dimming her surroundings. "Here's a bucket in case you have to…you know. Keep it close to you. I'll be back." John slid the bucket over to her, and it hit her in the knees.

He turned without a word and left the room. The door closed, plunging the room into total darkness. There were a few metallic slides and clicks that Lisa assumed were locks. Then there was only silence.

When sound never came and her eyes never adjusted to the darkness, she screamed for help.

CHAPTER 12

There was no way to determine what time it was or even what day it was. Lisa didn't know how long she had been unconscious. Holland told her it was two days. That could have been right. But he also could just be telling her that. She could have been out for only ten minutes, just enough time for him to chain her up and zip tie her hands. Then he gave her the bucket and left. That could have been right too.

The room was dark and silent. She heard none of the noises you would hear in a normal house. She assumed she was in the basement, but her basement was always making noise. Every time someone flushed a toilet or washed their hands, there was noise. Every time the heat kicked on, there was noise. Even someone just walking across the floor produced a sound in her basement. Yet, here, there was nothing. No sound of John walking back up the stairs. No sound of running water, of him walking across the floor. Just total darkness and total silence.

Lisa tried to let her mind wander, to think of other things so she wouldn't go crazy in her concrete room—cell. It was hard. She realized why solitary confinement was considered a punishment for people in jail. This was torture. She didn't know how long she had been there, but she counted the only thing she could. Meals. It had been four meals so far if she could call them meals. The first one was a slice of bread with some butter on it and a small glass of water. She hadn't eaten since before the gym, however long ago that was, so she ate and drank ravenously, not stopping even to breathe. The next meal was more substantial—a large plastic bowl full of rice. Holland must have seen how hungry she was after that first snack of bread and upped the amount of food he gave her. He didn't give her a utensil, but she didn't care and poured the rice out of the bowl right into her mouth, then used a finger to scoop out what remained, washed it down with another small glass of water. Rice again for the next meal and a bit larger glass of water.

Now she was just finishing her fourth meal, a bowl of ziti. John always stayed when she ate and took the bowl, the cup, and the light with him when he left. He stood over her now, just as he did all of the other times.

"I hope it doesn't taste too bad," John said in the same old man gravelly voice. This was the first thing he had said to her, other than telling her he'd brought food since he shut and locked the door on her for the first time.

Lisa didn't respond. She was too busy drinking the melted butter out of the bottom of the maroon plastic bowl. She heard him, though, and the thought crossed her mind to laugh. If the situation were different, she would have laughed, but she didn't. With her bowl empty, she grabbed the cup with both hands and drank down the water as fast as she could. She realized it was not the best way to eat or drink. She remembered hearing on one of those TV survival shows that eating and drinking too quickly when you had less calories coming in could give you gas. She didn't care. She was too hungry and thirsty to care. She slid the bowl and cup back over toward her captor and then looked up at him.

"I need you to clean out the bucket, too," she said. Her eyes looked over at the bucket. It was as far away from her as the chain would let her go, which wasn't far enough. Some flies must have found their way into the room because two were hovering over the top of it.

Holland nodded. "I wish you didn't have to do it that way. There's just no other way in here." There was a sad look on his face like he didn't want any of this to happen. She couldn't wait to get her hands on him. They always offered kickboxing classes at the gym—she'd always thought about going but then chickened out. When she got out of here, one of the first things she would do was enroll in one.

"Let me go, then." Lisa focused her eyes on his, trying to hurt him with just her look. "I could use a regular fucking toilet then."

Holland exhaled and shuffled over to the bucket. It was about half full—Lisa knew it was heavy. The man leaned over slowly, resting a hand on his knee as he did so, and then lifted with his legs and his back. The man that dragged her kicking and screaming across her front lawn groaned—not loud, but enough so that Lisa could hear him. She watched him, studying his every move the entire time. Then he struggled to bring the bucket back to the door, the contents sloshing around inside. John opened the door and set the bucket just outside. Lisa tried to look outside the room but still couldn't see anything beyond the doorway. He came back into the room and took the light.

"I'll be back with more food and a clean bucket," he said between long, heavy breaths and then closed the door behind him.

Four meals. She had no idea of the time or the day, but she knew it had been four meals. She guessed he fed her at least twice a day. It was so hard to judge time in the dark, but she felt like there was a longer time between the first meal and the second, and the time between the second and third was shorter. So maybe the meal she just ate was breakfast on the third day that she knew about. It sounded right in her head. There was lots of intermittent sleep mixed in with her waiting for food, so her timing could be all off. But for now, it was the only theory she had, so she decided to just go with it. She also needed to think of a way to get out of this place.

Holland always gave her a wide berth when he was in her room. He set the light down in the corner nearest to the door now, after putting it in the far corner the first time. The food was always slid across the floor—the same thing with the drink. He never got close enough to her for her to attack him, except when he took the bucket. The old man's slow retrieval of the heavy bucket could be the opening she needed. The problem was, if she attacked him, there would be no one around to help her out of the chains. If he died, she would probably die too. At least she would die with the light on. Maybe she would threaten to kill him. If he didn't want to die, he could let her go. They both lived, or they both died. She could convince him to let her get up and stretch her legs.

Lisa's head pounded. Her back arched, and her legs weren't much better. The zip-tie around her wrist dug into her skin. The darkness was driving her crazy. She knew she couldn't take much more of this.

Her mind began flipping from one thing to the next without reason. She thought about her escape and then about Matthew, Olivia, and Tim and what they were going through. If only they knew how close she was. She assumed she was in Holland's basement, but she didn't know for sure. If there was any indication she was inside his house, Tim would find a way to get to her. Even if the police didn't believe she was there, Tim would never stop looking for her.

How long would it take her to fill up the bucket again? She didn't know. She would want it to be heavier than before. Make him struggle a little bit longer before going after him and convincing him the only way he was going to live was if he let her go. That was her only play.

Definitely kickboxing class next time. Or karate, or jujitsu, or one of those fighting things. She was not going to be caught off guard again. The bucket, the bucket—she needed to concentrate. She needed to know exactly what she was going to do when he came back with the bucket. Lisa rolled on her side and stretched her legs out in one direction and her arms in the other, using her upper arm as a pillow for her head. She'd learned this was the most comfortable position. With her arm stretched out, the zip tie didn't hurt as much, and she liked the ability to straighten both legs at the same time. She wanted to think and prepare for Holland's arrival for what she could say or do, but her eyes began drooping. Before long, she was asleep.

***

The next sound she heard was the familiar click and metallic slide of the door locks. Lisa's eyes fluttered, but she didn't move from her stretched-out position. She hadn't had time to think earlier, and now she might have a chance to do something, anything to change the situation she was in. As the door opened, she decided the least she could do was change her attitude toward Holland. She tried to think back to the very first time she met him. He wasn't the scary monster back then. She would pretend she was talking to that guy. Maybe she could get somewhere.

John Holland stood in the doorway, her bucket at his feet, just behind him next to the light, a plastic bowl and cup in his hands.

"Rice," he said and slid the bowl toward her, then pushed the cup as close to her as he could.

Lisa didn't feel that hungry and wondered how much time had passed since he was last there. Was he just trying to mess with her again?

"Thank you," she said, trying out her new approach. She picked up the bowl in both hands and was about to eat but stopped herself and looked back up at him as he brought the light in and placed it in the corner. "John. I'm going to go crazy here in the dark like this. Could you leave the light and maybe a clock? I can't live like this for long."

"I wish I could," he sighed. "They won't let me."

"'They.' John, who is 'they'?"

"I—I wish I could tell you that too, Mrs. Ewing. But they won't let us do that either." Holland actually looked sad about the news he delivered. It was almost like he didn't want to be doing this anymore. She had to press him more.

"John, I think you're just losing it—" she started, but Holland interrupted her.

"No!" he shouted. It wasn't as loud as when she heard him shout in his backyard, but it was close to it. It echoed in her small cell. She jumped and almost dropped her bowl, not expecting the outburst. "I know what people around here think. You all think I'm just some senile old man."

Lisa shook her head. This was not the way she'd thought it would go. She needed to get it back on track, and a few lies wouldn't hurt. "John, my mother died a few years ago. She had dementia. Sometimes she didn't know what she was saying or who she was talking to. But they gave her medication, and it made her better. She remembered everything. She didn't get confused. It didn't kill her; she had a stroke. But the stuff that was going on in her head, it stopped." Lisa shed a tear. None of it was true—her mother was still very much alive with no signs of dementia. But the tear was for her mother anyway.

"I'm sorry for your loss, Mrs. Ewing. I really am. But this is nothing like that." Holland looked at her, then from one side of the room to the other, like he was waiting for someone to jump out of the walls at him. "They aren't just in my head. They're real. They aren't always in charge, but I always have to do what they say."

"Who are *they*? Can they see us?" Lisa felt like she was getting sucked into his fantasy world. She knew she was, but there wasn't much she could do to stop it. A voice in her head told her not to listen to him, but being locked in a dark room for who knew how long had done something to her brain. She felt her palms sweat and fought the urge to look around the room with Holland. She told herself to stick to her plan.

"I can't tell you more than that. Please eat, Mrs. Ewing."

Lisa put the bowl to her mouth and tipped it back, letting the rice fill her mouth. She did it three times, without another word between them. When the bowl was empty, she put it back on the floor and slid it over to Holland. She did the same thing with the cup of water, collecting her thoughts for one more play at him now that she had calmed down.

The bucket was still behind him, so she knew he wasn't leaving just yet. She wanted to see how close he would get to her. If he got close enough, she might try to grab him.

"John, I don't know if there is a *they* or not. I really don't. But I don't want to die in here."

Lisa looked up at him. With her hands bound together the way they were, it probably looked like she was begging or praying. She didn't think that could hurt her chances. More tears streamed down her cheeks; the salty fluid hit her lips. She stared at him. He picked up the bowl and cup, turned and put them on the floor behind him, then grabbed the bucket. Holland looked down at her again and tightened his lips. He looked like he wanted to speak but then stopped himself. He did it again, and this time words came out.

"They don't want that to happen either," Holland said. His eyes moved back and forth from one side of the room to the other, faster now. He was scared. "I don't want you to die in here, Mrs. Ewing. And...and neither do they. They told us to keep you alive."

Her bucket slipped from his hands and dropped to the floor. His fingers twitched, then she realized it wasn't just his fingers, but both arms. He was having a stroke or something. He was going to die in this hell room, and then so would she.

Holland's knees buckled, and he almost collapsed on the floor. His upper body slumped over, and his hands hung down, hitting the floor, but his half-bent knees managed to hold him up. It looked unnatural.

The contorted body in front of her stood up. There was a different look in his eye. They were harder somehow, more intense than the usual old man eyes he usually had.

"No!"

Holland's shout echoed again through the cell. This was the same shout she had heard in the backyard all those times. It seemed like so long ago, she was sitting on the stairs while this man yelled at her and slammed his shovel against her front door. She would have traded that for this any day.

"No! I don't want to!" he shouted again.

Holland kicked the bucket at his feet over to her. It slammed against her knee and rolled to the corner of the room out of her reach.

"John, are you okay?" she asked, knowing the answer to her question was a definite no.

"He is right, Lisa. We don't want you to die in here. In fact, you're going to help us," Holland said. He didn't shuffle but walked over to the corner to retrieve the bucket. "When we're ready for you, you're going to be our guest."

"John, who is 'we'?" she asked again, hoping to get a different answer since it was obvious something had changed with him. It was still his voice and his body, but there was no other resemblance to the man who had stood in front of her watching her eat five minutes earlier.

"We are in charge now. Sometimes John is in charge, and sometimes we are. But he always listens to us."

"But who are you?" Lisa said.

The change in John Holland made her curious and a little scared. She didn't know what was going on. She supposed he could be one of those multiple personality disorder people. But he seemed so much more different than before. There might be more going on, but she didn't know what.

Holland smiled down at her and dropped the bucket right in front of her. She knew she could grab his leg now if she wanted to—he was well within reach. But she didn't know if she wanted to grab this version of John Holland. It looked like it might be able to handle her fighting against him better than the other, older version.

"You will have all your answers soon, Lisa," Holland said as he backed up toward the door. "We will leave the light here for you."

"I...I hope you're telling me the truth." Lisa was scared and felt tears welling up in her eyes again, but she refused to let them drip down her cheeks. She stared up at him without blinking, hoping her eyes would dry up on their own. "Th... thank you for the light."

"You're welcome, Lisa. Oh, and it's two-forty-five in the morning."

Knowing the time made Lisa momentarily dizzy. She had been sure she had it figured out at least a little bit, and this revelation was not something she was expecting. Her entire internal clock was way off.

"What...what day is it?" Lisa asked, hoping to get a bit more information. Before Holland had said he couldn't tell her all of this information, but now he could. If he did have multiple personalities, this one was clearly the one in charge.

Holland smiled and laughed at the question, then shook his head. "You would like to know that, Lisa?" He wagged a finger at her. "Not yet on that one, we think. That will have to wait."

Holland backed out of the room, leaving the light on in the corner well out of Lisa's reach. He smiled as he closed the door.

CHAPTER 13

Chrissy Franklin couldn't see anything; she couldn't feel her body either. Was she dead? The last thing she remembered was the swarm of flies surrounding her, pushing her down into the puddle. She gagged and tried to spit when she thought about the flies that had pushed their way into her mouth. But she didn't know where her body was. She wasn't just in a very dark room. At least it didn't feel that way. It was more like her body was gone. She couldn't see because it felt like she had no eyes. Chrissy tried to move her legs and rub her fingers together, but there was nothing there. She couldn't feel anything other than what was in her head. She must have died. This was what happened when you died.

"Hello," she thought she said, but she couldn't hear the words and didn't know if she actually made any sound. Still, it was worth a shot.

There was no response. She didn't know what she would do if there was. She was stuck in the darkness. She had to be dead, and this was Heaven, or hell, or something in between. Chrissy's family was not very religious, and although she knew about what many people believed happened when you died, this was a whole new thing for her. She always kind of believed there was a God and Heaven and hell when you died. Her parents had never really talked to her about it, but it was something she just believed on her own. She supposed someday when she was older, she would have tried going to church, but in sixth grade, she wasn't about to start. It didn't really matter what her beliefs were—she had never heard anyone's idea of Heaven or hell as this black, bodiless space. No, she was sure that if people thought this was what the afterlife was like, they might be a little more scared to end up there.

"Hello?" Chrissy said again, still not sure if there were words coming out of her mouth.

"Hello," a voice called back to her. She hadn't been sure she was speaking, and she wasn't sure she heard the voice or if it was just in her head. Either way, it was not her voice.

"Are…are you real?" Chrissy said, not really sure what to say in this situation.

"Yes, of course, I'm real," the voice said. "I'm not you, am I?"

"No, I guess not. Well, where are you? I can't see anything. I'm just surrounded by blackness."

"Oh. Okay. Ready?" the voice said. Chrissy was sure it was a boy.

It sounded like a boy's voice. It made her think of Matt Ewing—he was probably worried because she never showed up for school. Her thoughts drifted for a second and then returned to her current problem.

"I'm ready," Chrissy said. It was reassuring having someone else to communicate with—it helped her feel less alone in the darkness. But it also sounded like this boy knew what he was doing.

"Okay, close your eyes," the boy said.

"But I—" Chrissy started, but he interrupted her.

"I know, I know. Just think about what you would do if you *could* close your eyes and do that."

"Okay."

"Now, you need to think really hard," the boy said. He slowed his words down, making each one seem like the most important one. "Think of the last place you were, right before you came here."

"The last place. I was being pushed into a big puddle," Chrissy said.

"Okay, but where was that puddle? The bottom of a hill, the top of a hill, a big grassy field? Wherever it was, just think about that," the boy said.

It felt as if he were right there next to her. It sounded like it too, but she still felt as if she had no body. She followed his instructions and thought about the Appletons' backyard—she knew it so well it was easy. The grove of trees, the early morning sky, and the puddle she had to jump over.

"Okay," she said.

"Keep thinking about it—don't let anything else inside your head. Only think of that place. Can you picture it in your head? As many details as you can remember. Put them all in there. Think about it all. But whatever you do, don't open your eyes."

The boy seemed confident like he knew what he was talking about, so Chrissy followed his instructions.

She concentrated on the Appletons' backyard. How many times had she been through it? All those trips to school, she walked through their yard every day. The back of the house. The rock she stepped on. The way the grass dipped as she walked toward the trees. The old fence along one side that belonged to the neighbors.

Then she felt it. Something was different.

Instead of thinking about what it felt like to close her eyes, it felt like her eyes were actually closed. Chrissy could almost feel the sun on her skin and the breeze in her hair.

"Are you there?" the boy asked.

"Yes, I...I think so. It feels like I'm there. Can I open my eyes?" Chrissy said.

"Wait, not yet," the boy said. He was closer than before.

"I'll wait until you tell me to," Chrissy said. There was a sense of nervousness and excitement. The fear of what happened to her was gone. She wasn't thinking about or worried about the flies or anyone from her life. She was lost in this moment, waiting to get her body back. Maybe it was Heaven.

"You're ready now," the boy said. "Open your eyes."

Chrissy hesitated. The wind blew. She was sure of it. Then, after a few short breaths, she opened her eyes.

The sun was bright. It was the middle of the day—not a time she would usually be standing in the Appletons' backyard, but it was beautiful. She looked around. It was like she was really there. The trees had leaves on them. It wasn't fall anymore, but late spring or summer. The end of the school year. She always associated the Appletons' backyard with school because it was the only time she was ever in their backyard, so she guessed it must be right near the end of the school year. It was warm, maybe even the very last day of school. That was always the best walk to and from school, knowing she wouldn't have to make the walk again until September. She smiled and looked up at the cloudless sky. Even if it wasn't the last day of school, she would pretend it was. The day was perfect.

"Just like you pictured it?"

Chrissy jumped, not expecting anyone else to be there with her. She put one hand on her mouth and another on her heart and bent over, staring at the ground. Her heart raced, but she didn't know if she should laugh or cry at being startled by the boy.

"Oh shit, you scared me," Chrissy said, regaining her composure.

"Oh, I'm sorry. I figured you knew I was here. I've never actually taught someone how to do that before, so it's cool that you could do it."

"Cool," Chrissy said, and smiled. She held out her hand.

"I'm Chrissy."

"I'm Brian," he said. He looked down at her hand but didn't shake it, then looked back up at her. "We can't touch each other here. This is in your mind — at least we think it's in your mind. I can visit it, but what I see is different than what you see. I'm in my own mind. If we touch, it's like combining the two worlds or something. Anyway, it doesn't let the world work, and we both end up back in the blackness."

"Ah, okay." Chrissy was confused.

"It's hard to explain. Just know we can't touch anyone else."

Chrissy nodded and didn't say anything. She had so many questions, and she thought Brian would be able to explain them. And he did know more than her, but still, he didn't have all the answers. After a moment, she decided just to ask her question.

"So, are we dead?"

Brian laughed. "No. We're pretty sure of that. Did you see flies?"

Chrissy nodded. "You keep saying we — are there others?"

"Oh yeah. I guess I should tell you everything we know." Brian smiled at her, but then the smile disappeared, and he looked like he needed to mentally prepare for what he was about to tell her. He looked like a normal kid about her age, but his clothes were certainly not anything boys her age wore to school. They looked like they were from the nineties or something.

"Okay, tell me everything," Chrissy said, eager to find out as much as she could about her current situation.

"Right. We all saw flies. There are four of us. You make number five. You, me, Barbara, Harry, and Tiffany." Chrissy could tell he didn't practice giving this speech because he jumped all around, but she followed what he was saying. "Anyway, we all saw flies. And we all, I think, thought we were about to die by some swarm of flies. But we didn't. The flies have talked to us. Barbara has been here the longest. She's talked to them the most.

They don't talk to us that much. I haven't really been here that long either. But the last time they talked to us, they said it would only be a short time until we would be about to leave."

"Leave? But where are we?"

"We don't know that. They just keep saying we will be able to leave once there is one more and then someone to make the bridge or something like that. We don't really know what they mean, but when they say so, we get to leave. We all kind of agree that is a good thing. I don't know if they mean a bridge back to the world or not, but it's better than the darkness."

"Well, why don't you just stay here?" Chrissy looked around and gestured with her hands to the world around her. The one she made up in her head.

Brian shook his head. "We can't stay here very long. We're not sure why. We don't even know how long we're here. Time is very strange here. You can learn more about that when you meet everyone. We think it's the mental exertion it takes to bring about this world. We can only do it for a short time, and then it goes away. Talking to others makes it go even faster. The rest of the time is spent in that darkness."

"Are we, like, prisoners? Because it seems like we are," Chrissy said. She scrunched up her nose and turned her back on Brian, looking at the rest of the world, wondering if she could imagine another place or if it was just limited to this place specifically because she disappeared here.

"I would say we're more like prisoners than guests. We don't need to eat or drink somehow. It's just dark, and we can talk to each other. Which is what we do most of the time." The image of Brian started to flicker in and out.

"You're...you're kinda disappearing."

"I know," Brian said, his voice more distant again. "I've been in my world a lot already. We didn't know you would be coming. You'll probably lose it soon. When you get back to the darkness, just call out to me."

"Okay. Can I...can I turn it off? Or does it just go away?" Chrissy said, realizing it didn't make much sense but unsure of how else to describe her thought world.

"Just close your eyes and stop thinking about it. You'll be back in the darkness. Call out to me like you did before, and we all can talk together."

It sounded like Brian was at the other end of a large empty gym. His voice echoed in her ears, and then he disappeared.

Chrissy stood alone in the Appletons' backyard and looked around. She didn't know when or if she would be back here in real life ever again. She hoped she would be, but it sounded like the others that were here with her wanted to get back to their homes too, and they didn't know either. Maybe, like Brian said, the flies or whatever they were would be done with them soon, and they really would let them get back with their families and friends.

Chrissy took in the world one last time. She knew she would probably be back, but just in case, she wanted to enjoy this view before returning to the darkness. She breathed in the warm fresh air and exhaled. Then she stood still, her arms by her sides, and closed her eyes. Her thoughts moved away from the warm, green world she'd just left and back to the darkness that had surrounded her. The feeling of her body left her. She was no longer hot or cold—there was just nothing. The warm breeze against her skin; gone. The smell of fresh air; gone. It was all replaced with nothing. She was trapped in only her thoughts again. She tried to open her eyes and realized she couldn't. She had returned to the darkness.

For a moment, she felt her anxiety rise, just as it had the first time. She was here in this nothing world, but she knew she was not alone, and that helped.

"Brian?" Chrissy called out. Her own voice sounded distant, but she knew she was actually just living in her thoughts. Still, her voice was her own.

"I'm here. We're all here, Chrissy," Brian replied. It was isolating because he sounded so far off, but at least she wasn't alone.

"Hi," a chorus of other voices echoed in her head.

"Nice to, um…meet you all," Chrissy said. It felt like she was smiling.

There was a long pause, and then a new voice spoke to her.

"Hi, Chrissy, I'm Barbara. I've been here since…. I've been here the longest," Barbara said. She sounded nice enough.

"Hi, Barbara, nice to meet you. How long have you been here?" Chrissy asked. She was just being polite, but there was still so much she didn't know about wherever they were. She wanted to know more. The thought crossed her mind, this could all be a trick, that somehow the flies or whatever they really were, were tricking her into believing that the others were here with her, but she was actually alone. She didn't want to dwell too much on that and trusted that the others were real people.

"It's hard to say, really. I can't explain everything. I was last alive in 1938." Barbara paused.

Nineteen-thirty-eight. That made Barbara almost eighty years old. But she didn't sound that old.

"I was surrounded by flies and then brought here, same as you," Barbara continued. "It seemed to me like a few hours later, and Harry arrived."

"Hi, Chrissy." A boy spoke, but it wasn't Brian. It must have been Harry.

"Hi, Harry," Chrissy said.

"So—so then I came. But when I left, it was the summer of…of 1960," Harry said. "Same thing as Barbara, really. This guy came walking through the woods. I didn't really get a good look at him. He broke all apart and turned into flies. They surrounded me, and I ended up here."

"It's the flies then? Brian and…I'm sorry, I forgot your

name. How did you get here? When are you from?"

"Well, it felt like a day or so. I don't know, it seemed like a long time, right Barbara?" Harry continued. "Barbara figured out how to visit the world in our heads, so she showed it to me. She had done it a couple times. That's when we started to realize you could only stay in that mind world for a little while. It just took so much energy or something."

"Okay," Chrissy said, realizing that although Barbara had been there for almost eighty years, it didn't feel like that long to her, and they were still learning as they went along. They knew more than her, but it felt to them like a few days maybe, at most. They were going to be in this together.

"We experimented with the trips into the mind worlds," Barbara added. "I tried to go into Harry's world and he came into mine. But we realized they were different worlds and we couldn't stay in them very long. But we really didn't know how long that was anyway."

"But it felt like a day maybe, and then Brian and Tiffany arrived," Harry said.

Chrissy tried to wrap her head around this story. There were so many questions. They all sounded like they were around her age, but somehow, they were from different times in the past. She let it sink in, and then her mind went immediately to their escape. Now that they knew the situation, could they figure a way out of this? It was like they were prisoners but stuck inside their own heads. How could they ever hope to get out of here?

"Hi," a girl's voice, Tiffany, said.

"Hi," Chrissy said. Now she had met them all. At least, until someone else came.

"So, I was um…ditching school with Brian," Tiffany said. Chrissy could hear the half-laugh in her voice as she spoke. It was funny how much of their speech came through, even though it was only their thoughts.

"Oh, you might get a detention," Chrissy said, hoping to

lighten the mood. There were a few laughs, but they died out quickly.

"Yeah," Tiffany said. "We ended up in the woods, and before we knew what was happening, we were being chased by a large group of flies. They surrounded us, and the next thing we knew, we were here. I guess it felt like a day or so since we got here. These guys explained everything to us, and we made a few trips out into the mind world. But mine was different than Brian's. Then you came, and we started all over again with you."

"Okay?" Chrissy said, not really sure what to say. It was a lot of information to take in.

"Chrissy, when are you from?" Barbara's voice asked. Chrissy realized they didn't know when she had left the real world. For Barbara, each time someone joined, it was further in the future. It had been almost a hundred years since Barbara came. Chrissy didn't know what she would think when she heard the year she was from.

"I'm from 2019," Chrissy said. There was silence. At first, Chrissy didn't say anything, then she decided to break the silence and hopefully get everyone focused on what they could do to get back into the real world. "Brian mentioned something about the flies talking to you."

The silence of the others lasted another moment. Chrissy remembered the *Back to the Future* movies she'd watched with her family a few years ago. Her dad said they were his all-time favorites. She couldn't remember the year they started in, but she did remember that they went forward in time and thinking the year they went forward to was not that far from the actual year. Maybe it was 2022 or something. But the fictional future world was a lot different from the actual future. She assumed the others were all thinking about the future at that moment.

"It's not really that much different from 1985," Chrissy said. "I've seen movies. The only real difference is the TVs are thinner, and the phones are smaller. No floating cars, I promise."

"Okay, good," Tiffany laughed.

"Not much different than my time either," Harry said.

"Yeah," Chrissy agreed. They all waited for Barbara. No one said she was the leader, but it was obvious to Chrissy that she was the one everyone waited for. She had been here the longest. She knew at least a little bit more about what was going on than anyone else. Everyone deferred to her.

"They told us they needed one more and then someone to bridge the gap. I don't know what that means," Barbara spoke finally. "I don't even know if it was just the flies. I just assumed it. There were many voices, not just one. You others have heard it too."

"We just wait then?" Brian asked.

"Is there anything else we can do? To get ready? Maybe we can try to fight back?" Chrissy said. She was amazed at how complacent they seemed to be. They told her the story, but none of them mentioned fighting back, trying to take their lives back instead of waiting for the flies to be done with them.

"I do not think that would be wise. I don't get the impression they are nice flies," Barbara said.

"You're saying they wouldn't like it if we fought back against them?" Chrissy said.

"Right."

"Whatever they want me to be, I'll be the opposite. I want to get out of here, and fighting them seems to be the best way to do that," Chrissy said. Why was Barbara against fighting them?

"Well, there is an alternative," Harry said. He must have sensed the tension between the two girls.

"Okay," Chrissy said. "Let's hear it." She hoped the others understood she was just doing what came naturally to her instead of just sitting back and watching what the others did. She always took charge. In group projects at school, she just became the leader. If no one stepped up, it was easy for her to take the lead role. But even when someone did try to step up, it was hard for Chrissy to sit back and not take some sort of leadership role.

"Well, they always talk to us right before someone new comes. Right, Barbara?" Harry said.

"Right."

"What if we try to get some more information out of them? What gap they are talking about. Stuff like that. Maybe we can get them to tell us something we shouldn't know. Then when that other person comes, when we start bridging the gap, we can plan something. Once things change, it might be easier to do something. Right now, there doesn't seem to be much we can do."

"Or we can piss them off and see what happens. Maybe they will make a mistake if they are mad at us," Tiffany said. It was clear she liked Chrissy's approach more than the wait-and-see plan.

Then Chrissy heard a soft buzzing, almost like bees were flying toward her. She knew instantly what the sound was.

"Looks like there won't be a whole lot of time to plan," Barbara said. "Here they come."

CHAPTER 14

Her lips were dry. She wasn't getting enough water—she knew that. Lisa ran her tongue across her lips, trying to moisten them, but there wasn't enough saliva, and it didn't do much to help her. She felt cracks on her lips and in the corners of her mouth and on the tip of her tongue. They hurt, and the longer she went with such a little amount of water, they were only going to get worse.

John had been better. He told her the time when he brought her food, and he left the light, except when the batteries died. Then he took the light with him and brought it back with new batteries the next time he came with food. The days didn't run together anymore. Lisa was able to keep track of them better now that she knew what time it was when she was fed. The days of the week still eluded her because she didn't know how long she had been in this room before he started telling her the time. But given his slight generosity toward her lately, she thought an extra glass of water or just a bigger glass wouldn't be out of the question. She would ask him the next time he came down.

She slept less with the light and knowing the time of day. It had been three days since he started telling her what time it was, and she tried to sleep just as she would during a normal day, sleeping only during the night and staying awake during the day. Keeping her mind sharp was important. She hoped there would be an opening for her to escape, and she needed to be on the lookout for any time she might have an advantage. If an opportunity presented itself, she needed to be ready for it.

Lisa played mind games to keep her thinking, trying to come up with riddles and even mentally writing short stories. Anything that kept her mind working was a good thing. She also tried to keep her eyes sharp. It was easy when there was nothing to look at, to just close her eyes. Staring at the same four walls in a nearly empty room made it hard to keep her eyes open, but she wanted to make sure her eyes were ready for anything. To keep her eyes sharp, Lisa would focus on a corner of the room, look away from the corner, and then look back at it, and try to focus her eyes on a single spot quickly. She didn't know if this actually did anything to her eyesight, but she could feel herself improving each time she did the exercise. It made her eyes tired after she did it for a while, but it also made her feel more alert.

The locks on the door clicked and then slid. It meant it was time to eat. Lisa couldn't count on her stomach to tell her when it was time to eat. She was always hungry; John didn't have a regular food schedule either. He just brought food whenever he felt like it.

"They're not in control now," the old man said quickly, catching his breath as he entered the room and moved toward Lisa. "They're gone. We can get you out of here."

Holland pulled keys from his pocket and stood over her.

This was her chance. The opening Lisa had been waiting for was here. She could knock down John and scream her head off. The door was open. Someone was bound to hear her eventually. Maybe she could even free herself. He had the keys out already. Could it be that difficult to get the chain off her legs? But she didn't do any of that. His voice was weak, the voice of an old man, and she trusted him.

Holland unlocked her legs and helped her unwrap the

chain. Lisa snatched the keys from Holland and groaned as she stood up for the first time since she was brought down here by the same man who was now helping her. Holland got up from his knees just as slowly as she did.

"Go!" He looked up at her and shouted in his gravelly voice.

Lisa turned to run, then stopped and looked at the light in the corner of the room. She took two quick but painful steps toward it and picked up the light with both hands, still bound together. It wasn't too heavy, but it was heavy enough. With the light in her hands, she went over to Holland, who had just arrived back on his feet. She looked at him and hesitated for a moment. He'd just helped her, unlocked her legs and set her free. Why he helped her, after going through all the trouble to keep her there, in that cell, she didn't know. At least not yet. Part of her wanted to leave him there and run away, but she knew she couldn't just leave him. He was the same man who'd held her captive. No, she couldn't just leave. She pushed him back and knocked him off balance.

"No," John said. "They'll be back. You need to go."

Lisa shook her head at him. She didn't care about him at all, really; only about Matthew, Olivia, and Tim. She only wanted to get back to them, to see them again, and she didn't want him to have the chance to stop her.

"Sorry, John." Lisa slammed the light down hard against the old man's skull. He toppled as his knees buckled and fell in a heap on the floor of the small cell.

She looked down at him, wanted to turn to leave, but lifted the light back up above her head as high as she could and slammed it down again, just above his neck. Blood spilled out of the old man from a cut along the base of his skull. It flowed out of him, covering his back and spreading on the floor underneath him.

Lisa stared for a second. She wanted to feel bad, but she

didn't. She knew she should have felt some remorse for what she did, but there was nothing. No feeling at all. Just the need to get out of there as soon as possible. To get back with her family.

She dropped the light and left the room. The hall outside the room was dimly lit, and concrete stretched in both directions. The only sounds were the echoes of her breathing. She didn't know which way to go, so she picked one, heading right as she exited the room. Her cell. Her heart beat loud and fast as though it was about to break out of her chest. Lisa tried to slow her breathing, to calm herself down so she could think, but she was too worried, or scared, or excited. Or maybe it was a little bit of everything. There was nothing but this hall between her and her family now.

She took a few staggering steps down the hall. There didn't appear to be doors in either direction, but she remembered Holland telling her that her cell was more than just a room in his basement, so she kept moving forward. With each step, her legs loosened up. She realized she should have been trying to move and exercise them as much as she could while she was chained up. Of course, that didn't matter now — she wasn't planning on getting chained up again any time soon. She reached the end of the hall, and there was only another hallway, just as dimly lit as the first. She looked back behind her, second-guessing her original choice, but it was too late to change her mind. The last thing she wanted to do was walk back past the dying or dead John Holland on the floor of her old room if she didn't have to.

Lisa pressed on, ignoring the pain in her hips and back that came with each step forward. She stumbled and fell against the cold concrete floor of the hall. There was no way this could fit underneath Holland's house. She pushed her hands back against the wall and forced herself upright, took a few more steps, and saw a doorway along the right side of the wall, about halfway down.

The exit. It had to be the exit. Her pace quickened. Her

knees clicked with each step, but she didn't feel any of the pain. Her eyes focused only on the door that drew closer with each step. Finally, she reached it. Her hands, still bound together, groped at the doorknob. She was able to grasp it, and with her entire body, turned the knob she hoped to lead to her freedom. It was locked.

She fumbled with Holland's keys. There were only four keys on the ring, and two of them were small keys for padlocks — the two bigger keys looked like door keys. She managed to get one out and into the keyhole. It slid in easily, but when she turned the knob, it didn't budge.

"It must be the other one, Lisa, come on," she encouraged herself.

She quickly switched keys and slid the second one into the hole. Again, she turned with both hands, and the knob twisted. Lisa smiled, expecting to see a set of stairs leading up out of Holland's cement nightmare of a basement and back into his house. Then it would be a quick stroll through his house and back to her house next door. Her family. Tim was probably home with the kids; they would be happy to see her. She would collapse on the living room floor, and Tim would call the cops. They'd search Holland's house again and find him dead in the basement as a result of her escape.

Lisa leaned her shoulder into the heavy metal door and pushed it open. As it opened, she realized she'd made a huge mistake, but it was too late. The sound of a swarm of flies filled the room. Initially, she just thought there were lots of flies in the room, but then she saw them. Along the far wall were five people. Five kids. But she could only see them from the waist down. From the waist up, the children were covered in flies. Each of the five kids' heads, arms, and legs was covered in a mass of crawling, buzzing flies.

"No!" Lisa shouted.

She wanted to run but knew she had to help those kids. Instead of leaving the fly-filled room, she went in. She looked for something to prop the door open but couldn't find anything. She let it close gently behind her, hoping it wouldn't close all the way and lock her in, but she had the keys just in case. There were flies everywhere. Most covered the children. The rest hovered over the floor, circling. As she entered, they seemed overly interested in her. They began to fly around her head and arms, buzzing toward her face even as she swatted them away. Lisa reached one of the kids. She couldn't tell if it was a boy or a girl, and she pulled on the kid's pant leg.

"Hey, can you hear me?" Lisa shouted over the buzzing that seemed to grow louder each second she was in the room.

There was no response from the child. Lisa moved to the next one and repeated the process, but there was no response from this one either.

Lisa stared up at the fly-covered children and tried to figure out how she was going to get them down. There were so many flies crawling over one another—just a mass of flies. She looked too long, and the image of that many flies made her gag. She fought the urge to throw up and gagged again, looking down and away from the flies for a moment.

A slam from behind her made her jump, and she turned back toward the door, thinking it had slammed shut.

It hadn't shut. In the doorway, looking very much alive, was John Holland.

"You should not have done that, Lisa."

He smiled at her, the blood still dripping out of his neck and down his shoulders. The rasp was gone from his voice. This wasn't the old John Holland. This was the other John Holland. The one who pulled her across her front yard and into her house. The one that didn't shuffle across the room. The one that banged on her front door that first time. She still didn't understand it, but she knew there were two of him. This one looked old, frail, and weak but wasn't.

"No, please. I'm sorry. Let me help them. Just...just let us go. I don't know what happened to you, John, but we can find you help. We can get help for you and them." Lisa looked at the kids still surrounded by flies. The flies that swarmed her head a few seconds ago were gone. The air around her had cleared. The noise in the room died down with the entrance of this version of Holland.

Holland just laughed at her. He looked down at the ground, and she followed his gaze. The flies circled his feet but stayed low to the ground.

"We were nice to you, Lisa." He stared at her, his dark green eyes almost looking through her as he spoke. "I left the light in there for you. We told you the time. I was never going to do that. But you didn't seem like the type who would try to escape. I guess we were wrong. Plus, the old man likes you. We tried to be nice, and look what it got me."

Holland reached behind his head and then showed her his hands, crimson and dripping on the floor. There was a small puddle of blood behind him, and Lisa was sure there would be a trail down the hall. She would find out if she ever got out of this room, though that was becoming increasingly unlikely. She tried to follow what he was saying, but he kept shifting back and forth between we and I, us and me. It was hard to keep track of what he was saying.

"What are you going to do with me? With these kids?" Lisa wanted to turn and move toward the kids, grab one of their legs, and try to get away, but realistically she knew she wasn't going to get past the strong version of Holland.

"We need them, and you," Holland said. He stepped toward her, the flies moving with him, still circling his feet. "It was just a matter of time before I would have had to bring you in here anyway. I needed you in here before we could be done with you. This was inevitable. I guess we just thought it would happen a few days from now. We still need some more time to get ready. But it's okay. We can get ready with you in here instead of the other room."

The corner of Holland's mouth twitched up into a half-smile. It made her want to scream.

"No. I'll...I'll go back to the other room. Please, not in here."

She tried to push past him, but he grabbed her upper arm and held her firmly in place. Lisa tried a few times to push him off her, anything to break his grip, but of course, she couldn't move him. Holland pushed her back, and she stumbled toward the wall with the kids on it. Her back hit the legs of one of the kids and disturbed the bed of flies surrounding them. She looked up, not realizing what she had hit, and then dropped to the floor away from the flies.

"The good news is if you're in here, I won't have to chain you up. And we can take that off your hands too." Holland looked at the zip tie, still holding her hands together. He reached into his pocket and pulled out a knife, went over and knelt down on the floor next to her, and ran the knife through the plastic of the zip tie with ease. "Don't try anything funny now. We are watching you all the time now. We'll see everything and know everything, and we can stop you."

Lisa rubbed softly at the raw, bloody skin on her wrists. As Holland turned and left, Lisa got a glimpse of the gash along the back of his neck. She didn't understand how he was still upright, but she realized there was a lot about the entire situation she didn't fully understand. A glance around the room told her it was empty except for the light at least fifteen feet above her. That and children. And the flies. The insects were quieter. The sound wasn't totally gone, but much different from when she first entered the room. Her eyes kept looking up at the kids attached to the wall. How were they eating or drinking? Were they even alive? They looked alive. It didn't look like their bodies were decomposing or anything. Even if they were only dead for a few days, Lisa knew, the room would have a distinct smell.

"It's okay." She sat on the floor near the feet of the children. "I'm going to figure out a way to get us all out of here. Just hang on until then."

The flies that were not part of the blanket of flies swarming the children didn't like something she said because they swarmed around her head again. She waved them off a few times, but they didn't relent. Lisa stood up.

"What do you want from me?" she asked the flies, realizing how she looked. This only made the flies buzz and fly around her with greater speed and more agitation. Then they got together and formed a wall between Lisa and the children.

"What the fuck?" Lisa said out loud but spoke mostly for herself. The wall of flies moved toward her slowly, and she backed up a few steps. The flies continued at her, tightening the distance between them. Lisa backed up again two more steps, and then two more as the flies advanced. The mass of flies curled around her as her back hit the cement wall behind her. There was nowhere else for her to go. The flies rose up and then moved down toward her at an angle.

"No!" Lisa stared up at the flies in defiance. She knew they wanted her to crouch or kneel down on the floor here, but she didn't want to. She wanted to show them she was in charge, not the other way around. But the flies drew in closer and tighter together. Lisa didn't move and stood, staring back at them. The flies drew closer, pressing themselves against her head, and she felt the strength of the tiny insects. The pressure on her head forced her down to the ground. She had no choice. Once she was sitting on the ground, the flies backed off.

She knew what would happen if she got up, so she stayed in her spot, her eyes focused on the kids across the room from her. Her mind was still thinking of a way out. She had been so close to her family, but it was ripped away. At least this time, she would be able to save these kids too.

The flies hovered around her as her mind worked. She

could move her arms and legs, so that was a plus, but the flies were not going to let her do much of anything. Maybe she could offer herself in exchange for the children. What did he need them all for? Maybe she could get him talking and figure out what he was doing.

The flies swarmed around her. They didn't touch her but got close. It was an uncomfortable feeling knowing the insects were watching her. With no real ideas as to what her next move would be, Lisa's eyelids started to close. She kept them open as long as she could, but eventually, the exhaustion of her near escape caught up with her, and she fell asleep.

CHAPTER 15

"Time to wake up, sleepyhead."

Holland's voice snapped her awake. Lisa didn't know how long she had been out, but it was the first time she'd seen Holland since he left her. She blinked a few times and turned her head to either side, loosening herself up. It was the most comfortable sleep she'd had in a long time. It was difficult sleeping in the other room, chained and bound. In there, when she moved, the chain rattled or pulled at her legs, or the zip ties dug into her wrists, making it hard to stay asleep. Although in here she'd slept sitting up with her head against a cement wall, it was the more comfortable of the two places she slept since becoming a guest of John Holland.

Lisa looked up from her seat on the floor. The children had not moved. They were still plastered to the wall by the mass of flies. The rest of the room was filled with flies, although they were not paying as much attention to Lisa now as they were before she fell asleep. She tried to move her feet and realized both of them had fallen asleep—there must have been a severe lack of blood flow from this particular position. Holland didn't even glance down at her from what she could see. His attention was focused only on the five kids stuck to the wall. Lisa moved her legs back and forth and bent her knees, trying to get rid of the pins and needles running from her hips all the way down to her toes, but she couldn't get her legs moving fast enough to stimulate blood flow.

"Can I stand up, please?" Lisa knew better than to just do it. She didn't want those flies touching her again. The feeling was bad enough the first time. She could only imagine what it must feel like to be those kids.

"Yes, of course," Holland said as if there was no question that she should be allowed to stand up. As if she didn't get backed into this wall by a swarm of angry flies. As if she wasn't chained to a pole in a room just down the hallway for who knew how many days.

She thought of a few things she would like to say to Holland after his response, but she kept them to herself. There was no reason to be a pain in the ass to him. He already knew she didn't want to be there. Holland, at least this version of Holland, was too strong for her to make any kind of escape following a physical attack. It was almost like his strength was inhuman. Something more than just the strength of a man, even a strong man. Lisa thought back to when she was dragged across the front lawn. She tried as hard as she could get away from him, but there was nothing she could do. With one hand holding her in place, he'd pulled her into his house, and she didn't even get him to budge. That, and the flies were intelligent. Something was different about all of this, but the more she put the pieces together, the more scared she became.

She got up, stretched, and twisted her body. The sound of cracks from her legs and back filled the room as she turned her shoulders to either side, doing a short version of the stretching she did before getting on the machines at the gym. She had to get out of here, and the more she knew about the situation she was in, the better. Holland didn't seem to be paying too much attention to her. He just stared up at the children, so she decided to see how far she could push him.

"What do you need them for?" she asked, taking a slow step toward Holland. She tried to sound casual in spite of her fear.

"Them?" Holland said. He didn't turn to look at Lisa when he spoke to her but pointed up at the kids trapped against the wall. "They're the key. We need them to finish our conquest."

Lisa was right behind him. The cut along the back of his neck where she slammed the light was still there. It wasn't bloody anymore, but there were no bandages on it. She could see the red flesh beneath the cut, but there was no blood. Just the sliced skin of an old man who was a lot stronger and more agile than he appeared.

"I don't underst—" Lisa started, but Holland cut her off.

"You should not understand. This would not make sense to you. It is not your world. It is not their world either." Holland nodded toward the children. "It is *our* world, and we're going to take it back from you."

He paused. Lisa wondered if he was done or just getting going. It seemed like he was ready to make a speech. She didn't know, but she let the silence hang for a moment. When he didn't continue, she prodded a little bit more.

"Then what do you need them for? Me? Why do you need us?" Lisa knew she didn't have the whole story. She was going to pick at pieces of it until she had enough to put the whole thing together in her head. She didn't know why she felt the need to do this—probably for the same reason she'd decided to research other disappearances in Medville. She was just too curious to do anything else. Maybe her curiosity would pay off.

"We need you to help us get control. You think you are in control, but with their help." He turned to look at Lisa, a smile across his face. She didn't like the smile. It made her want to be as far away from him as she could. In that one glance, she went from caring about the children and wanting to help them to not caring at all. Her only thought in that second was to get away. She backed up against the door and tried to pull on it, but it was locked—she couldn't even twist the doorknob. Holland didn't seem to care, and he, thankfully, turned back to look at the children and continued. "We were going to have to explain all of this to you at some point, so we might as well explain it now. Your little half-assed escape attempt only moved up the timeline a few hours, you know. You still would have ended up in this room."

Lisa felt her stomach drop. He needed her in here, and she had come right where he needed her. All she did was piss him off. If she had run the right way, she would have been long gone by now. Her only mistake had been the direction of her run. She took offense to the fact that he called her escape half-assed.

"I took you down long enough to get in here, didn't I? What if I went in the other direction? What if I got away?"

Holland didn't turn to face her but threw his head back and laughed.

"You did not take *us* down. You took Holland down. That weak old man. There was barely anything left of him when we got here. That was before you knocked him out cold. Now he is gone. If we ever decide to leave him, his body is dead. We left him alone for a few minutes, and he tried to set you free, and you killed him for it."

"What do you mean? If you're not John Holland, who are you?"

Lisa was afraid to ask the question. She looked around the room at the flies swirling along the floor, zipping past her legs and weaving in and out of Holland's legs. At the flies covering the wall opposite her. She didn't want to hear the answer, but she was afraid she already knew it. Her lips pulled back, and she fought back the tears as they tried to drip down her cheeks. But she steeled herself—she didn't want to appear weak in front of Holland.

"You do not pick up on stuff too well, huh, Lisa?" Holland

stood for over a minute, silent. She knew what he was going to say. She just didn't want to hear it. "We are the flies, Lisa. The same ones that get in your house. The ones that huddle on the dog shit on the curb a few houses down. The ones that flock to the dead squirrels like a magnet. You think we are a pest, a nuisance, something you can just get out of your house because we bother you. But we are so much more than that."

Lisa tried to listen to him, but the volume of the buzzing within the room increased. The flies flew around her faster, more agitated with each second. Holland turned back to her, his smile gone. He opened his mouth as if to speak again, but instead, a burst of flies flew out of his mouth straight for her. Lisa backed up against the wall. The flies swarmed around her but didn't touch her. She could feel the air moving around her arms as she covered her face, hoping to keep them as far away from her as she could. The sound of the flies persisted around her, and she shrunk down to the ground, curling up into a ball, waiting for them to stop.

"Please. Okay, I'll help you. I'll do what you need me to do. Please, just leave me alone. And when I help you, I want to go home," she said. That was it. The tears came. For a few seconds, the buzzing and swarming continued. She didn't know what else she was going to be able to do other than let them do what they wanted.

The flies stopped. She could still hear their wings as they flew around her ankles close to the floor, but the buzzing was not deafening like it had been a few seconds earlier.

"Maybe," Holland said. When he opened his mouth, some of the flies returned to the warmth there. He continued speaking, hardly noticing. "We'll have to see how good a job you can do, then we'll make a decision."

"So, what do I need to do?" Lisa said. She realized the chances of Holland actually letting her go once she helped him were very slim, but if she was going to help him—them—she wanted to get it over with as soon as possible. There was no sense in sitting around in this disgusting room if there was a chance, even a slim one, she could get out of it soon.

"You just want to get out of here. If that is true, then you'll probably do a good job for us. That's a good thing for all of us. We need to talk to the children first. The kids know we are the ones who took them. They could trust us eventually, but that would take too long. We need to send someone in that they will trust right away. You, Lisa."

Lisa looked at the kids on the wall, the flies crawling all over each other, covering the upper half of their bodies.

"Like that?" Lisa said, just staring at the wall, not making eye contact with Holland.

"It is not as bad as it looks, Lisa. We are not as bad as we look. We can assure you we have no diseases, and we are all very clean. It must be done, Lisa. You cannot leave without going in to talk to the kids and convincing them to follow you back out into this world. Then they will start their part, and yours will be done."

"But why me? Why did you pick me?" Lisa asked.

Holland was sharing more information than ever before. Maybe because it was almost time for the flies to finish this thing they had started, and they were as anxious to get on with it as Lisa was to get out of Holland's basement. She was going to keep him talking, and hopefully, she would have some sort of revelation she didn't think about before that would help her get herself and the children out of here uninjured. It was a long shot, but the bad guys always said too much in James Bond movies—maybe it would work in real life too.

"It wasn't going to be you, Lisa. It was going to be Tim. For some reason, kids respond better when their hero is a man. At least they always have in the past. It's been a while since we have needed to do this. Maybe they will respond more to you." Holland turned back to look at her, and for a moment, she thought she saw a glimpse of the nice John Holland in his eyes, but the look vanished.

"Why?"

"Why the switch to you?" Holland laughed the evil smile back on his face. He turned completely around and stood with his hands behind his back. Still stuck in the body of a frail old man, she could see the strength of the fly-controlled old man. How had she not seen it before? "It is your own fault, really. You were just so nosy. Always watching us even when you were pretending not to, but we knew you were watching. Looking up stuff about the other disappearances, that did not help either. You were not the only one doing that, just the closest one. So we decided you would be the better target to help us this time around. Plus, if we knew where you were you would not be able to watch us."

Lisa stared back at him as he smiled at her. A fly landed on his cheek and walked into his mouth as he stared back at her.

"Does that answer all of your questions, Lisa?" Holland asked. He turned back around and motioned for her to stand next to him. At first, she didn't move, but the flies still in the room began to get louder and rise back up around her. As the swarm formed on either side of her, she stepped forward reluctantly until she was standing next to Holland. The flies stopped and returned to their area close to the floor.

"No. I still don't really know what it is you want me to do," Lisa said, standing next to him. He stared at the children plastered to the wall and wanted her to do the same, she could tell. But she had a hard time looking at the mountain of flies. She kept her eyes down, focused on what was still showing of the kids' bodies as opposed to the fly-covered parts.

"Ah yes. We guess that is true. The children are in a place called The Darkness. Others have called it similar things over the years. Dark World. The Nothing. In that world, they exist only in their thoughts. They have no physical body. They can still think and even communicate with each other, but they have no bodies. If they use a tremendous about of mental energy, they can create worlds and what seems like physical bodies to them. But they cannot stay there long because it takes too much energy to sustain it."

Lisa continued to just watch the kid's legs, wondering what it must feel like to be there and how long they had been this way.

"We are going to tell them you are coming to help them get back to the real world. They will be waiting for you. Then we will return here and bring you into the darkness. Once you are there, you need to convince them all to come with you. When we return, we will explain how you get back here. Children's brains are different than adults'. Children experience time differently from adults, and they make decisions differently than adults. The children could know exactly where they are right now and not be able to get back because of the differences in their brains. That's why we always take children for this part of it." Holland gestured toward the wall, then toward Lisa. "We always take adults for the other part of it because adults, once they know where they are and how it works, are always able to get back to the real world on their own, as long as they know all of the information, which is why we're telling you everything. The kids, we could explain everything to a hundred times, and they would never get out. Same thing for adults who do not know what happened. They are just stuck until they are reborn. But only we need to worry about that. That will come soon."

Lisa had trouble following him, but her task seemed straightforward enough.

"I go in there, in the darkness. I get them. And then I bring them back, and I go home," Lisa said, breaking the totality of what Holland explained into the simplest terms possible.

"More or less." Holland scrunched his face and waved his hand back and forth. "We cannot let you go until the kids have finished their part of this. But once they are done, then yes. You can go back to your home."

"Already changing the deal," Lisa said. She knew Holland, or the flies, whoever she was talking to, had no intention of just letting her go. Maybe she would get out, but she would find her own way out. It didn't feel like she had much of a choice. Holland didn't respond. Either the flies didn't get sarcasm, or they just didn't like it or want to respond to it. "So, how do I do it? How do I bring them back?"

Holland shook his head. "We cannot explain that. We have never done it, nor would we be able to do it. You will feel yourself coming back here from the other place, the place where the children are when you get there. Our world. And you'll know, then you just convince them to follow you, one at a time."

"They are not going to be in the…The Darkness?" Lisa tried to recall what he'd called the world the children were in.

"No. We are going there now to move them to our world. It makes for an easier transition if they come from our world into this world. It is harder on their bodies if they come from The Darkness into the real world. We will move them, and then you will join them. We must go now." He turned back and looked at her, the grotesque smile back on his face. "We will still be here watching. Do not try to leave."

Holland didn't wait for a reply from her and turned back toward the children. Lisa crouched down to the floor and scooted away from him. Holland opened his mouth and vomited up a large group of flies. The insects continued to pour out of his mouth. Lisa watched in horror, gagging and covering her mouth as the flies filled the air. She couldn't look at his face anymore but saw his body break apart and change into the flies. The bugs swirled in the air and added their mass to the blanket of flies that already covered the children. Lisa felt her breath get faster. Her heart pounded; she could feel it in her chest. She wiped the sweat from her hands on her pants as the last of the flies landed on the wall. Holland was gone. Lisa was in the room alone again with the children and the flies. Many of them still buzzed and walked around on the floor, being sure to give her a wide berth. She stared down at them, knowing if she were to make a move to leave the room or take the kids off the wall, they would stop her.

She could do nothing else but wait.

CHAPTER 16

Brian still wasn't used to not having a body. He tried to turn his head in the direction of the approaching sound of the flies. He couldn't, of course, but he could hear them. The faint flutter echoed throughout the darkness. If the voices of the other kids here with him felt as if they were far away, the approaching flies felt twice as far. But he knew they were on their way. The flutter got louder and then changed into a different noise altogether. When they arrived, it was a loud buzzing cutting through his head. He had only met the flies here once before, and the sound of their approach terrified him as much now as it did that first time.

"Here they come," Barbara said. She had spoken to the flies the most but didn't sound any less scared than the rest of them.

"That's what they sound like?" the new girl, Chrissy, said.

"Yes," said Harry. "But only when they first arrive. It's just as scary when they talk. It's not like just one person talking, like when we talk. It's like thousands of voices saying the same thing at the same time. But they are all around you. You'll see."

Brian could hear the fear in everyone's voices when they spoke. No one wanted the flies here. They were all happy, he was pretty sure, to just stay here in the darkness without any more

visits from the flies. They could get them back to the real world
or do whatever they wanted with them without talking to them,
couldn't they? There was no need for this.

"I wish they would just go away," Tiffany said what they
all were thinking.

"Let's see what they want," Chrissy said. Brian could still
hear the fear in her voice, but it was mixed with something else.
Curiosity? It surprised him because this was her first meeting
with the flies, and she sounded less scared than the rest of them,
except maybe Barbara.

The buzzing of the flies got louder. It reminded Brian
of when the flies had taken him and Tiffany. He was sure the
others heard a similar sound just before the world went black.
The thought reminded him of the flies pushing their way into
his mouth. If he had a body, he would have gagged. Then the
buzzing stopped. They were there.

"Hello?" Barbara said moments after the buzzing stopped.

"You are all here now," the flies said. Their voices echoed
throughout his head. Some of the voices seemed far away,
others close by. They were everywhere. Their words surrounded
him like the buzzing. It was as if the flies were inside his head.
Everywhere.

"Yes, I'm —" Chrissy started to say, but the flies interrupted
her.

"Chrissy Franklin, we know you all. We know everything
about all of you. We have been inside your heads. We know
your memories and your thoughts before you arrived here in the
darkness. You do not need to tell us about yourself, Chrissy," the
flies said. It was the same speech Brian had heard when he and
Tiffany first arrived. He assumed the others heard it as well when
they first got here.

"Well, we're all here now," said Tiffany. "What do you
want with us?"

Tiffany seemed emboldened by Chrissy's arrival. Maybe

she didn't agree with the way Barbara was willing to sit back and let things happen. Now, Tiffany had someone else who was willing to be more of a fighter, something that any of Tiffany's teachers would have said was part of her character.

"In time, Tiffany, you will find out. The good news is you will not have to spend much more time here in the darkness," the flies said. It felt as though they moved with each word. Some words felt like they were spoken close to him. Others felt far away. The flies words were slow and deliberate.

"Where? Where are we going then? If we're done here, but you're not ready for the job you have for us, where are we going?" Brian said. His fear was real, but Tiffany's more defiant attitude gave him a boost of confidence as well.

"To our world. Not really our world, but it looks like our world. It will be easier for the person assisting you to bring you back to the real world from a copy of our world instead of this darkness or any of the worlds you are able to create with your minds. You will all be able to exist in our world together, physically, like in your own mind worlds. We will keep the world together for you—all of our mental energy will go toward keeping you in that world."

"What if we don't want to go to your world? What if we want to stay here, in The Darkness?" Chrissy said.

There was a sound that followed. Brian didn't know what it was, but he could only describe it as a snort of a laugh by the flies. It was not something he wanted to hear again. The vicious sound reverberated inside his head long after the initial snort. It was a sound he wanted to forget but knew he never would.

"You will come with us, Chrissy Franklin. Or you will never leave this place. This is your only chance to ever get back to your world," the flies shouted into Brian's mind. And everyone else's, he assumed.

"Chrissy, don't fight them," Harry said.

"There is no reason to think they won't just let us get on

with our lives once they send us back. Who knows what they want? I don't know why they took us, but if they say they are going to send us back to the real world, why wouldn't we just let them do that? We might be able to get on with our lives like this never happened," Barbara added.

Brian didn't have to see or hear Chrissy to know she would be frustrated with the reaction from Barbara and Harry. He sort of understood her frustration. She went from being on her own to being a part of this group she'd only known for a few minutes. Now they were asking her to do something different than what she would do on her own. But she didn't really know them that well. Brian didn't know these other kids that well either. Were they really a group working together against the flies, or were they just five individuals? He guessed that was about to be determined. He heard Chrissy sigh.

"All right, let's see this fly world," Chrissy said, the sarcasm in her voice easy to hear.

"Close your eyes," the fly voices demanded, knowing full well they couldn't actually close their eyes.

Brian hesitated. Chrissy's idea to fight at all costs floated in his head, while Barbara's plan of compliance to get what they wanted also swirled around in there. He didn't know who to believe or who was right. Either one of the plans could be the right one. Either plan could be wrong. Or the scariest prospect about all of this, neither plan would get them what they wanted, and they didn't really have a chance in hell of changing anything. They would all die as captives of these flies, and there was nothing they could do about it. None of them had bodies anymore, and they didn't know where their bodies were. The flies already had control of them—even if their thoughts were still free of the insects, their bodies weren't.

He became aware of the fact that he might not be the only person in their little group hesitating to close their eyes when the flies spoke again.

"Close your eyes, now!" There was no anger in the fly voices, but the volume of the voices was raised. Maybe he was the only one with his eyes still open, so they moved closer to him, or the others were thinking the same thing he was. He had a feeling Chrissy Franklin's eyes would still be open, too, if they had eyes.

Brian relented and thought through the act of closing his eyes. There was silence, and he waited. At first, there was nothing, just the silence of the area he had come to know as The Darkness in such a short time. Then he thought he felt it melt away from him, and although he didn't dare open his eyes, he could have sworn he felt a change in his surroundings. Then, the stench. It was the blend of two smells that he hoped he would never have to smell again. The foul air filled his nostrils, and he felt the physical clenching on his stomach and throat that, if he had a body, he might have puked.

The smell was not hard for him to place. When he was in third grade, there was a mouse problem in the basement of his house. Brian remembered his father going down in the basement to get a screwdriver because he wanted to change the doorknobs on one of the bedroom doors because it was loose. Brian wanted to see how to change the doorknobs because he was always interested in knowing how to do projects like that with his dad, so he followed him into the basement. As they got to the bottom of the stairs, Brian's dad flipped on a light, and they both saw, scurrying across the floor of the basement, three mice. Brian jumped when he saw the movement.

"Shit," his dad said. It was also the first time his dad swore in front of him. "All right, Brian, looks like we have a new project before we get to those doorknobs."

On one of the shelves in the basement, way up top in a brown paper bag that looked like it hadn't been open in years, were mousetraps and sticky paper. Brian's dad set to the task of showing him how to set the mousetraps. Brian nearly caught his finger once but managed to set three traps on his own without losing a single appendage. Brian's dad set four of his own. Then they set out the sticky paper, got the screwdriver they needed for the doorknob, switched off the light, and left the basement. They finished the doorknobs and returned the screwdriver but still hadn't caught any mice. The next day Brain had school, and his dad worked late. No one checked the traps. The day after that, Brian's dad was home from work early, and after they ate dinner, he called Brian to check the traps with him. Brian didn't mind checking the actual traps but was worried about the sticky paper. The traps would kill the mice instantly. The sticky paper wouldn't kill the mice at all. Those mice would, Brian assumed, die from starvation. They would just be stuck to the paper until they died for some other reason. The last thing he wanted to see was a live mouse stuck to the paper, struggling to get free as it slowly died.

When they got to the bottom of the stairs, Brian's nose burned.

"We got at least a few, Brian; you smell that?" his dad said.

"What is it?" Brian asked. He first covered his mouth and nose with his hand but then pulled his shirt up to cover both instead.

"Death, son."

Brian would never forget that smell and never forget the way his dad was so quick to point it out. The smell in the basement that day had been bad, but nothing like the assault on his nose he felt now. The smell of death was overwhelming, and this time he didn't have hands or a shirt to cover up his mouth and nose to ease the smell a little bit. He just had to endure it.

"Oh my God," he heard Tiffany groan as she smelled the same horrible smell.

"Death," Brian repeated the words his father had spoken to him just a few years earlier. But death was just one of the two smells that filled the air of this horrible place that he was yet to see. The second, while not nearly as horrible as the stench of death, was also easily identifiable. Most people might have said dirt did not have a smell. Brian, and anyone else who spent as much time outside as he did, knew there was a definite odor that was unique to dirt. It was hard to explain because the smell of dirt changed with the seasons and with a person's location. In the spring, it was an earthy smell that mixed with the smell of fresh-cut grass because everything was just beginning to grow. The summer gave more of a dry, dusty smell as the ground dried out from the heat of the sun. Fall produced an earthy smell as well, but it was altogether different as the leaves fell from the trees and decomposed on the ground, changing the smell of the dirt. Even through the smell of death, Brian could point out the damp smell of earth here as well. He didn't know what time of year Chrissy was taken or when they were going to be brought back to the real world, but he knew here, in the fly world, it was early spring.

Brian remained motionless for another few seconds and then realized he was hearing again. There weren't any real noises other than Tiffany's exclamation at the smell, but he could sense that his ears were working. He also realized he was rubbing his fingers together. He was here. They were here in the fly world. Their bodies were back with them, just like when they brought themselves into their own mind world. Except this world was not inside any of their minds. It was inside the minds of the flies. It would be nice to have his body back, even if it was not in the real world. It was also nice knowing that he would not lose his body when his mind got tired. According to the flies, they were here until they were brought back to the real world.

Brian opened his eyes. He caught a quick glimpse of the others and knew they were just opening their eyes as well and taking in their new surroundings.

"Wow!" Chrissy said.

Brian had to stop himself from saying the same thing as he looked at the fly world.

They stood in an underground cavern. The roof stretched up over their heads and out of sight, and from what he could see of it, it was made from a hardened form of dirt. It was not rock, at least not any kind of rock he'd seen before. The floor was dirt, wet dirt. He could see it glistening in the light as he let his eyes follow along the ground in front of him. The walls were what caused the exclamation from Chrissy and the scream that Barbara let out at just the same time Brian looked at the walls. The group was in one far corner of the cavern, but it stretched out around them. Just as he couldn't see the ceiling of the massive room they were in, he couldn't see the far end of the cavern either. The walls started behind them and just went off until they were out of sight. If there was light, maybe he could see more of the cavern, but he couldn't even figure out where the light was coming from. The walls were not just there, though. They were moving.

Brian took a step forward when he realized the walls were covered with millions, or maybe even billions of flies crawling over and under each other.

Tiffany let out a yelp as she must have realized what the walls were made of and grabbed onto his arm, pressing herself against his back. He tried to hold in a smile, but it was hard. It felt good to feel the touch of someone else again. In the darkness, time seemed to move quickly, but when he could use his eyes and feel his body, he realized it seemed like forever since he'd felt the touch of someone else.

"Welcome." The voices of the flies surrounded them and echoed throughout the cavern as the walls spoke to them.

"This...this is really where you're from? This is your world?" Barbara asked, stepping forward and turning around, looking at the massive underground space.

"Yes, and it is getting smaller every day. This is not real, but it is, in every way, our world. We die in here, and more of us are born. Slowly, over time, we are filling this cavern," the flies responded.

Brian looked around, wondering how long the flies had been here and how big the cavern must have been when they first got there.

"I don't really feel sorry for you," Chrissy said.

Brian smiled—he liked her.

"We are not asking you to feel sorry for us. We are not giving you a choice, Chrissy. We will help you return to your real world, and you are going to help us," the flies said.

Brian thought they were going to continue their explanation of what was going on in this world, tell them what they were looking at, but they went silent instead.

"Are you looking for a bigger space?" Harry asked as he walked over next to Barbara. Brian looked back and saw Tiffany had moved next to Chrissy. Whether they had done it on purpose or not, it seemed they had taken sides in the short disagreement between Barbara and Chrissy. Brian took a few steps toward Tiffany. The best chance of them getting out of this alive was for them to work together. But he also agreed with Chrissy. They needed to fight back against the flies, not just go along with everything they said. Maybe it was because of the time period they were from. Barbara was from the 30s, and Harry grew up in the 50s. They were taught more or less to listen to anyone who was older than you. A "respect your elders" kind of thing. Brian understood it, but it didn't mean you were supposed to respect a group of evil flies after they kidnapped you. Brian blew air out his nose and shook his head, realizing how ridiculous that thought was.

"No. We need to leave here. And you will help us do that."

"How? How can we help you leave here?" Brian asked. It was strange hearing his voice through his ears. His voice echoed throughout the cavern, but it didn't echo inside his own head like it did in the darkness.

"Do not worry about that. When you are in the real world, you will know what to do. It will be an instinct," the flies responded. The walls shimmered as the flies all moved in unison. Brain watched as the wave moved across the wall, into the distance, and out of sight.

"So now what?" Chrissy took a few steps forward out in front of the rest of them and turned around, looking at the walls and then at the other kids. She shrugged her shoulders and kicked a few times at the dirt beneath her feet and then sat down. "You just want us to stay here in this place while you figure the rest of this shit out? We have our own lives we'd like to get back to."

"You can do whatever you would like, Chrissy Franklin. We know you don't want to help us, but it will be the best thing for you. We hope you come to realize that when this is done. You will be better off because of it. You hate it now, in the short term, but in the long term, it will be the best thing for you." The flies shimmered again as if turning along the wall. "We must leave you now. We will be back soon with the one who will help return you to the real world."

The walls shimmered once more, and then the flies all pushed off from the walls and flew around. It didn't seem as though any of them left. They just moved away from the wall and then resettled against the wall a moment later. Brian watched them, staring at the walls and trying to figure out when they would leave or if they would actually leave. He realized, since this was not the real world, only the consciousness of the flies had to leave. Their actual bodies could remain here because this was simply a mental projection and not the real world.

"Are you still here?" Brian asked. They all waited in silence for a few seconds. When there was no response, they all assumed the flies had gone.

"Is our only plan just to let them, whoever this person is, just take us back to the real world? We don't know that they will do what they say they will do. We need to get there ourselves. We need to do this on our terms," Chrissy said. "I'm not trying to be the difficult one. I just don't want to die or stay with them forever. And if that happens, I don't want to look back and think I did absolutely nothing to try to help myself get out of the situation."

No one said anything, but Brian caught Tiffany nodding. Brian nodded also.

"I think we need to at least try to do something. If they need us so bad for whatever they say they need us for, they won't kill us if we fight back. So they have to keep us alive," Tiffany said, looking to Harry first and then to Barbara.

Barbara nodded too.

"Part of me wants to think you're right. Another part of me wants to think they are in trouble and they need our help. They don't know how else to ask for help, so they do this." Barbara gestured around them with her hands.

Chrissy shook her head. "No, I don't think so. There is something more evil than just the fact that they need help. Why would they take us the way they took us? *Something* is not right about all of this. I'm not going to just let this person who's coming take me."

"The person is probably a hostage, just like us. Maybe they know more than we do or different stuff than we do. We should see what that person has to say. I just don't want to upset the flies too much. What if they took extra of us in case something happened? What if they don't need all of us?" Harry said. A tear dripped down his cheek, and Brian saw his top lip start to quiver. When Brian and Tiffany first arrived, he thought Harry was the tough one and was going to be the leader of the group. It was clear that wasn't the case. Chrissy and Barbara were struggling over who would lead them. Brian and Tiffany were solidly behind Chrissy, even though they never said it. It was pretty obvious. Even Barbara might be doubting her plan a little bit. Harry still held on to the belief that the flies were just going to let them go. Harry was scared, but he did make a good point.

"You're right, Harry. Whoever, or whatever, shows up to

take us back to the real world might be a hostage just like us. It wouldn't hurt to find out what they know before we just go with them. Maybe we can all come up with a plan together," Brian said, looking at Chrissy first and then Barbara.

Chrissy opened her mouth to speak but didn't get the chance to. Off in the distance, there was a new voice.

"Hello?"

CHAPTER 17

At some point, Lisa fell asleep. Was it called falling asleep if you just passed out from mental and physical exhaustion? She didn't know, but that's what it was. She didn't want to sleep, but the longer she sat and thought about what her body had been through and the things she had seen and done, her mind felt like it was on overload. She couldn't think about the situation she was in for another second. Finally, her eyes became heavy, and she fell asleep. It could have been minutes or hours later, she had no idea, but she woke up to the sound of the flies coming off the wall and rematerializing as John Holland in the same spot he disappeared in when he left.

Lisa opened one groggy eye and tried to focus it, but Holland and the room were still blurry. She closed her eye and squeezed it shut, then opened both eyes, hoping the world in front of her would clear. It didn't. She blinked a few times as Holland turned toward her. She tried to straighten her exhausted body from its position leaning against the wall of the room opposite the fly-covered children, but her muscles were slow to react to her request. Everything hurt in a way she had never felt before. Finally, she got her eyes to focus. Holland was a whole person again. He stood over her and looked down, the evil smile plastered on his face.

"Your turn, Lisa," Holland said.

"No, I don't want to. I...I'm not ready," Lisa said. The words barely escaped her dry mouth. She felt her lips crack when she spoke. How long had it been since she had any water? She didn't know. How long had Holland been gone? She didn't know that either.

"You would never be ready for this. It just has to happen." Holland opened his mouth, and flies poured out of him.

"No, no."

Lisa couldn't move her body and had just enough time to cover her face with her hands before the flies surrounded her. The insects crawled along her skin. Lisa pressed her hands against her face as they surrounded her. She closed her eyes so she couldn't see what was happening. The buzzing was deafening as the flies swarmed around her head. They pushed their way into her ears. The urge to scream was overwhelming, but she kept her lips pressed closed tight. She curled her lips inside her mouth and bit down on them, determined not to let them in her mouth even as she felt more of them crawling inside her ears. The copper taste of blood filled her mouth as her teeth broke through the skin of her lips. A scream of terror filled her throat when the flies worked their way between her fingers and forced their way up under her clenched eyelids. The flies moved down her face toward her nose. Lisa used her hands to pinch her nose shut while still keeping her mouth covered. This worked momentarily, but she couldn't breathe and needed to move her hands to get some air. The flies used that to their advantage, and she felt them fly up into her nose.

It was only then that she realized her entire body was covered in flies. They had just not been able to get into her mouth yet. She wondered if that would be enough to keep her out of the darkness. But it didn't matter. The flies in her nose had cut off her air supply. Lisa was going to have to open her mouth to breathe or pass out from lack of oxygen. They seemed to stop, as if knowing she was going to have to open her mouth eventually, and they waited. Lisa held her breath as long as she could, but she was terrified, and the pressing of the flies against her body made breathing difficult. Her chest burned, aching for oxygen.

Lisa couldn't wait anymore. Her lips slipped from between her teeth, and she pressed her hand tight against her mouth, hoping she could take a breath without letting the flies in. She drew in a soft breath from between her slightly parted lips, but somehow, they knew. They pressed against her hand and force her fingers apart. Her lips were sealed shut, but she wasn't biting down on them, and it was the opening they needed. The first fly entered her mouth, and then her lips were pried open. More flies entered and pushed her mouth open wider. The vibrations of them against her tongue made her gag. Her body went from tense to relaxed, and then she felt nothing.

"Lisa." Holland's voice echoed inside her head the second she lost feeling in her body.

Lisa tried to blink, she tried to look around, but she couldn't see anything. The Darkness, she remembered.

"What...what is this?" Lisa tried to speak, but she had no mouth. Somehow her words echoed in her head anyway. It felt as though her mouth was not close to her, though. It was like hearing herself speak in a large empty room and only hearing the echo.

"This is it, Lisa. The Darkness. You did not have to put up such a fight, you know. We will keep you safe. We need you. You are important to us." The voice had changed. It was no longer Holland's voice. There were many of them, talking at the same time from all around her. They were not using Holland's body anymore. This was them. This was the flies.

"I won't stop fighting you," Lisa said. She tried to sound determined to stop them but realized it probably sounded weak and amusing to the flies who had been able to do anything they wanted with her thus far. Lisa would have tightened her mouth if she had one. In her head, it made sense, but it was still hard to comprehend. She was still laying there, on the floor of that room covered in flies, just like the kids on the wall. But somehow, when they entered her, they were able to create this thought world where she could live, not feeling the pain of the real world and still sharing thoughts with the flies. This was how those kids had lived for however long they had been like that.

"You can fight all you want, Lisa, but if you want to save those kids, you still have to help us. We told you, we cannot bring the kids back to the real world. Only you can do that. Those kids can live a long time on the wall like that, a very long time, but they will die there eventually. The only way to save them is to bring them back one at a time. And only you can do that, Lisa."

The evil left the voice of the flies in her head. They were more conversational than they had been. It was the first time since John Holland tried to help her escape that she felt like she was actually talking to another person and not some evil creature. It was probably just a trick, though. They were acting that way to get what they want. It occurred to her they might be able to read her thoughts. She had no way to tell, so she just assumed they couldn't.

"Of course, I'll help them," Lisa said, knowing that didn't mean she wasn't still going to try to stop the kids from doing what the flies needed them to do, which remained unclear.

"Good," the flies said. Lisa pictured Holland's smile when the flies spoke. "From here, the children are able to create the mind-worlds we told you about. It gives them a body and something to look at instead of just blackness. It is hard for the human mind to survive totally isolated, so we made them able to create their own mind-world to go to on occasion. We even taught the first one, Barbara, how to move from the darkness into the mind-world. She hasn't told the others how she learned about the mind-world yet, which we find interesting. But she did teach the others how to get there. They have even visited the others in those mind-worlds." The fly voices echoed through her head. Some felt like they were inside her ears, shouting at her—others seemed far off. They spoke in unison; it was almost overwhelming to her brain to hear that many voices at the same time inside her head.

"So one is named Barbara. How long have you had her? What are the others' names?" The name rang a bell, but Lisa couldn't put her finger on where she'd heard the name before. She wanted to get away from the flies and get the kids and herself out of this place as soon as she could. She had other questions she wanted answers to, but none of that was as important as getting everyone out of there safely. If she got to ask those questions later, she would. If she never got to ask those questions, as long as the kids were safe, she would be okay never knowing the answers to them.

"Barbara has been with us a long time. But we will let her tell you how long if you cannot figure it out. The others, Harry, Brian, Tiffany, and Chrissy, have been with us for less time. You are already familiar with them. We will bring you to them now. To our world, our thought world, and then leave you to it. Just remember, the way you get back is the way they will get back. One at a time, or you might well lose one of them."

Lisa knew immediately why the name Barbara, and the other names, were so familiar. They were the kids who had disappeared in the neighborhood over the last one hundred years. But how could that be? Those were the same kids who were stuck to the wall in that room? She was too involved with what was happening to her, with John Holland and flies, to make the connection between herself and the missing children. Chrissy. Chrissy Franklin. She wasn't dead or missing. She had been taken by John Holland, just like Lisa had been. And the other kids had apparently been taken by him, or by the flies, and held here in stasis like this since the day they were taken. It must have been awful to live in this darkness for that long, Barbara for almost one hundred years, stuck inside her head like this.

"Now close your eyes," the flies said.

There was a long pause. She had no idea what they wanted her to do. She had no eyes.

"I can't. I have no body. No eyes," Lisa said.

"Think about when you do have a body. Pretend you have a body and think about closing your eyes. Do it now," the flies commanded, but again in a nice, conversational tone. They just wanted her to go along with what they were saying and figured this was the best way to get what they want. In a way, they were right.

Lisa concentrated and thought about what she would do if she had a body and how she would close her eyes. She could almost feel the muscles on her face clench as she thought. She could feel her eyelids close, covering her eyes, even though neither of them were actually there.

There was a silence, and even in the nothingness of this place, the silence grew and surrounded her. Then the silence was gone. She breathed in through her nose, and she could smell. It wasn't a good smell, but after being without a body, though just for a short amount of time, it was good to be able to use her nose again.

"Now open your eyes," the flies said.

This time she didn't protest or hesitate. She just opened her eyes. She found herself in a huge cavern. She assumed she was underground, but she couldn't see the ceiling, so she could have been outside. There was no wind, and the stench of death that enveloped her told her she was indeed inside a cave or cavern of some sort.

"Now what?" Lisa asked. She looked at the walls of the cave, and they appeared to ripple. There was no response from the flies, and she didn't want to get much closer to the walls of the cave to find out why they were rippling, though she guessed they were covered with flies.

The first few steps across the dirt covered floor of the cave were strange. They felt like real steps and real feet, but she knew they weren't. She tried to process this and turn it into something that made sense in her head, but she couldn't, so she ignored the problem. Lisa moved forward, listening to the sounds around her. There weren't many. The only thing she could be sure she heard was the sound of her feet shuffling along the dirt underneath them. She took a few more steps, knowing she had to find the kids somewhere in this cavern and get them out, but she was afraid to yell. She didn't know what else was in here with her, and she didn't want to give away her position.

The words Holland spoke to her back in the fly room were all she could think of: *you will feel yourself coming back from the other place.* The problem was she didn't feel herself going back to the real world. And neither Holland nor the flies had been very specific about how to do what they expected her to do. Maybe she would know what to do when she found the kids. She had to find them.

Lisa picked up her pace. Instead of slow, exploratory steps forward, she walked with quickness, with a purpose. She went about thirty or forty yards, she guessed at an almost running pace. Since it wasn't her real body, her aches and pains were gone, and it felt good to be moving again, even if this wasn't real.

There was a noise. She stopped. It sounded like whispering. She held still for a moment and listened. The low murmur was there again, in front of her. Either they were whispering, or they were really far off. The kids.

"Hello?" Lisa called out into the darkness in front of her. The sounds stopped. Silence. Lisa called out again. "Hello?"

There was still no response from the kids. Lisa would have done the same thing if their places were reversed. She wouldn't have been able to trust the voice she heard in the darkness, either. The only reason she knew the kids were real and not just something made up by the flies was the fact that she had seen them with her own eyes. She knew they were real, and she knew she needed to get them down off that wall. She needed them to make noise for her to know which direction to go. She had to get them to trust her.

"I…I know you probably think I'm them, the flies, but I'm not. They took me too. They told me I have to help you."

More whispering in the darkness. It was still in front of Lisa, but she couldn't tell exactly where they were, just that they weren't behind her. They didn't respond, but Lisa kept moving forward, talking, almost yelling into the darkness as she walked.

"If I were you, I wouldn't trust me either. I can't make you believe me. I was just in the darkness, and they brought me here. They can't get you out of this place for some reason. Only I can. At least that's what they told me. Please believe me." Then she paused. There was still no response back from the kids, just more whispering back and forth. She could almost make out some words now. She definitely heard Chrissy's name. Lisa didn't know if telling Chrissy who she was would help her case or make the kids more suspicious, but she didn't have too many other choices. "Chrissy? I'm Lisa Ewing, Matt's mom."

The words hung in the air for a moment without a response from the group of five children somewhere in the vastness of the cave she was in. She stood still, listening for the whispers, but there were none.

Lisa took a few steps forward and then stopped in her tracks again when a voice called out from the darkness.

"Mrs. Ewing?" the voice said. She assumed it was Chrissy's, but she had never seen or met the girl.

"Yes," Lisa replied, walking in the direction of the voice.

"I…we want to believe you, but we aren't sure if it's you or a trick," the voice said.

"I understand that. I would say the same thing about you, but I've seen your bodies, so I know it's really you," Lisa said. She wanted to reach out to them and make them trust her, but she knew it would take more convincing. They were only kids, and given what had happened to them so far, they had a right to be suspicious.

"What kind of phone does Matt have?" The voice Lisa now knew was Chrissy's called out.

"An iPhone." Lisa smiled, thinking of how Matt did that to her, then she added to her response, wondering how much Chrissy knew. "An iPhone 8, but he wants the X. I won't buy it for him, though."

There was another long pause and whispering, then Chrissy broke the silence.

"We're over here. This way!" Chrissy called.

Lisa could hear the smile in her voice. It was obviously enough to convince Chrissy, and maybe Chrissy had enough pull with the rest of the group to convince them that she was really there to look out for them and help them out of there.

CHAPTER 18

Lisa approached the group. They looked happy and healthy. One of the kids was out in front, dressed in modern clothes. The rest were back only a few feet behind her but still shrouded somewhat by the shadows of the cave.

"Chrissy?" Lisa asked, and pointed at the girl in front.

Chrissy nodded. "It's me. We were kind of split on this. I didn't want to trust you until you said Matt's name. Then, the iPhone thing did it for me."

"Everyone is so worried about you, Chrissy. There have been news stories and search parties," Lisa said.

"What?" Chrissy looked confused. The others moved up, and Lisa got a better look at them.

"Well, since you've been gone. Matt was so worried. The rest of the school really has been too. It's been a tough few days for everyone. Or at least it was before I was taken. However long ago that was."

"What...what do you mean?" Chrissy's eyes squinted. "I've only been here...." She trailed off.

"Time is different here," a girl's voice said from behind her.

Chrissy looked back and took a half step to the side. A girl, about the same age as Chrissy, stepped forward. She had a long dress on, and her black hair pulled back. She gave a weak smile.

"Barbara?" Lisa looked at the girl, knowing who she was. The girl nodded. "Do you know me?"

"Well, no." Lisa shook her head. "Not really. I don't know any of you, really. But since...since Chrissy disappeared, I've done some research. There was one story about Chrissy's disappearance that mentioned other disappearances. I just got curious and looked into the rest of them. That's how I learned about all of you. I was taken by our neighbor John Holland shortly after that. I didn't put two and two together until just now. I was thinking too much about my own kidnapping, about being taken. I never stopped to think that they might all be related."

"So, this guy, John Holland," a boy said. Judging by his clothes, Lisa guessed he was Harry. "He helps the flies like you do?"

"No, no. I don't think he helps the flies. And I certainly don't want to help them. I think he *is* the flies. They use his body or take over his body. They haven't taken over me." Lisa hoped they felt like they could trust her.

"We've been trying to figure out what to do," Chrissy said. "We want to trust them because we can get back that way, but we don't know if we can. They say you can get us back to the real world."

Lisa nodded. She wanted to tell them she didn't think the flies would let any of them just go, but she also wanted to give them hope. She was torn about telling them the truth or giving them some version of the truth that would make them fight that much harder for their freedom.

"They've told me that too. They said only I can bring you back to the real world, so if I want to help you, I need to do this," Lisa said. She spread her arms out around her and shrugged. She looked past Barbara, Chrissy, and Harry at the two still standing behind them in the shadows. "Obviously, I want to help you, all of you. I...I've seen your bodies. They look relatively healthy, though I don't know how they haven't aged at all." She didn't think mentioning the blanket of flies covering their bodies would be all that helpful at the moment.

"We still look like kids, even Barbara?" Brian said, finally speaking up.

Lisa nodded. "Yes. I don't know what will happen when you are allowed to get up and moving again, but from what I saw, you all looked like kids. They told me they can't bring you back, only I could. They also told me they would let me go once you're back and have completed whatever task it is they need you to complete."

"But you don't know what that is?" Barbara said.

"No," Lisa shook her head. "The only thing I could think of that made any sense to help you was to get you out of here, and then when we are all back in the real world, in physical form, we can try to fight them. It's hard to fight them here—they are controlling this whole thing. The darkness and everything else. I don't like doing what they want us to do, but I really don't see any other way until we're all back in our bodies."

Barbara turned and looked at Harry and then Chrissy. Chrissy turned her back to Lisa and looked from Barbara to Brian and Tiffany. They all exchanged a glance. There wasn't much talking, just a few nods and a couple of shrugs. There must have already been some discussion about what they would do. That was probably the whispering Lisa heard earlier. The kids already had an idea of what she was there for and wanted to hear what she had to say before they made a decision. Whatever they decided, it was clear they were going to stay together. They were in this together. She was still an outsider.

"Okay," Chrissy said. "We'll go back. But then, once we get there, we do whatever we can to break free from them. There are six of us now. We're all together."

Chrissy seemed to be the one rallying the group together, and she stopped just short of having them put their hands in a circle and shouting, "Go team!" Maybe she even thought of doing that but realized this wasn't the right place to do something like that. Lisa smiled, though, thinking back to Matt. He had basically told them he wanted Chrissy to be his girlfriend. From talking to him, he thought Chrissy wanted him to be her boyfriend. She was glad he picked a girl like her to be his first girlfriend, even if it only meant they would text or talk on the phone a little bit more than they did already, and maybe a few more trips to the movies. Still, she was the kind of girl she hoped Matthew would end up with. Chrissy turned and caught Lisa staring at her and smiling.

"Mrs. Ewing? Are you okay?" Chrissy asked.

"Oh yes," Lisa shook her head quickly and let the smile drop away. "I was just thinking about how happy Matthew will be to see you. He was pretty upset."

Chrissy smiled. It was the first real smile she had seen from any of the kids. "I'll be happy to see him too. He is…he's a great friend."

They all stood looking at each other for a few seconds. Then the kids turned their eyes to Lisa. She just looked back at them and smiled, assuming they were happy to have come to this decision to let her in, trust her, and get out of this together.

"So how do we get out of here?" the only one who hadn't spoken yet, Tiffany, said.

"Oh, I don't actually know," Lisa said.

"What?" Brian said. She could see the anger on his face.

"They only told me I would know when the time was right. Because you're younger than me, you wouldn't be able to do it without help. I would be able to do it, and then I could show you how and bring you back one at a time."

"But they didn't tell you how?" Harry asked.

"No," Lisa shook her head. "They only said they can't do it, and neither can any of you on your own. They can't tell me how to do it. I will just figure it out."

"What do we do now?" Harry said.

Lisa hadn't really thought this part through. She assumed that when they told her she would know how to get out, it would be obvious. It was clear it wasn't. She took a step back, away from the group of kids, and closed her eyes. She thought about her conversation with Holland before he left to speak to the kids and move them from the darkness. She tried to remember everything he'd told her about how to get them out, but the only thing she could recall was that he said she would feel herself leaving this world and going back to the real world, and she had to convince the kids to go with her, one at a time.

She opened her eyes, disappointed.

"I…I don't know. There's nothing, no clues that they gave me."

The kids were all staring at her, mouths open.

"How did you do that?" Brian said.

"Do what?" Lisa was confused.

"Mrs. Ewing, you like, faded in and out while you were standing there. You were gone for a second and then came back," Chrissy said.

"I don't know. I was just trying to think about what John Holland, the flies, told me. I didn't know anything happened."

"Do you think that's it?" Barbara said. The excitement in her voice was clear. She may be almost a hundred years old, but she was still a girl and had been here in this place for a long time. She was ready to leave.

"I don't know. Let me try again."

Lisa closed her eyes and took a step back away from the kids, giving herself space like she did the first time. She thought back to the fly room. She thought about Holland and tried to remember the details of what they were talking about. She felt like she was floating above the room. She could look down and see herself, flies swarming around the upper part of her body. It would have grossed her out, but she was too focused on trying to get herself back to that world. She concentrated harder and thought about moving herself down to her body, and then she floated there, closer to the floor. She looked out of her eyes again. Flies crawled along the floor in front of her, and she could again hear them buzzing inside her ears. Past the flies in front of her face was her hand, no longer covered by the flies. Lisa looked at it and rubbed her fingers together. It worked. She could feel that she wasn't fully inside her body, though. A part of her was still back with the kids.

"You've done it," millions of voices echoed in the room. "Now, bring them back."

Lisa didn't know what to do at first, but then closed her eyes and thought, this time of the dark cavern that smelled of death. She opened her eyes again, and she was back there, the kids standing in front of her, watching her.

She couldn't move her body or smell death in the air like she was in-between worlds—part of her in the fly room, the other in the cave. Then her senses came back to her. She blinked her eyes and breathed in; the smell of death once again filled her nostrils. She rubbed her fingers together like she had in the fly room, and she knew she was fully back in the cave.

"Did it work?" Chrissy asked.

Lisa nodded her head. "Yes. All I really have to do is think about where I need to be. I can see myself floating down and then entering my body."

"So, how do we do it?" Brian asked.

"I don't know. They said I need to go with you. And that I need to do it one at a time. I think if we hold hands or something, I can help guide you. I don't really know. That just feels right." Lisa looked at them and frowned. She wished she could be more definitive, but she had only a little bit more information than the five kids did.

"I guess it's all we've got to go on," Barbara said. "Does anyone want to volunteer to go first?"

"I'll go first," Harry said right away. He stepped forward, his lips pressed together, looking like the protector of the others in the group. "Someone has to go first. Then, if anything happens to me when I go back, the rest of you can come up with another plan."

"Nothing is going to happen to you, Harry," Barbara said. Her words were matter of fact, but her eyes hopeful.

"Yeah. We've got this, right, Mrs. Ewing?" Chrissy said.

"Yes. You'll be fine, Harry. And Chrissy, I think we're past you calling me Mrs. Ewing. Lisa will be fine from now on," Lisa said with a smile, trying to show the kids that she wasn't worried. She hoped this worked the way she thought it would. "Ready, Harry?"

"You got this, Harry," Brian said, pumping a fist at the only other boy in the group.

Harry looked over at Brian, nodded back, then tightened his lips together again and took a deep breath.

"Yeah, this is going to work. I'm done with those fucking flies. Let's do this."

The entire group, Lisa included, smiled. None of them had known each other long, Lisa realized, and if there was ever a situation where swearing would be allowed no matter who was around, it was this situation.

"Yeah." Lisa smiled at Harry and looked him in the eye. "Let's fucking do it."

He smiled back at her and held out both his hands. Lisa stood facing him and crossed her arms, grasping his hands tight while Harry did the same.

"Here we go," Lisa said when she felt like they were in a good position. She didn't really know what she was going to do with Harry once they were in the fly room together, but she hadn't known how to get back into her own body either—it just kind of happened. She figured she would make it up as she went along, assuming she could get Harry back there at all. "Now, close your eyes."

Lisa watched Harry close his eyes, then she did the same. She thought of the fly room again. She pictured herself laying on the floor again, but this time also the kids plastered to the wall and tried to think about which one was Harry. It was his jeans that gave him away. The bright blue jeans of the 1960s were different than the jeans of the 80s, or even the present day. With the jeans at the front of her mind, she tried to put herself back in the room. Just like before, she found herself there, floating above the floor near the ceiling. She looked at her hands as she tried to maneuver herself closer to the floor. Harry's hands were still there, gripping hers.

"Are you still with me, Harry?"

"Yes, what…what happened to us?" Harry said. His voice echoed through her head.

"I didn't want to tell you all what happened to you. The flies said they needed to do that to you to keep you safe. To keep you alive all this time. You would have died without them on you like that. Just think about entering your body. As soon as you're in there, I will leave and come back with the next one." Lisa felt them move above the bodies. She looked down at them and saw Harry was directly above his body.

"Okay. Thank you," Harry said.

She wanted to let go but didn't know if it was the right time. She thought about moving lower to the ground, and they moved lower. She held Harry's hands tighter, and as they moved lower, Harry moved into his body, and Lisa felt his hands release. The jolt of losing her grip on Harry sent her flying backwards to the other side of the room, against the wall just above where her body lay on the ground. Harry's body shook for a second as if he was having a seizure, then stopped, and he fell to the floor, the flies moving off him. She stayed for a second and watched Harry's body move, first his hands and arms, then his legs and feet. He was back.

Lisa floated back up toward the ceiling and thought about the cave again. The flies zipped around the room, and the form of John Holland began to take shape. He looked up at where she was and nodded. He smiled at her and then turned his attention to Harry, who was pushing himself up to his feet.

Lisa focused her thoughts on the cave and returned there to the four hopeful faces looking back at her. It took her a moment again to regain her full presence in the cave.

"Did it work?" Tiffany asked.

"Yes," Lisa said, out of breath. She felt like she had just been to the gym for a few hours, and she had to do it four more times. She didn't know if her body would hold up. She reminded herself that she didn't have a body, and it was only mentally exhausting, but it didn't help. But now that she knew she could get the kids out of there, she had no choice but to save them all. She knew if it was one of her kids that had been taken, she wouldn't want the person saving them to stop after just one. No, now that she knew she *could* save them, she knew she *would* save them all.

"Who's next?" Lisa asked. Without hesitation, Tiffany stepped forward in front of Lisa.

"I'm ready," Tiffany said. She held out her hands and crossed them like Harry had done. Lisa gripped the girl's hands tight and repeated the process she had done with Harry. Before long, they were floating above the fly room, looking down at the four bodies still along the wall. Lisa gave Tiffany the same explanation about the flies covering their faces when she asked. Then both Lisa and Tiffany focused their attention on Harry and the man standing next to him.

"Who is that?" Tiffany asked.

"That's John Holland. He's my neighbor," Lisa said. The flies took over his body. Holland was looking up at them, and Harry stood next to him, looking at the bodies along the wall, probably waiting for one of the others to join him.

"Harry looks okay," Tiffany said. "I think I'm ready."

"Think about being inside your body. I don't know how else to describe it. Just think about it, and your hands will be free of mine. Harry fell off of the wall and onto the floor. He looked stiff at first but seemed to pop right up."

"Okay." Tiffany took a deep breath and closed her eyes again.

The two of them drifted lower to the ground, hovering right over Tiffany's body. Then, just like before, her hands disappeared from Lisa's, and her body shook and fell to the floor.

Lisa watched until she saw Tiffany begin to push herself up off the floor and then closed her eyes to return to the cave. She opened her eyes and took a deep breath once she was back with Chrissy, Brian, and Barbara. She felt dizzy and took a few more, long deep breaths.

"Are you okay, Mrs. Ew— Lisa?" Chrissy asked.

"Yes, I can do three more trips. We're almost out of here," Lisa said. She smiled but could feel the exhaustion on her face. "Who's next?"

CHAPTER 19

Harry floated down from the ceiling, and his hands left
Lisa's. At first, it felt like he was falling, but there was no end in
sight. He fell slowly into his own body. It was strange at first to
be back. He had little control over his body at first, but he knew
the change was taking place. His mind and his body connected
again for the first time in a long time. Harry blinked. The flies
surrounding him burst into the air, and he crashed to the floor.
Harry blinked a few more times—he had trouble focusing, and
everything was blurry. Then he moved his hand. The fingers
of his right hand curled when he wanted them to. Each finger
clenched and unclenched. It worked. Lisa had brought him back
to the real world. He pushed himself up and turned to look back
at Lisa, but she was already gone to get the others.

Harry tried to sit up, but his entire body was sore and stiff.
He groaned and managed to push himself up to his knees.

"It is okay. Your body has been there, stuck to that wall,
for a long time. It will not take long for it to feel normal again," a
voice said from behind him.

Harry turned and sat on the ground next to Lisa's fly-
covered body.

"Who are you?" Harry said, but he already knew who it
was. It was them. The flies, in their human form.

"You know who we are," the flies responded. "It might be easier for you to refer to us as John, though, since we look human."

"Am I...are we free to go now?" Harry asked, still just sitting and looking up at the old man.

"No, Harry." John laughed. "You are just getting started. We need you and the others now. Then you can go free."

"What could you possibly need me for? What year is this? Why did you need kids from so many different times?" Harry might not have discussed all of his thoughts with the rest of the group, but he needed his questions answered, and he had the person, or things, that could answer them for him.

"Time is just different for us and different for you when you're in the darkness, Harry. We did not bring you through time. When we took you, time just moved...faster. It is just how it works. Now that you are here, time will move at a normal speed for you. We just needed four of you. Tiffany came along for the ride. Now you can do what we needed you to do from the beginning. Spread our message across the earth." John moved closer to Harry and knelt down next to him.

"What? What do you mean to spread your message? What message?"

Harry tried to back away from the old man and his evil grin. He pushed himself away against the floor with his feet, but John placed a hand on his shoulder, keeping him from moving.

"The message that we will get rid of all humans on this planet and take it for ourselves."

The old man opened his mouth, and flies poured out of him. They swirled around Harry's head. He lifted his arms and covered his face, but the swarm disappeared.

The world around him changed. He could see, but not in the same way he could before the swarm of flies. Everything was blurry. He tried to blink, but he couldn't. He tried to rub his eyes, thinking one of the flies had gotten in them, making his vision blurry, but he couldn't move his hands. The room was different. Like a mosaic, he saw many versions of the room at the same time. He could still sense John kneeling next to him, but it was more than just eyesight that let him know he was there.

What happened?

Harry wanted to stand up, to get out of the room and get away from John, but his body wouldn't respond. It wouldn't listen to his brain. He knew what was going on, but his body was frozen. Or so he thought. His body did move, but not the way he told it to. He stood up, and John looked at him, smiling.

"Join us over here, Harry," John said. Harry did not want to go next to John, who was standing in one corner of the room gesturing for Harry to stand next to him. The door was right there next to him — he could reach for it, pull it open, and leave. But his body didn't respond. Instead, he stood and moved over next to John in the corner of the room.

"Very good," John said, adding a nod to his grin. "Now we just wait for the others."

A few minutes passed, and Harry still had no luck moving or controlling his body. Then Lisa and Tiffany appeared above them. John turned his head toward the ceiling, Harry did not, but he could still see the two of them floating down towards the bodies below. He wanted to stop them, tell them it wasn't safe, but there was nothing he could do.

"Stop! Don't do it!" he tried to shout. His voice echoed throughout his own head, but nothing came out of his mouth. He was trapped in his body, and it was too late to help the others. They were all going to end up like him.

Tiffany's body dropped to the floor.

"Stay right here," John said to him. He had no choice but to listen. To obey. Harry remained motionless and watched as John let loose the swarm of flies around Tiffany once he determined that she was okay. Then, just like him, Tiffany's mind was separated from her body. She joined Harry and stood next to him. He knew she was trying to talk to him, trying to get out of the room just like he was, but there was nothing either of them could do. He wondered what John, what the flies, had in store for them. What were they going to be forced to do?

Brian's body dropped from the wall, and he joined them, then Barbara, and finally Chrissy. They were all there, all stuck, just like before, under the control of the flies. At least before they were in the darkness and felt as though they had some control. And they could communicate with each other. Now they were stuck. Trapped in their own brains without a way to communicate with anyone.

Lisa's body twitched on the floor, and her eyes opened. His first thought was that she would join them, be trapped in her body just like they were. But the flies did something different with her. Instead of releasing the swarm that circled her head for just a moment, John released a larger swarm covering Lisa's entire upper body. Though she was laying on the floor, she looked a lot like the others had when they were trapped by the flies against the wall. Lisa was in The Darkness. Harry wanted to help her, but a new thought entered his brain. A darker thought he had no control over. He wanted to go to her, to surround her, like the flies had done to all of them. He needed to do it. Although he didn't want to, Harry moved toward Lisa. His face felt strange, but he didn't know why. He felt a hand on his shoulder.

"Not her, Harry," John said, holding him in place. "We may need her again. There are many more you can convert. Follow us. All of you."

John opened the door to the room, and the five children unwillingly followed him out. Harry wanted to look back and make sure Lisa was okay, but his body didn't let him. Harry led the way as they maneuvered down one long hallway and then another, and still one more. Eventually, John led them to the stairs. They followed him up into a house and then out onto a street. The street looked somewhat familiar to Harry, but not really. He didn't know what year this was, but it wasn't 1960 anymore. He thought Chrissy might recognize the street better than any of the others, but he couldn't ask her. The sun was low in the sky. Middle, late afternoon? Harry wasn't sure.

"Now, Harry, and the rest of you too," John said, standing in front of them, his smile wider than ever before. His dark eyes turned a bright, brilliant green as he spoke. "Go out into the world and bring our kind back to power."

Harry didn't want to, but at the same time, he couldn't resist the urge. His head snapped to one side, and his blurry eyes focused on a man down the street checking his mail. Harry didn't know the man or care who he was. His body took him to the man. He was running but moving much faster than he had ever run before. His legs were stronger, and they pushed him effortlessly across the yards and down the street toward the man. Harry thought he looked the same as he always had, but the man's reaction told him that might not be true. The man screamed as Harry approached, and his face curled back in a grimace when Harry got even closer.

"No!" the man shouted. "Help!"

By that time, Harry somehow knew that it was too late. His arms spread, and his mouth opened. He felt larger than ever before. He surrounded the man and saw flies swarm him from every direction. Harry felt himself break apart into a million pieces, then wrapped himself around the man and collapsed down on him. A second later, Harry got up, whole again, and the man was gone.

Harry stood up, feeling happy with himself but also terrified. He looked around, confused.

Do not worry, Harry, John's voice filled his head. *We have made a nest for him in the backyard. He will remain there until he has matured.*

Harry smiled and looked around for the next human.

CHAPTER 20

Lisa brought the rest of the kids back to the real world, ending with Chrissy. As Chrissy's hand disappeared from her own and her body dropped to the floor, Lisa, still floating above the room, looked down at the kids. They all stood motionless in a line, with Holland standing next to them, looking down over them and smiling. She wished there was more she could do for them, but they were left at the mercy of the flies, who no doubt told them to stand there and stay still until they all were there together. When Lisa saw Chrissy move her hand and begin to push herself up, she knew she had done what she needed to do. She smiled. The first part was finished. She had taken the kids from The Darkness and back into the real world. Now all she had to do was get them and herself, free from John Holland. It wasn't going to be easy, but at least she had some help this time around.

Lisa thought herself down toward her own body and then felt her consciousness drop back into her own head. The cold of the floor felt good against her face even as flies buzzed around her. The odor of the room told her she was back. The flies backed away from her, but she still couldn't open her eyes. Her body twitched as she fully reentered it. She didn't move for a few moments, just breathed in slowly through her nose. The thought crossed her mind that Holland had no intention of keeping his side of the deal. He could and probably would kill her the second she got up. She didn't really have any other options, though. He was the flies, so he probably already knew she was back inside her body. Lisa held her breath and listened. She listened past the sound of the flies zipping past her to the children and Holland. There were no sounds from them. No one talking, not Brian or Tiffany or even Chrissy, who she thought would be protesting or asking questions by now. Nothing. It worried Lisa, and she opened her eyes.

They were open just in time to see the swarm of flies descending back down on her. She didn't even have time to scream—they covered her, and she plunged back into The Darkness.

"Son of a bitch!" Lisa shouted into the empty space that was The Darkness. Her voice echoed around her. If she had a body, she would have slammed her fist down against a table or the wall or something. The darkness and loneliness in this place were eerie and uncomfortable.

"Well, I'm trapped now," Lisa thought or said—she couldn't be sure which, but the words echoed in her head again. She still had conscious thought and felt like she had her own body with her, but of course, she didn't. She was still in the fly room covered with flies, and who knew what Holland and the flies were making those kids do. Something was wrong with them. Lisa knew it. They were just too quiet. She had to get back there. She had to get back to them and help them or stop Holland. Or both. But she didn't know how.

Then, like turning a corner and seeing someone you weren't expecting there, she jumped. Or she would have jumped if she had a body. She remembered the words Holland had said to her. Adults, once they know where they are, know how to get out. His words echoed through her head as clear as her own. Of course, she could get back to the real world the same way she had brought the kids back. It didn't matter that she was there in The

Darkness instead of in the flies' cave. They were always in the darkness — what they saw didn't matter.

The flies must have been too distracted with their plan for the kids to realize they couldn't keep her trapped in The Darkness the way they could keep the kids there. Lisa thought through the act of closing her eyes. It would be different going back to the real world from The Darkness instead of from the cave, but she was sure she could still do it. She had just done it six times. It took a lot out of her, but she was sure she could do it one more time. Once back in the real world, she could help the kids, and maybe together, they could stop Holland and end it all.

With her eyes closed, Lisa thought. She visualized the fly room, remembering every detail. The worst thing would be to end up in a version of the fly room that existed only in her mind — she wanted to be in the real fly room. The one where her body was. The one that would bring her one step closer to helping the kids and seeing Tim, Olivia, and Matthew again. She thought of the room and of all the people she needed to see again. At first, there was nothing, then she felt like she was flying again.

Lisa opened her eyes and looked down on the fly room. The room was empty except for her body lying on the floor near the door and a small blanket of flies, just barely covering her upper body. The rest of the room was empty. The flies must have been needed elsewhere because there was just a small number of flies there to make sure she didn't get away. And, more importantly, the door was open. Lisa tried not to get too excited when she saw the door had been left ajar. She didn't want the flies to realize what happened. In their haste to leave with the children, they'd given her an easy escape. This was the advantage she'd been waiting for.

Her thoughts moved her down closer to the floor and then finally into her body. She was there but didn't want to move. Just above her head was the open door. Lisa needed to get through the door and slam it shut before the flies could stop her. There were so few flies on her body, she didn't know if they could stop her even if they wanted to, but she didn't want to chance it. Did they realize she was no longer in The Darkness? She was going to assume they did and work quickly to get out of the room, and the basement, before they sent some kind of fly signal to the others.

The flies were not near her legs, so she slowly moved her feet until her toes were pressed firmly against the floor. She waited in that position, eyes still closed. She took one long deep breath, and then her eyes shot open. Everything happened fast. Lisa pushed herself up on her hands, and with her toes already against the floor, she shot herself forward through the open door. The flies flew off her and buzzed around in what she could only describe as shock. She barrel-rolled once out into the hall and then turned quickly onto her knees, slamming the door shut behind her. A few flies managed to get out of the room with her, but the five or six that were there could do nothing but fly circles around her head.

Lisa waved a hand at them like they were ordinary house flies. "Get outta here," she said to them, hoping there was nothing they could do to her. For some reason, this brought a slight smile to her face.

Lisa stood up, her body still aching. There was no time to worry about her soreness now. She needed to get out of the basement, this time for real.

Her movements through the hall were slow at first, cautious, unsure of who or what might be just around the corner. Around the first turn, there was nothing. She passed the door to the room where she had first been held. It was still open. Holland's blood stained the ground, but it was dry now, almost black. Past the room, the hallway stretched and then turned sharply to the right. Lisa picked up her pace and followed the hallway to the end. There were two doors, one on her left and then just a few feet past it was one straight ahead of her. One of these doors would take her to a stairway and out of the basement if it was the basement. And the other would lead somewhere she didn't want to be. She took a deep breath, looked back and forth at the two doors, exhaled, and stepped straight ahead. She grasped the doorknob of the door directly in front of her and turned. It opened.

The door was heavy, and Lisa strained to push it open. It moved an inch and then another. She planted her feet against the floor and leaned into it, driving her feet as hard as she could, trying to move the heavy door. It moved another few inches, and she kept pushing harder, forcing it to open against its will. She stopped pushing and tried to slip her body through the thin opening, but it wasn't quite big enough. She caught her breath and readjusted her feet, then leaned in again, giving what she hoped would be one final push. The door opened another few inches, and she turned her body sideways and slid through the opening.

The back of the door was cement and fit tightly against the cement floor. She was in a small, dark space. She realized it was Holland's basement, and it looked like the heavy door had been somewhat camouflaged so it wouldn't be easy to spot in the dark basement. There was a fake wall in front of her, just another trick to help keep the door hidden, she thought. The wall was held up with just wood brackets leaning against it, but there was a hallway in front of her. She followed it around until she came to a wooden door. She pushed it open and came into what she assumed was John Holland's finished basement. She had been in basements like this before. Sometimes water would get into the basement around the edges, so to make sure it didn't happen in the finished part, people would leave the outside few feet of the basement unfinished to minimize water damage. The outside edge was usually poorly lit except for the areas where the water heater and furnace were. It would make an easy place to hide a door, which was exactly what Holland had done.

She walked out of the dark and into the basement. It was

JOE SCIPIONE

finished, as she thought, though not very nice. There was an old couch in the corner, piled up with dusty boxes and old books. In the opposite corner was an old TV that looked like it had been in the same spot since 1975, with a wooden frame surrounding the screen. On top of the TV sat seven or eight lamps of various sizes. Most of them were dusty as well, but a few looked new. Those must have been the ones Holland brought back with him, Lisa thought as she turned her head back toward the door she had just come out of.

She looked toward the stairs. It was only then that she realized she was out of breath. The prospect of getting out of this basement after however long was not lost on her, and her excitement was almost too much. Lisa felt dizzy. She needed to get up and out of the house to escape and also to help the five other kids that had been trapped down here with her, but she wasn't even sure she could climb the stairs.

She leaned on the railing that would lead her up and out of the house for good. She put her head down and rested it against her arm. The sweat from her forehead felt cold and slimy against her arm.

"This is it," she whispered to herself. "Finish this, and then you can go home, be with your family and sleep for a week. But you've got to finish this first."

She forced herself up step after step until she got to the top of the stairs. She looked around with some vague memory of seeing the inside of Holland's house when he first took her. It didn't take her long to find the front door. She opened it and stepped outside.

It was her first breath of fresh air since Holland had taken her, but she didn't have time to enjoy it. She checked the front yard and looked down the street — there was no sign of Holland or any of the kids. Then, her attention turned toward her own house. There were no cars in the driveway, but that didn't mean no one was home. She didn't know what Tim and the kids had been doing since she disappeared, but she was sure their schedule would have changed dramatically from what it was before she was taken. They could be anywhere or doing anything. She didn't even know what day of the week it was.

With one more quick glance down the street to check for Holland, Lisa turned and sprinted toward her house. She could see her family, call the police, and get those kids away from Holland. Once the police got there, it would be over. She ran as fast as she could, but it felt like she was running through water. Her legs just couldn't push her forward as fast she wanted to go. A voice stopped her in her tracks.

"Lisa?" It was Marie Shaw. Lisa's head snapped around, and she looked over at the Shaw's house. Marie was standing next to her car with the door open.

"Help." Lisa tried to yell, but the word barely made it past her lips. She swallowed and tried to yell again, this time with a bit more success. "Help."

Marie's eyes widened. "Are you okay?"

"Call the police," Lisa said in the loudest voice she could muster.

Marie turned back to her car and fumbled around for a moment, probably looking for her cell phone. Lisa slowed her pace and started to jog across the street.

She looked up at Marie and then stopped in the middle of the road. Marie was still digging in her car and didn't see the figure turn around the side of the car. It was Tiffany. The face was undoubtedly Tiffany's, but something had happened to her while she was stuck against that wall by the flies. Tiffany moved up behind Marie. Lisa broke out into a full sprint. She needed to stop whatever was about to happen.

Tiffany was directly behind Marie now. Lisa wasn't going to make it. Tiffany spread her arms, and Lisa could hear a low growl, followed by the familiar buzzing of flies. Marie started to turn around just as Tiffany's body broke apart. She turned into a giant swarm of flies.

"No!" Lisa shouted, but it was too late. The flies swarmed around Marie. They wrapped themselves around her legs and her chest and then filled in the spaces, covering Marie until all Lisa could see was a group of flies in the shape of Marie's body. The buzzing got louder, and Lisa stopped moving forward, unsure if she should run to help Marie or run away because she might be next. The flies seemed to squeeze Marie, the swarm got tighter around her, and it looked like they were shrinking around the young mother.

Lisa just stood in the middle of the street watching until the swarm disbursed. Marie's body was gone. The flies moved around for a few seconds as if they were reorganizing themselves. Then they reformed back into the shape of Tiffany. She couldn't see the girl's face when she reformed. Lisa backed away slowly, realizing she needed to be far away from Tiffany or any of the other kids. She didn't know what the police would do, but she needed to get in touch with them.

Lisa continued to back away, her eyes still glued on Tiffany, hoping the girl wouldn't notice her. Tiffany's head snapped around and stared at Lisa. Her lips were pulled back against her teeth, and her eyes were wide open, unblinking. It wasn't Tiffany anymore. It was something else inside Tiffany's body. That much was clear. Just like Holland, the flies had taken control of Tiffany, but this time with a much darker purpose.

Lisa turned to run, sprinting toward her house but afraid to turn her back on the monster that was once a twelve-year-old girl. Her chest heaved as she reached the middle of her front yard. A quick look back told her that Tiffany was following her but not running after her. She glanced up and down the street. No one else was out, and there was no sign of Holland or the other kids. She ran the rest of the way up to the door. So close now, she just had to get inside and make the call and lock Tiffany out while she waited. Lisa grabbed the doorknob and turned. It was locked.

It must be a weekday. The kids back at school? Maybe. Tim at work? She banged on the door, hoping someone was home, but she didn't have a lot of time. She looked back. Tiffany was running now, already at Lisa's side of the street, still staring at her, the low growl escaping her lips. No one answered her knocks, and she needed to move.

Lisa breathed in and coughed as she felt smoke from a fire in her lungs. Lisa's head whipped around in the direction of the guy who burned once a week. She knew watching the neighborhood would pay off one day. It must be his fire—he was always outside when he burned, usually smoking a cigar. He must be out there now. Lisa ran along the porch as Tiffany made it to the top of the driveway and toward the steps of the porch. Lisa got to the end of the porch and hurdled over the railing, her foot dragging along the top of the shrub planted on the other side, and she fell to the ground. She rolled once and popped up, looking back to see Tiffany running back down the stairs. Lisa turned and sprinted toward the fire. It looked bigger than normal, but maybe it was just because she was closer to it than usual. She could hear the fly-Tiffany gaining on her as she ran across the street and toward the roaring fire.

White smoke filled the air, and Lisa tried to glance back to see where Tiffany was, but when she did, her foot clipped a stone that was part of a walkway in the backyard. She lost her balance for a second, her legs kicking out behind her, but she was able to regain it. There was no one in the backyard. Where was this guy? Lisa continued toward the fire. She didn't need to look back to know Tiffany wasn't behind her anymore. She could hear the buzz of the flies she had turned into.

Lisa drew nearer to the fire and could almost feel the flies against the back of her legs and on her neck as she ran. They were faster than her—there was no chance for her to outrun them. The fire brought back a memory of her brother throwing bugs in it. It gave her an idea. Lisa continued her sprint toward the fire.

She judged the height of the fire as she was less than three steps away. There were a few good-sized branches on top, and the flames reached about up to her waist. But it would only be a few burns—she didn't want the flies to get her. She adjusted her last few steps. Her foot landed as close to the fire as she could get it, then she took off, jumping over the fire. She felt the heat against her legs when she took off, flames licking the backs of her thighs and calves. She landed on her feet and looked back. More than half of the swarm of flies flew into the flames. They burned up, small sparks flaring up and then disappearing. Lisa caught the small flashes of fire lifting up into the air as the flies were then incinerated.

The flies that were not burned up flew up into the sky and then back down toward the ground. Lisa caught her breath and watched the flies that looked like they didn't know what to do next. They flew around in a circle close to the ground. Lisa moved closer to the fire in case they came after her again, but they just circled and weaved close to the ground a good ten feet away from her. Then they left, flying off in the direction of John Holland's house.

CHAPTER 21

With the immediate threat gone, Lisa sat down to catch her breath. The fire crackled and popped next to her. It was a nice day out, with no clouds and sunny, though a little cool. She realized she could see her breath as she sat there, letting the warmth of the fire help relax her aching muscles and bones. Tiffany had turned into the flies. Was that what they needed the children for? To get more people and turn them into flies as well? Lisa tried to wrap her head around everything she had seen and done since being forced into Holland's basement, but there was too much to comprehend. Tiffany had taken Marie Shaw and had almost taken her as well. There were four other kids out there probably doing the same thing — taking people, bringing them someplace. If Tiffany was close, the others couldn't be far. How could she call the police with this? She didn't think they would believe her or know what to do. Lisa barely knew what to do. The only thing she knew for certain was fire killed the flies.

She stood up and looked at the fire. The old man was always out there while it burned, but he was nowhere to be found. Lisa didn't know for sure, but she figured the flies had gotten him. She pushed aside the thought that the kids, who were really just being used for their bodies now, were the same ones she had met inside the cave. Those kids were gone. In all likelihood, they had been gone since they were taken. Chrissy a few weeks ago — however long it had been since she was taken — and Barbara almost a hundred years ago. Since the time they had been taken, they would never really exist in this world again. For a while, maybe their families held out hope that their children would return. Lisa knew Chrissy's family still hoped their daughter would come back. Matthew too. She was sure there was a part of her son that just assumed Chrissy would walk back into school one day like nothing happened. She needed to push all of those thoughts aside to do what needed to be done. Those kids, the ones that were taken, were long gone. The flies were just using their bodies to try to take over the earth from humans. They turned them into these fly monsters to help spawn more of them, she assumed. They probably had the same super strength John Holland did. But they were not immune to fire, especially in their fly form.

Lisa got an idea. She looked back across the street at her house. Tim was probably at work and the kids at school, but there was no way of knowing for sure. The neighborhood was deserted, but maybe it was because of the flies and not because it was the middle of the day in the middle of the week. There was no way to know that either. But she would keep telling herself everyone was at work and school until she believed it. She looked at her house again and then around the backyard she was in. Lisa walked around the fire. Laying on the ground next to it was a lighter. Not a small cigarette lighter — the long kind used for starting fires or lighting a grill. She picked it up and pulled the trigger. Red hot, nearly invisible flame was expelled from the end of the long tip. It wasn't a regular lighter but a butane one. Even better. This one wouldn't go out with a gust of wind.

The old man had a shed in the backyard, and she walked over to it. There was a lock on the latch, but it was unhooked. Lisa tossed the lock to the ground and opened one of the doors. It let loose a high-pitched squeak as she pulled on it. Inside, she found a small hatchet with a leather cover over the blade—she tossed it to the grass outside the shed. On one of the shelves along the back of the shed, she found what she was looking for, a can of lighter fluid. She shook it. It was mostly full. Lisa smiled and left the shed. She didn't really have a plan beyond finding the fly monsters and lighting them up. There was no way to know if it would work when the things looked like humans or if she had to wait until they were in their fly form. But she didn't have any other ideas.

Lisa surveyed her supplies laying on the ground and picked up the hatchet first. It wasn't very heavy, but the leather cover on the blade made her think it was sharp. She pulled off the cover and found out she was right. The end of the blade glistened in the sun. This was just in case. The handle of the hatchet went into the back of her pants, and she tucked her shirt down between her skin and the sharp blade of the small ax. Next was the lighter fluid and lighter. Lisa flicked open the can and gave it a slight squeeze, sending a stream of fluid up into the air. It worked perfectly.

Lisa was as ready as she would ever be. She had no destination in mind. The fly monsters were probably just out looking for people. Hunting. Lisa would hunt them. She hobbled in the direction of her house, the toll the past few weeks had taken on her body just now becoming evident to her. Adrenaline was the only thing keeping her going. The monster that used to be Tiffany was no longer chasing her or going after her neighbors, and Lisa felt the results of being shackled and sleeping on floors and against walls for multiple days. She tried to walk normally, but her legs, back, and neck were sore and stiff, and each step sent pain up and down her body. When this was over, and she was back in her house with her family, she would sleep well for a long time.

Lisa crossed the street to her front yard and approached her front door, then stopped and looked down, pausing to think.

She couldn't go back into her house – she'd lose her edge, the edge she needed to take out the rest of these things. A call to the police would require a lot of explaining on her side, and even then, they wouldn't believe her. She didn't feel like explaining anyway. Lisa wanted to end it herself. Who knew how many neighbors the flies had already taken? She was going to stop them all.

Without a real idea of where to find them, she walked across her yard. There was no way she was going back into Holland's house, but it didn't mean she wouldn't go into his backyard. It seemed like as good a place as any to start her search. Most of the yard was visible from her own. The grass was all dug up, and dirt covered the entire area from one fence to another. She didn't see any of the monsters, but that didn't mean they weren't there. If they were, she was ready.

While still holding the lighter, Lisa opened the gate into John Holland's backyard. The first thing she noticed was the smell – the same earthy smell as the cavern in the mind world. The Darkness. Then she saw them. Bodies.

Lisa let out a short scream when she saw the bodies, mostly buried in the ground with a small group of flies covering their faces. There were at least ten of them. Lisa recognized Marie Shaw in the group. Her eyes scanned for anyone that resembled Tim, Matthew, or Olivia, but none of them did.

There was a movement to her left. She didn't see what it was because she was focused on the bodies. She turned fast, looked in that direction, and readied the lighter and the lighter fluid. Harry, what used to be Harry, moved at her from around the far corner of the house. His eyes were wide, unblinking. Lisa had never gotten a really good look at Tiffany because of the distance, and then she was behind her. Chasing.

The fly monster moved slowly toward her, staring at her as it crossed the backyard. Lisa held the lighter and the can of fluid low against her body. She didn't know if the flies that survived the first attack managed to communicate with the others. If they did, they would know exactly what she was up to. As the monster drew closer, Lisa noticed the bright green eyes. They were not human eyes—she could see the many different lenses, like looking into the wrong end of a kaleidoscope. They were the eyes of a fly. Harry drew closer still, and his pace picked up. Lisa wanted to run, but she held her ground.

The monster smiled at her, and Lisa fought the urge to run back out the gate she had come through. But she stayed. She waited and watched as the monster drew closer. The legs started first. They broke apart and changed from a human form into flies. That was her cue. Lisa squeezed the can of lighter fluid hard, and it sprayed all over what was left of Harry's body. She drenched him as much as she could. He broke apart more into flies. They swarmed toward her, and she clicked the lighter on and held it out in the direction of the oncoming flies. The proximity from one fly to the next was perfect. Covered in the accelerant, one fly caught on fire and ignited almost all of the others, turning the cloud of flies into one big fireball heading straight for Lisa. The burning flies tried to pull up and away from the flame of the lighter. Lisa dropped flat on the ground as the fireball lifted up just over her head, the heat of the flames grazing her back. The smell of the burning lighter fluid filled her nose. The flies were incinerated, and the fireball disappeared. Lisa exhaled and couldn't help but smile to herself as she stood up. Two down, she thought. It was a gruesome thought, but the way she saw it, it was her or them.

She examined the bodies closer, this time making sure to check her surroundings as she did so. If one of them was here, there might be more. She still didn't recognize any of the other people, other than Marie Shaw. She didn't know if she would be able to get them out or what would happen to them. Holland told her adults could find their way out of the darkness—maybe Marie and the others here could find their way out. Lisa was worried that if she tried to pull them up, it would kill them. She debated her next move. When no other monsters arrived, Lisa knew she needed to keep moving to find the others. Then she would find Holland and help the people in the ground.

There were three of them left — Barbara, Brian, and Chrissy. Lisa didn't know what she would do when she saw Chrissy. She didn't know the girl that well, but she knew Chrissy was important to Matthew. How could she face him knowing what she had done to her? She pushed the thought aside; she would deal with it when she had to.

Lisa walked down the street in the direction of Roberts Elementary School. She didn't really know why she went that way. It just felt right. She still hadn't seen any of her neighbors. There were ten in the ground that Lisa assumed lived in the area. They were unlucky enough to be outside when the fly monsters passed by. It must be a weekday, she thought. It would explain the lack of people in the area a little better since it was clear they all weren't in the ground behind John Holland's house.

She turned down a side street and heard a noise between two cars parked in a driveway. Lisa jumped at the noise and turned to face it.

"Oh, I'm sorry I scared you," an older woman with gray hair said as she pulled a bag of groceries out of the passenger seat of her car.

"Oh no. It's fine. I was just out for a walk," Lisa replied and smiled at the woman. She suddenly became aware of how she looked, dressed in gym clothes that hadn't been washed since before she was taken — a week or two, at least. She probably had dirt on her face from sleeping on the floor and being in the awful room with the flies for so long. Her hair was most likely a mess — she hadn't seen a mirror in a long time. She was carrying a hatchet, a lighter, and lighter fluid. Maybe the old woman had bad eyesight and didn't get a good look at her. Lisa put her head down and kept walking without making eye contact with the woman again.

Lisa made it a few steps down the street past the woman and thought she was in the clear until she heard the woman call to her again.

"Don't I know you?" the old woman asked.

Lisa stopped but didn't back up. "Maybe. I live a few streets over," Lisa said, not really lying but not telling the whole truth either. She was missing, and she was sure her face had been plastered on TV as much as Chrissy's. Maybe they were even shown at the same time — two disappearances that close together, the police were bound to link them. She still didn't back up. She didn't want the woman to get a good look at her and was content to let the woman shout at her from between the cars.

"Oh, maybe that's it," the woman said, and then continued. "You kind of look like that woman who went missing. Leslie, I think her name was."

"Oh." Lisa pushed out a laugh that she hoped sounded real enough. "No, that's not me. I hope they find —"

She stopped. From around the corner of the house came Brian. His teeth were bared, and he darted toward the old woman. Lisa wasn't close enough to get to him before he got the woman.

"Run! Run toward the road now!" Lisa shouted. She broke into a sprint toward the woman, her lighter fluid ready to go.

"What?" The woman looked up at her and then back toward the fly monster running toward her.

"No!" Lisa shouted.

The fly monster began to break apart, feet first. Always feet first, Lisa thought in her head. She raised the can and started to spray while still a few feet away from the woman. The fluid shot over the woman and landed on the upper body of the thing. Brian was flies from the waist down, and Lisa hit the only part of it that she could have hit at that distance. The old woman didn't move but instead dropped to her knees in the middle of the driveway. It wasn't the best spot for her to be, but at least she was partly out of the way.

The flies swarmed down around both of them. Lisa continued to spray the fluid onto the swarm of flies as they surrounded both of them. She clicked the lighter, but it didn't catch. The swarm of flies tightened around them. Lisa knelt on the ground, wanting to keep as much distance as she could between her and the flies. She clicked the lighter again. Still nothing. She dropped the can and swatted at the flies with her hand, hopefully buying herself another second or two. She clicked the lighter for the third time. It lit. She waved it around, knowing she just had to catch one of the fuckers with the flame.

One caught, and the flap of the flame as it spread out around her and the woman cowering beneath her filled her ears. The flies tried to pull away, but they were so tight together it made their escape impossible. The heat from the fire surrounded the two women and then dissipated. A small group of flies flew away, and few remaining burning embers dropped onto the driveway and on the hoods of the cars on either side of them.

"Are you okay?" Lisa caught her breath and pushed herself back up to her feet.

"I...I think so. I don't even really know what just happened." The old woman stared at her, blinked a few times, and then continued to stare.

The woman didn't say anything, but Lisa could see the recognition in her eyes. She knew who Lisa was. There wasn't a whole lot of time to explain.

"It's kind of a long story, but I think I just saved your life." Lisa tilted her head to the side, hoping the woman would understand. Lisa had two more monsters to find. "If you could — not mention this to anyone, that would be great. I think you know who I am. I'm okay now. We can just keep this to ourselves."

Lisa smiled and hoped that was enough for the old woman.

"I...I think I can do that." The woman exhaled and gave a knowing smile to Lisa.

Movement caught Lisa's eye, and she looked up.

Barbara was sprinting down the street.

CHAPTER 22

Barbara watched from around the corner of a house across the street as Lisa helped the old woman up. She hadn't seen what happened before that, but she could only guess one of the others had gone after the old woman, or Lisa, or both of them, and Lisa figured out a way to stop them somehow. Good for her, Barbara thought. She knew she didn't want to be this monster anymore. She could feel its instincts and knew what it was going to do before it did it. But it was not her. Her brain was in there. She still had her own thoughts, but they were stuck, and she couldn't control her body anymore. The flies controlled everything but her thoughts.

She hoped Lisa would be able to kill her.

She didn't understand what was happening. Whatever the man — John — said, her body did. She thought he was controlling her mind or something. But when she watched Harry go after the man checking his mail and then turn into a swarm of flies, Barbara realized the same thing had happened to the rest of them. Chrissy had been right all along; they never should have trusted the flies.

Barbara's body pulled her toward Lisa and the old woman. She saw Lisa look up and see her. That was a good thing. She wondered how Lisa had been able to stop the other monster if that was what happened. When Lisa looked up at her, Barbara heard her own mouth let out a long, high-pitched shriek. It was a noise she was sure no human could ever make. It hurt her ears. Lisa and the woman jumped at the sound.

Lisa directed the old woman up toward the house behind them, but Lisa did not go with her—she turned back toward Barbara. It looked like she was waiting for her. Barbara tried to think of what Lisa was going to do.

Barbara had already taken six people in this neighborhood. The strength her body now possessed was incredible. She was faster than she had ever been in her life, and she felt stronger like nothing could stop her. There was a guy getting in his car who she'd found less than ten minutes after John told them to go hunt. He was twice her size, and she could see his muscles through the shirt he was wearing. She didn't want to go after him—she was sure he would stop her or hurt her. But he didn't. He couldn't. The guy with the muscles didn't stand a chance. She ran him down, but he didn't really try to run away. He didn't realize how strong she was either. She broke apart into a million pieces and flew at him. He tried to push her away, all the parts of her, but she was too strong. She pinned him down to the ground and enveloped him. Then he was gone. There was nothing he could have done.

The strength she didn't mind. In school, no one ever thought of her as the strong one. She only just now realized that school was almost a hundred years ago. The world looked different, with strange-looking cars everywhere. The people dressed differently, and there were more houses and less open space. It was a different world than the one she had left, and she knew she would not have wanted to live here, even if she was not this monster. There was only one thing Barbara could hope for now, and she hoped Lisa could give it to her.

Her body moved toward Lisa. She felt herself gaining speed. Lisa just stood there, waiting. Lisa had something in her hand, but Barbara couldn't see what it was even as she got closer. If there was one thing about this monster body she didn't like, it was the eyesight. She could see everything, much more than she could with her old eyes. But it was hard to focus on things. Instead of one image to focus on, there were hundreds, thousands of images maybe, and none of them were as clear as they would have been with her old eyes. So she knew what was going on all around her, but she couldn't focus enough to get a good idea of everything that was happening. The objects that Lisa had in her hands were a mystery. So was the reason Lisa started running toward her.

Lisa wasn't sprinting, but she was closing the distance between the two of them. Barbara still didn't know why; this monster was stronger than Lisa and could take her away just as she had done to the others. Lisa must know that. What was she doing?

There was wetness on her. It splashed on her face and her clothes. It wasn't rain. It smelled funny. She didn't know what the odor was, but it was something she had never smelled before. Barbara could taste it in her mouth, and the smell filled her nostrils, getting stronger by the second. She was almost at Lisa. Was this part of Lisa's plan? What was she doing? Barbara felt her body start to break apart again. It always started in her legs, and the sensation moved slowly up her body. She wasn't herself anymore. She was them. The flies. Hundreds or thousands of them, she didn't know. All she knew was that she was them. She was the flies. All of the flies individually were her. The wind blew past her as she flew toward Lisa. The flies' urge to surround Lisa was overwhelming, just as it had been with the others she captured. She could see everything that every fly could see, and it was almost too much for her brain to process. But she maintained her sight and kept her eyes on Lisa. She still couldn't really see what she had in her hand. She was almost right on top of her now.

Barbara only wanted one thing. She wanted Lisa to kill her.

Then a flash and the heat. So much heat.

Barbara's vision changed. She couldn't see much, and then she was looking straight up at the sky. The flies had pulled away. She had set them on fire?

There was less of her somehow. She saw the ground again, but there were only ten sets of eyes for her to see out of. They gathered together and tried to reform.

"No," Barbara tried to shout, but of course, she wasn't able to speak. She wanted to die. Lisa had killed most of the flies but not all of them. Now Barbara was stuck in these few flies. They tried to reform again into her single body, but they couldn't.

"I just want to die," Barbara said. If she had a body she could control, tears would have been running down her face. She was going to be stuck in these few flies for who knew how long. Maybe forever.

Barbara caught one final glimpse of Lisa slumped against one of the cars catching her breath. Then the flies took off and headed back in the direction of John's house.

CHAPTER 23

"One more," Lisa said under her breath. She leaned against the old woman's car and watched the small group of flies that used to be Barbara zip away. She could never get all of them, but she got most of them. Enough that they weren't able to transform back into human bodies or take anyone. Maybe they needed the whole group to take people, but she was stopping them one at a time.

"Is...is it okay to come out again?" the old woman called from just inside her front door.

Lisa turned and saw the woman had cracked open the front door and was yelling through the small opening. The sight almost made Lisa laugh, but she stopped herself, like the first time she heard four-year-old Matthew swear. He dropped the cup of water he was holding, and it spilled on the floor.

"Oh fuck," the toddler said. Lisa was standing right there. She couldn't really get mad at him. Just two days before, she'd dropped a plate after getting it out of the dishwasher, and it shattered on the floor. The same expletive young Matthew said was the one she used for her own case of the dropsies. She turned away from him and covered her mouth so he wouldn't see her smile. Once she composed herself, she turned back around, a more serious look on her face.

"Matthew, that is a very grown-up word, and you shouldn't be saying it," Lisa told him.

"But you said it, Mommy," the four-year-old replied as most four-year-olds would have.

"You're right. I did. But Mommy shouldn't have said it either. Understand?"

Matthew nodded. Lisa picked up his cup and refilled it for him, and then wiped up the water on the floor.

The old woman was yelling through her door because she was scared. Two fly monsters had just chased after the both of them, and she didn't know if there would be any more. But the idea of the woman cracking her door, mixed with Lisa's near exhaustion, was funny to her. Lisa composed herself the same way she had done ten years ago. She turned away from the woman, pretending to look up and down the street for more fly/human combinations, then turned back around.

"I think it's okay," Lisa called to the woman.

There was a long pause, and then the front door opened. The woman came out with something in her hand. Lisa couldn't tell what it was until she got a little closer. It was another can of lighter fluid.

"I'm Martha Rosewood," the woman said. "I know where you live, but I can't remember your name. You were on the news every day for at least a week. I guess it's a good thing I remembered your face." Martha smiled and looked up at Lisa.

"I'm Lisa Ewing. Yes, I live right around the corner."

"I obviously don't know what's going on. I'm just going to stay inside, and I won't call anyone. This...this is to say thank you, I guess. You should go finish whatever it is you're doing." Martha handed Lisa the full can of lighter fluid and then turned back around.

Anyone would be uncomfortable with what Martha had just seen, and Lisa didn't blame her one bit. She must have known Lisa was trying to help, though, and that was why she gave her the fluid. It was a good thing, too, because her original can was nearly empty. She only had one more of the kids to get, and then she had to do something about John Holland, but she didn't know if the fire would work on him the way it worked on the others.

"Thank you," Lisa shouted as Martha reached her front steps. "Please keep all your windows closed, Mrs. Rosewood."

Martha didn't look back but threw her hand up in recognition of Lisa's request.

Lisa shook the almost empty can of lighter fluid, and was about to toss it on the ground, then noticed Martha's trash barrels off to the side of the driveway. Lisa walked over and dropped the can in. She pulled the plastic seal off the top of the new can and flicked the top open. With a slight squeeze, a little fluid came squirting out of the top. She was good to go.

Other than the shrieks and yells from the fly monsters, the neighborhood had been quiet all afternoon. No cars drove by. This was not unusual. Most of the families had both parents at work during the day. The people who lived alone, like John Holland, were older and didn't get out much during the week. She didn't know everyone, but she knew enough that the afternoon, just before the kids got home from school, was the quietest time in the neighborhood.

Lisa's back was to the road, and she didn't see the school bus come up from behind her. From the side road the monster that looked like Barbara had also come down. It turned right and passed behind Lisa. She closed the top of the can of lighter fluid and looked up as the bus made its way by her and took a left down Molly Lane. After that came the unmistakable squeak and hiss sound of the bus braking.

The entire thing didn't connect with her right away. She usually picked up Matthew and Olivia from school — they didn't need to take the bus. Then she put it all together. Tim still needed to work. The bus must pick the kids up in the morning and take them home in the afternoon. It wasn't the best situation, but it was the only way it could work for Tim by himself. She took a few walking steps down the street and then broke into a run, then a dead out sprint. It was probably a quarter of a mile, and she would have never been able to sprint for that long, but her body continued to surprise her. The wind felt good against her face, sweaty even in the cold late fall air as the houses flew past her in a blur, her eyes focused on the corner of the street just ahead. Lisa turned the corner just as the bus pulled away down the road. Her eyes went to the front of the house, where Matthew was just climbing the steps to the porch.

"Matthew!" Lisa shouted, breathless. She felt wetness on her cheeks, a mixture of her sweat and her tears.

Matthew whipped around and stood at the bottom step of the front porch, looking down the slight hill at her, obviously recognizing his mother's voice before even seeing her.

"Mom?" he looked back, confused.

She didn't really know how long she had been gone. She guessed a few weeks, but it could have been longer than that. Time had been a blur since Holland took her. She was passed out for a while and didn't know how much time passed, and she could never really tell if Holland was telling her the truth or not. But she didn't care—she was going to have her family back.

Matthew watched her and then ran toward her, his eyes focused on her. She stared back at him; she had never been so happy to see his face. Then his gaze shifted off to her left behind her. The look of happiness on his face changed to one of confusion.

"Chrissy? What happened to you?"

Lisa jerked back and turned her head around. The fly monster was charging at them, Chrissy's snarling face recognizable as the young girl, but just barely.

Lisa turned back around to look at Matthew.

"No, Matt. It's not her. It just looks like her. Get down!"

Lisa readied herself to take out the last of these things. The

monster was still a good thirty feet from her, and Matthew was
another thirty or so feet from Lisa. There was enough distance
to keep Matthew safe from the flies and the fireball that would
follow. The monster ran a few steps, and Lisa realized its angle
was off. It wasn't headed for her; it was going toward Matthew.

The monster picked up speed. Lisa had never seen
anything move as fast as the thing that inhabited Chrissy's body
moved, closing the distance between it and Matthew faster than
Lisa could react. Lisa broke toward the monster, trying to cut off
its angle, and sprayed the fluid as she ran. She caught some of
the front of what used to be Chrissy's body as it passed by her,
along with some of her side and most of her back. She chased it
as Matthew stood still, a look of fear and confusion on his face.

Lisa continued to spray the lighter fluid, clipping the back
of Chrissy's heels as it ran. She couldn't get between the monster
and her son, but she knew what was about to happen, and she
had to stop it. She watched it intently while she ran behind it,
the space between them getting further and further apart. Then,
the feet and legs of the monster started their transformation. She
knew it was coming. It was what she had been waiting for.

Lisa reached out with her right hand and clicked the
lighter. Nothing. She ran as hard as she could and clicked the
lighter again. Still nothing. The body of Chrissy Franklin broke
apart. She was nothing but flies now, barreling toward Matthew,
who was crouched down low to the ground, watching as the flies
surrounded him. The swarm of flies got tighter around him. Then
tighter. It looked as if it had shrunk with Matthew underneath it.
Was she too late? Lisa clicked the lighter again, and the flame
shot out of the tip. She waved it at the tight ball of flies.

"No!" she shouted, hoping the lighter fluid she managed
to get on them would be enough. She caught a few of them on
fire finally, and the flies that surrounded Matthew were replaced
by a ball of flame. The fireball shot back toward her and up into
the air. Lisa fell back to the ground after feeling the heat of the

burning flies against her face.

As the fire dissipated, Lisa's eyes dropped to the ground. Matthew was still there curled up in a small ball, his sweatshirt smoking and a little charred. Lisa got to her knees and then dove toward him. She wrapped her arms around him, ignoring the smoldering sweatshirt, and hugged him, her body pressed against his smoking sweatshirt.

"Mom?" Matthew said after a full minute. "What the fuck was that? Where have you been?"

"I thought it got you, Matthew," Lisa said, not really hearing his question at first and then registering it in her brain. "I'll explain, but not right now. We've got to get inside. Where's Olivia? Is she taking a bus too? What time does she get home?"

She helped him up without waiting for a reply. He could talk while they walked inside. Holland was still out there somewhere, and she didn't know what the deal was with the people in his backyard.

"Uh. Um, yeah, she takes the bus," Matthew stammered. He still looked confused. "We had to because Dad couldn't just be home forever, and we needed to—"

"I know. I get it. Let's just get inside. When does she get here?"

"About ten minutes. I usually don't even go in. I just wait for her on the steps here. She's one of the first stops. Are you okay?"

"Okay. Yes, I'm fine. Do you have a key?" she said to him. She realized he had millions of questions, the first of which was probably where she had been for however long she'd been gone.

Matthew pulled a key from his pocket and opened the door. Lisa put a hand on his back and gave a gentle push through the door, and then followed right behind him. She shut the door behind her and went to the side window, watching for Olivia's bus, which could come at any time.

"Mom, where were you?" Matthew said as they both

watched for the bus out the window.

"Not right now, Matt. Let's get your sister safe in here first," Lisa said. She didn't look back at Matthew, just watched out the window. She had to get them both inside. Tim was safe in the city for now. She hoped it would all be over by the time he got home from work.

"Well, I missed you. I'm glad you're okay," Matthew said. She could hear that he was crying, and she turned just for a second to look at him. He had dropped his bag and was just looking at her, tears in his eyes and streaming down his cheeks.

"Matt. You have no idea how good it is to see you." She put her arm around him and squeezed him tight to her, her eyes back on the road outside. "It's just...it's not safe yet out there—Olivia isn't safe yet. So I just want to get her in. Then I can explain everything if there's time. I missed you guys more than you could ever know." She held him close until she heard a bus around the corner. She looked over at Matthew. "Is that them?" she asked.

He nodded.

"Go out there. If the bus driver sees me, it might slow everything up. Just get her inside as fast as you can."

"Okay, Mom."

She let go of Matthew, but she didn't really want to. She didn't want to send him back outside, even if it was just a few steps out onto the porch. She didn't want either him or Olivia outside until she was sure it was safe. She had to get rid of Holland.

Olivia got off the bus, and the sight brought a smile to her face. There was a figure off to the right. Lisa looked away from Olivia for a moment and focused on the figure down at the far end of the street. It was John Holland standing and watching. Her heart skipped a beat, and she felt her stomach drop when she saw him, but he made no movement toward them at all—he just watched.

"Liv, come on! Hurry up!" She heard Matthew yell to his sister from the porch. Olivia made a face at him. "Hurry up!"

Matthew repeated. This time she grudgingly complied.

Lisa kept one eye on Holland and the other on Matthew and Olivia. The door behind her flung open to a shouting Olivia.

"What the hell was that, Matt?" Olivia said. Lisa could tell her voice was half serious and half kidding. She didn't care what the words were. She was happy to hear her daughter's voice again. Lisa pushed the door closed, and Olivia turned around.

"Mom?!" The girl took one falling step into her mother's arms and squeezed. Lisa could tell just from her breathing that she was crying. She looked up at Matthew, and he fell against them too. She knelt on the floor, hugging the children she hadn't been sure she would ever see again.

"Where have you been? Are you okay?" Olivia asked, showing the same concern her older brother did.

"Listen. Matt, I know I said I would tell you everything, and I will. But this isn't quite over yet. When it is, I will tell you the whole truth. I promise. But I've got to finish this first."

"Mom, why don't you just call the police?" Matthew asked.

Lisa shook her head. "I will. But they wouldn't understand all of this. Like that out there, Matthew. You know?" She looked at Matthew, and he nodded. "Don't open the door unless I say it's me and that the coast is clear. If I don't say the coast is clear, don't let me in."

"Mom. You're scaring me," Olivia said.

"I know. It's okay to be scared of this. But if I don't take care of this, we'll be worried for a long time. If I do take care of it, we won't have to worry." She gave Olivia another hug, wondering if she would actually be able to tell her everything that had happened. "Do you trust me?" Lisa looked at both of them and then quickly looked over her shoulder and through the window. Holland was still out there but now walking slowly in the direction of his house. Or theirs.

"Yes," both kids responded. There was a seriousness in

their voices, especially Matthew's. He had seen the flies. He had more of an idea of what she was up against. Though he didn't know the whole story, he knew enough to understand why she needed to finish what she started.

"Okay. We have to let go. You two are going to the basement. Keep quiet. Keep the TV off. You'll be able to hear me from there if you're quiet. I'll say it's me, and the coast is clear. If I don't, don't open the door." Lisa didn't know if the flies would be able to take her over or if Holland would make her get her children since she had taken away the ones he already had. He might need more. She still didn't have all the answers, but she knew what worked against the flies now.

"Okay, Mom. We love you," Matthew said first, hugging her again.

"I love you, Mom." Olivia joined in the hug.

"I love you too. That's why I have to go now. Basement."

The kids turned away from her and went toward the basement. She heard the door open and listened for their feet against the stairs on the way down. Then, satisfied that the kids were as safe as she could make them, Lisa turned her attention to the window. Holland walked up the front walk to his house and went inside.

"This is it," Lisa said under her breath.

She didn't have a plan, but she was most concerned with getting the others out of the backyard if that were even possible. She took a deep breath and went to the garage. The gas tank they used for the lawnmower looked like it was full, but she picked it up and shook it just to be sure. She took that and a few of the long lighters they had sitting on a shelf. She tucked the lighters into her pants, next to the hatchet that she was happy had not moved since she first put it in there. Then she opened the garage door, lugged the gas tank out onto the driveway, and closed the door behind her.

Lisa heaved and lifted the heavy gas can in one hand, and

her trusty can of lighter fluid in the other and headed down the slight slope back to John Holland's house.

CHAPTER 24

She thought about just going into the house, finding Holland, lighting him on fire, and watching him burn. That would have made her feel great, but she needed to try to help the people buried in the backyard first. Lisa dragged the heavy gas can down the hill and into Holland's yard. She took a quick look at the windows on the back of the house and didn't see him in any of them. She was set, at least for the time being. She lugged the gas can and shook the lighter fluid can. It was still mostly full, even after taking care of the fly version of Chrissy Franklin.

Lisa hadn't stopped to count the first time she was back here, but it looked like there was only one more body here now than there had been before. And she didn't think there were going to be any more bodies added to the…nest was the only word she could think of to describe it.

She put the lighter fluid can down and knelt down in the dirt next to the body of Marie Shaw. It was the only body she recognized. She might have known more of the people buried under the blanket of mostly harmless-looking flies, but she didn't know. The bottom of Marie's dress gave her away, though. She looked around for a way to get Marie out from under the flies, but there didn't seem to be an easy way to do it.

"All right," Lisa said, looking down at where Marie's face

should be. "I guess I have to do it this way."

Lisa plunged her hand into the swarm of flies that surrounded Marie. A few of the ones on the top flew off because off the disturbance, but most of them stayed, unaffected by Lisa's hand pushing them aside. She felt them crawling on her hand as she reached around and pushed further down through them. Then she felt what she was looking for—Marie's hand. It was not limp, which was a good thing for Lisa, and when she closed her fingers around the hand, she felt Marie grip hers back. This was a good sign. She was probably stuck in The Darkness or wherever Holland put these people and had some control of her body.

When she felt like she had a good enough grip on her, Lisa pulled. She felt Marie's body move under the weight of the flies, but she couldn't get enough leverage to pull her up with just one arm. Lisa dug her feet into the dirt to get more traction and pulled again. Marie's body shifted, but she still wasn't able to get the body out from under the flies. Lisa dug her other hand in next to the arm that was already buried deep in the flies. She found Marie's hand again and grabbed it with both hands now. She stood up and pulled, letting all her weight fall backwards at the same time. This was enough. The body came up out from under the flies. Lisa could see she was still breathing as she dragged her onto the dirt just next to the flies. The docile flies that had covered her just shifted over and covered the others in a heavier, thicker blanket.

"Marie," Lisa said, leaning in close to her neighbor. There was no response. "Marie," she repeated.

There was movement under her closed eyes. Lisa waited to see if Marie opened her eyes, but she didn't. Lisa reached up and lifted an eyelid. Two flies flew out of Marie's eye and joined the group. Lisa let out an audible groan and then lifted the other eyelid, releasing two more flies back to their group.

"Marie?" Lisa said a third time and then pulled open Marie's mouth by putting her thumb on her chin and pushing down. A small group of flies flew out of her mouth, swirled around above Lisa's head a few times, then also rejoined the group.

Maire let out a long breath through her nose. A few more flies left her body. Her whole body shook. It scared Lisa, who jumped and backed up, still kneeling on the ground. Lisa stared at Marie as she shook and then shot up, first to a sitting position and then all the way to her feet. Lisa stood also, snatching the can of lighter fluid at the same time and then crouching down, waiting to see what would happen next.

At first, there was nothing. No movement, no recognition at all from Marie. She just stood there, unblinking and staring off at nothing in particular. Then she spoke.

"What happened?" Marie said, still staring.

"Marie?" Lisa relaxed a bit and walked around in front of Marie to meet her gaze.

"Lisa, What...what happened?" Marie finally blinked. There was recognition in her face.

"Do you remember anything?" Lisa asked, exhaling. She was going to be able to save all of them before she got Holland.

"I...I remember seeing you and then getting my phone, and then...flies?" Marie said.

She looked like she was about to pass out. Her body rocked back and forth, and Lisa could see her eyes roll. Then she went rigid again, and her eyes changed from the dark brown to an even darker green. Lisa backed up when her face started to change. Her lips curled back, and she bared her teeth.

"No," Lisa said to herself, watching the transformation occur before her eyes. "No."

Lisa sprayed the lighter fluid on Marie as her body shook and convulsed, changing from a normal human into another of Holland's fly monsters.

"I'm sorry, Marie. I wish there was something else I could do for you," Lisa said. Having drenched Marie's still unaggressive body in the fluid, Lisa took two steps backwards, dropped the can of lighter fluid at her feet, and pulled two lighters from her waistband and waited for the inevitable. The convulsions slowed and then stopped. Lisa waited and watched. Marie's body stood still for a moment, and then its head snapped in Lisa's direction. She held the lighter tight, bent her knees, crouched, and waited. The monster that used to be Marie Shaw didn't make a move toward her but turned directly into flies, feet first. Lisa waited as long as she could and lit both lighters as the flies converged around her. They exploded in a huge fireball. There were no surviving flies.

Lisa took a deep breath and then looked down at the other bodies still covered by flies. Was the same thing going to happen to them? She assumed the answer was yes, and knew she should just get rid of them all before they became fly monsters too and tried to take out humanity, or whatever it was they hoped to accomplish. She started to spray the rest of the lighter fluid over the flies and the bodies in the ground.

"You are right, you know." John Holland's voice made her jump. She'd forgotten he was even in the house. He had no doubt heard the fly fireball she'd just ignited.

"What do you mean?" Lisa asked, still spraying the fluid on the bodies until the can was empty but keeping her eye on Holland the whole time.

"You have to kill them. We told you if we bring an adult into the darkness, they can find their way out. When those spawners, the children do it, they become one of us almost immediately. Our spawners are much more powerful than we are at creating new flies, at bringing new life into this world. Our world," Holland said, the evil smile having returned to his face.

"I didn't want to kill them. I wanted to save them all," Lisa said. The lighter fluid can was empty, so she dropped it on the ground and stared back at Holland. The fear she felt for the man, whatever he was now, was gone. It was replaced with pure hatred. She couldn't wait to watch him burn.

"We know. We wish you hadn't done that, Lisa. Nothing can stop us. Not you or anyone else. All you can do is slow us down."

Lisa heard what he said but didn't care. She stepped toward Holland and lit the flame of the lighter in her hand. Holland jumped back a step into the house. The gas can she'd dropped was just a few feet away, and the flies were drenched in lighter fluid less than a foot behind her. First, she had to take care of Holland. That much was certain. He couldn't be allowed to get away, but if she made a move toward the gas can, he would see it and probably just leave through the front of the house. She had to keep him interested in her while she figured something out.

"You just want to turn everyone in the world into...into those things?" Lisa said and gave a quick glance back over her shoulder as she took another step forward. She was right at the entryway to the house now, the gas can almost touching her left foot.

"No. Eventually, we want to turn everyone into us. We outnumber you, and we are stronger than you when we work together. There is no reason we should not control this world. One day we will. What will happen to Lisa Ewing? Perhaps she will live. Perhaps she will die. In the end, it does not matter. *We* will live!"

Lisa clicked the lighter once more, and Holland jumped again and took another step back. His eyes were focused on her and the lighter — she wasn't sure he realized where he was in the house. The kitchen table was just behind him. She might be able to get him off balance. It might give her enough time. Eyes focused on Holland, Lisa slid her left foot to the side just enough to make sure the gas tank was still there. She wanted to look down just to be sure she knew where the top was but was afraid if she took her eyes of Holland even for a short glance down, he would realize what was happening and run for it.

"You won't," Lisa said.

"What?" Holland looked back at her.

"You won't take over the world or get rid of us or anything you think you're going to do. You might as well give up now, you son of a bitch!" Lisa clicked the lighter again, and Holland jumped back, the back of his leg slamming into the table behind him. Lisa turned and grabbed the heavy gas tank. She spun the top off and looked up. Holland had just turned back toward her. He tried to get away and take off through the house, but he ran into the table for a second time, losing his balance. He pushed himself up, but Lisa had pushed over the gas tank, covering the kitchen floor with gasoline.

Holland stood up, his pants and shoes soaked, some of it dripping off his hands. He backed away through the kitchen toward the front door, but Lisa could see the gas spilling all the way to the door. Lisa scrambled backwards out the door to the backyard, hid around the corner of the house, reached in, and clicked the lighter. She felt the force of the air and fire push back against her arm, throwing it back out of the doorway. The sound was not as loud as she expected it to be, just a low thud of the gas igniting. She knew Holland didn't have time to make it out, even with his superior strength and speed, and wouldn't have been able to make it all the way to the front door before the house was engulfed in flames.

She leaned back against the wall of the house and could feel the heat on the other side—she had to move. The original flame must have ignited the flies and people buried in the ground because when she looked back, they were on fire too. The flies burned up in little individual sparks. Lisa dropped the lighters and the hatchet that was still in the back of her pants. She didn't think she would need either of them now. The vinyl siding started to melt from the heat on the inside. The same crackle and pop that she heard at the fire pit not that long again filled her ears. At first, she could only smell the burning scent of gasoline, but as the fire continued to rage, the smell of burning wood overpowered the odor of the gas. Through the windows, the flames looked almost like a painting or a video of a fire on TV. But this fire was real, and that thought made her smile.

The black smoke rose up from the open door she'd just left, and she still couldn't fully get rid of the grin on her face as she walked back up the hill toward her own house. The fire now crackled louder, and the distant sound of sirens grew closer. Lisa gave the house a wider birth, not wanting to be too close in case anything exploded. She went to the front. There was no sign on Holland on the street. He wouldn't have been able to get out of sight that fast. He was incinerated for sure.

Lisa collapsed on the hill of her front yard, looking down at Holland's house. The flames poured from the downstairs windows, and she assumed they would be traveling upstairs sooner rather than later. Lisa rested her head against her arm as the sirens got louder. She already knew the story she would tell them. The house grew hotter, and the flames pushed up and broke through the roof as the first responders arrived. It was a policeman first. She heard him shut the door to his cruiser but didn't take her eyes off the house. A large group of flies left the house through the chimney and disappeared into the sky.

"Ma'am, ma'am. Are you okay? Was there anyone in the house?" she heard the officer ask her. She didn't look at him, just watched the house burn.

"I'm Lisa Ewing," she said. "I don't know."

CHAPTER 25

It was Halloween again; Lisa had been looking forward to this holiday for the last three months. What used to be her least favorite holiday had become her favorite. Whenever she went to a store, she was always on the lookout for new Halloween decorations for the front yard. It was only their second Halloween at the new house, but it felt like they had been there a lot longer.

"All right, guys, let's go!" Lisa shouted upstairs to Olivia and Matthew. Olivia had stopped eating breakfast downstairs and was on the Matthew plan, spending most of the morning up in her room. Lisa and Tim didn't care all that much. Both kids' grades were good, and they were happy, so as long as it worked for Olivia, they were good with it.

Olivia came bounding down the stairs first with a smile on her face, her hair pulled back in a ponytail, just like her mom.

"Get all your homework done?" Lisa asked, already knowing the answer. She handed Olivia a sweatshirt. "You might not need this later, but it's cold now."

"Okay." Olivia took the sweatshirt from her, set her backpack on the floor, and threw the sweatshirt on. Then she pointed at the pile of Halloween decorations that filled the living room. "You're gonna do all that today, Mom?"

Lisa nodded and smiled. "Yup, Liv, that's the plan."

"What's the plan?" Matthew said, arriving down next to his sister.

"Mom's doing all the Halloween decorations today."

"Yup. Anything you want me to save for you guys to put up?" Lisa said, looking over her large collection and wondering if there would be enough room on the front lawn.

"No, go ahead. You're looking forward to it, so you might as well go all out," Matthew said.

She had been getting a lot of this from everyone since her abduction. She felt like people were appeasing her a lot more than they did before. Her mother always gave her shit about not visiting with the kids enough, and as soon as the ordeal with John Holland was over, the nagging stopped. It wasn't just her mother, though; everyone was nicer to her. No one really knew the full story. The people that knew the most were Matthew and Martha Rosewood, the old woman down the street, who knew more than anyone else.

Even Tim was left in the dark. Lisa wanted to tell him but thought it was easier just to give him the same story she gave to the police. She didn't know anything about the bodies in the backyard or the fire. She managed to escape, and he set his own house on fire just as she left the house. She didn't know why he did that—he was obviously crazy. She told them about the hidden part of the basement and the two rooms she was in. She had seen Chrissy Franklin's body down there, but that was it. The story worked for everyone. Matthew knew a little more than all of that, obviously, but she made him promise never to ask questions.

The police and her doctors and basically anyone who knew her told her she needed to go to therapy after something like that, so she did. But she just told the therapist the same story she told everyone else. It was easier that way. She was surprised by how little remorse she felt after taking so many lives. Maybe she'd convinced herself it wasn't really her who took the lives.

She felt bad for Chrissy Franklin's parents, but she wanted them to know she was there so they could have some closure. They were able to identify the bodies in the backyard, many of her neighbors. She felt bad for Marie Shaw's husband Mike and their twins. She really thought she had saved Marie at first. But she didn't feel bad about anything else. Not the people who died — it was just their bodies. Their minds were already gone.

"All right, here we go." Lisa swung her arm toward the door, and the kids went outside to the car. She pulled the door shut and followed them.

Work had started on the new house next door. Lisa and Tim had seen the plans a few months ago when the contractor came by to take some measurements. It was going to be a nice house. The frame was up right now. The best part of the whole thing was that it wasn't going to look anything like the house that used to be there. Holland's kids didn't get any insurance money from the fire because Lisa said he set it himself. They didn't even have the remains of the house torn down. They sold it as it was for less than $10,000, a steal for that size lot in this neighborhood. The contractor who bought it knew about the history the house had, and wanted to meet Lisa as soon as he had possession of the lot. She was happy to meet with him. He was a nice guy and wanted to make sure she was okay with him putting a new house there. The sight of it still made her stomach drop every once in a while when she stepped outside, but she would get used to it.

The kids got in the car, and Lisa glanced over at the frame of the new house. She wondered what her new neighbors would be like — they couldn't be any worse than the last one.

She got in the car and drove off, taking Matthew and then Olivia to school.

Her phone rang on the way home.

"Hello?" Lisa said, at first not recognizing the number.

"Hey." It was Tim, on a work line.

"Oh, hey. I didn't recognize the work number," she said.

This was part of the new normal for them too. She used to just be on her own once the kids were dropped off at school, but now she had a few different check-ins every day. Tim usually called right after he knew the kids were off and again in the afternoon at some point. Her mother would call at least once a day, though the time varied. And friends would call or text her throughout the day. If she didn't return a text, it became a thing, even after only an hour. It was just the new routine. She understood it, and she let everyone worry about her a little bit. It wouldn't last forever, she hoped.

She still went to the gym every day unless she had something going on. Today was one of those days. She wanted to get all of the Halloween decorations out. The other neighbors had put them out this weekend, but she had been planning to put them out today for a while, so she didn't rush it. When she got home, she let herself into the house and got a bowl of cereal. She would eat and then bring everything out to the front yard. Hopefully, she would be done by lunchtime so she could shower and start the laundry before it was time to pick up the kids. Another ordinary, busy day.

Lisa sat at the kitchen table with her bowl in front of her. She took a few bites and stopped every now and then to look out the window, and people watch. It was the one habit she couldn't break. She heard a small noise at the window off to the right. She got up and pushed the curtain back. A single fly was flying into the glass, trying to get back outside. Lisa smiled, grabbed a magazine from the kitchen table, and folded it in half. It didn't matter to her if she had read it or not. The fly crashed itself into the window twice more and then stopped to rest on the white edge of the window. Lisa pulled the curtain back further so the fly wouldn't get on the fabric. She watched the fly, and it didn't move. She didn't wind up but instead flicked the folded-up magazine hard against the windowsill. The fly splattered, most of it sticking to the cover of the magazine. Lisa dropped the curtain back into place and threw out the magazine. She took an anti-bacterial wipe and wiped the remnants of the fly from the window. She washed her hands and returned to her bowl of cereal, taking a bite. It tasted better than any of the others.

THE END

Joe Scipione lives in the suburbs of Chicago with his wife and two kids. He is a Senior Contributor and horror book reviewer at Horrorbound.net. He has had stories published in several anthologies, including "Stories We Tell After Midnight: Volume 2," "Satan is Your Friend," and "Throw Down Your Dead: An Anthology of Western Horror." When he's not reading or writing, you can usually find him cheering on one of the Boston sports teams or walking around the lakes near his home.

Made in the USA
Monee, IL
03 September 2021

77326442R00152